THE AUTHOR

'The Great Gladys', as Philip Larkin has described her, was born Gladys Maude Winifred Mitchell in Cowley, Oxford-shire, in 1901. She graduated in history from University College London and, in 1921, began her long career as a teacher.

Her first novel, *Speedy Death*, was published in 1929 and introduced Beatrice Adela Lestrange Bradley, the heroine of a further sixty-six crime novels, whose eccentricity was to become Gladys Mitchell's hallmark as a writer. She also wrote short stories, nine children's books and a number of novels under the pseudonyms of Malcolm Torrie and Stephen Hockaby.

In 1961 she retired from teaching and, from her home in Dorset, continued to publish at least one novel a year, as she had done for most of her life. Gladys Mitchell died in 1983.

Surreptitious slaughter, and the reasons behind it, have never lost their power to enthrall. Old ladies' wills and wilful old ladies, the sleuth in evening dress, the eccentric village squire and the portly butler (who either saw, or did it) continue to exert their fascination. Some detective stories have worn rather better than others – as a rule, those in which playful-ness, assurance and ingenuity are well to the fore.

The Hogarth Crime series, in reviving novels unjustly neglected as well as those by the justly famous, offers a new generation the cream of classic detective fiction from the Golden Age.

THE SALTMARSH MURDERS

Gladys Mitchell

*New Introduction by Patricia Craig
and Mary Cadogan*

THE HOGARTH PRESS
LONDON

Published in 1984 by
The Hogarth Press
40 William IV Street, London WC2N 4DF

First published in Great Britain by Victor Gollancz 1932
Hogarth edition offset from original Gollancz edition
Copyright the Executors of the Estate of Gladys Mitchell
Introduction copyright © Patricia Craig and Mary Cadogan 1984

British Library Cataloguing in Publication Data

Mitchell, Gladys
The saltmarsh murders.
I. Title
823'.912 [F]   PR6025.I832
ISBN 0–7012–0560–1 Pbk

Second impression

Printed in Great Britain by
Redwood Burn Limited
Trowbridge, Wiltshire

INTRODUCTION

'Gladys Mitchell's classic *The Saltmarsh Murders*' (Nicholas Blake's description) was first published in 1932. It was the fourth detective novel in a series of sixty-six; Gladys Mitchell (1901–83) increased her output from one to two books a year in the final period of her life. All her detective fiction features the same central character, the redoubtable Mrs Bradley (later Dame Beatrice), a distinguished psychiatrist who, for maximum effect as an investigator, combines 'extraordinary pothouse accomplishments' with an old-fashioned elegance of speech.

There is nothing ordinary about Mrs Bradley or the way she goes about her investigations. She looks like a reconstituted pterodactyl and behaves like the Cumaean Sibyl. It is her habit to keep suspects on the alert by poking them in the ribs. Her percipience is frightening and her humour prodigious. From the moment of her first appearance, in *Speedy Death* (1929), she imposed herself on author and audience alike. Gladys Mitchell, actually, had intended to create a male detective but in the course of writing this novel she found herself vanquished by Mrs Bradley. The irresistible old lady moved to the forefront of the action and has stayed there ever since.

The Saltmarsh Murders, like everything in the earliest group of detective novels by Gladys Mitchell, is an exceptionally stylish and high-spirited piece of work, with strong comic overtones. One of the author's practices is to poke fun at a minor convention of detective fiction by pushing it to an extreme; in this novel she has a go at the cosy village setting from which so many detective writers gained their most pointed effects. The village of Saltmarsh, where Gladys Mitchell's clergyman–narrator has his first unfortunate curacy, is peculiarly prone to disturbance. It is a place where the vicar may be taken for a goat and tethered to a stake in the ancient pound, while his wife remains in a state of outrage over various licentious goings-on. In certain respects it bears a resemblance to the *Cold Comfort* hamlet of Howling. Adultery, high jinks, horseplay, an illegitimate birth, a hidden baby, rumours of infanticide, exhibitions of lunacy, a couple of murders, a lost corpse, an illicit trade in pornography, even a spot of incest all keep things lively for Gladys Mitchell's benighted villagers before Mrs Bradley gets to the bottom of the imbroglio.

The literary ancestry of the blithe young curate who tells the story can be traced back to Dr Watson via Captain Hastings, but Noel Wells's mannerisms are all his own, and all agreeably ingenuous, down to the repeated use of the phrase 'of course'. He isn't exactly an admiring acolyte: 'I like old women to be soothing,' he declares, while the gnomic detective, of the eldritch cackle and outlandish actions, goes out of her way to unnerve everyone around her. In the interests of justice, naturally, as well as bedazzlement; Mrs Bradley's integrity is never in question, any more than her wits or her wit.

It takes great confidence and aplomb, as well as technical expertise, to go in for singularity and convolution on such a scale; and Gladys Mitchell deserves credit for possessing all these qualities. Her originality cannot be too highly praised. *The Saltmarsh Murders*, long out of print, is wonderfully eccentric and entertaining.

Patricia Craig and Mary Cadogan, London 1983

CHAPTER I

MRS. COUTTS' MAGGOT

There are all sorts of disadvantages in telling a story in the first person, especially a tale of murder. But I was so mixed up in the business from first to last, and saw so much of it from all conceivable angles and from nearly everybody's point of view, that I can't very well stand outside the story and recount it in a detached manner.

I had taken an arts degree at Oxford, and was intending to read for the Bar when a bachelor uncle died and left me thirty thousand pounds on condition that I went into the Church. Well, my mother and sisters were living on about two hundred and fifty a year at the time, and I owed my father's friend, Sir William Kingston-Fox, for my University fees, so I took the will at its word and did three years slum curating in the South-East district, Rotherhithe way. After that, Sir William recommended me to the Reverend Bedivere Coutts, Vicar of Saltmarsh, and I became the curate there.

I didn't like Mr. or Mrs. Coutts, but I liked Daphne and William. Daphne was eighteen when I first knew her, and William was fourteen. I fell in love with Daphne later, of course. Well, not so much later, really. Daphne and William were surnamed Coutts, and were old Coutts' niece and nephew.

As I look back over the whole thing, I can see that

the match laid to the train of gunpowder must have
been the day upon which it became known to Mrs.
Coutts that our housemaid, a quiet, softly-spoken,
rather pretty country girl called Meg Tosstick, was
going to have a baby. I think Meg herself had known
for about three months that the thing was going to
happen, and had kept a shut mouth and a demeanour
of great calmness. Awfully creditable, at least, I think
so, because I imagine it must be a rather hysteria-
making—(Daphne's word, of course, not mine)—thing
to be carrying a baby when one isn't married and has
a boss like Mrs. Coutts.

The net result of Mrs. Coutts' discovery that the
poor girl was with child, was as may be imagined. Out
went the girl, in spite of the fact that she told Mrs.
Coutts her father would thrash her and kick her into
the street if she lost her place—the old devil used to
turn up regularly at both the Sunday services, too !—
he was our verger—and Mrs. Coutts told the vicar that
public prayers would have to be said for the girl.

If there's one thing for which Coutts was to be
admired it was for the fact that, afraid of his wife as he
was, he never allowed her to dictate to him where his
job was concerned. In the home she reigned supreme,
but in the church she became as other women are, and
had to cover her bally head. He replied, on this
occasion, that it would be the time for public prayers
when the girl herself asked for them, and then he turned
to me and asked me whether I was going to visit the
girl's home and soothe her father, or whether he should
go himself. I left it to him, of course. In the end, the
innkeepers, Lowry and Mrs. Lowry, who were extra-

ordinarily alike to look at, by the way, decided to take
the girl in, and promised to see her through. I didn't
know at the time whether Coutts paid them for it, but
I supposed that he did. I didn't like the chap, but he
was very decent where the parishioners were concerned. Besides, I think his wife's attitude got his goat
rather. At any rate the next we heard of Meg Tosstick
was the news that she was a mother.

Mrs. Coutts was one of the first to get hold of the
tidings, of course.

" It's happened," said Mrs. Coutts. She came into
the study where Coutts and I were working, removed
her fabric gloves, folded them and laid them on the
small mahogany table which had belonged to her
mother. The table was inlaid on the top surface with
squares of ebony and yellow oak for chess, but no one
at the Saltmarsh vicarage played chess, and so the table
supported a small cheap gramophone and two cigarette
tins containing gramophone needles. The blue tin with
the gold lettering held the unused, and the yellow tin
with the scarlet lettering held the used, needles. I was
sentimental, rather, about these tins because Daphne
and I used to dance to the strains of the gramophone.
Mrs. Coutts took off her rather frightful dark brown
hat, shoved her hair this way and that, as ladies do,
and laid the hat on top of the gramophone case. She
was a tall, thin woman with eyes so deep in her head,
that, beyond the fact that they were dark, you couldn't
tell their colour. She had thinnish lightish eyebrows
and a nose whose attempt to give an expression of
benevolence and generosity to her face was countered
heavily by an intolerant mouth and a rather receding

chin. She seated herself in the only comfortable chair, of course, sighed and began to drum nervously on the broad leather arm. I think her rotten nerves were what got on me, really. Her hands, though, were really rather fine. Long, thin, strong-fingered hands, you know. She was rather a fine pianist.

As usual, she started straight in to bait the great man, who, to my quiet delight, had taken no notice at all of her entrance beyond clicking his tongue in an irritated sort of way.

" Have you nothing to say, Bedivere ? " she demanded.

" No, my dear, I don't think I have," her husband replied. " Would you mind not tapping like that ? I can't concentrate upon my sermon."

" If you are not able to improve upon last Sunday's performance, it won't make much difference whether you concentrate or not," replied Mrs. Coutts, sharply. It was justified, mind you. His previous effort had been well below forty per cent.

" Oblige me, my dear, by not referring to my preaching as a performance," said the old man. He laid down his pen, scraped his chair back and turned to look at her. I rose to go, but he glared at me and waved me to my work. I was checking his classical references.

" I suppose I shall get no peace until I hear the news, whatever it is," he added, " therefore open your heart, my dear Caroline, and do please be as brief as possible. I *must* get my sermon ready this afternoon. You know I've that match to umpire to-morrow."

He stood up, removed his pince-nez and bestowed

upon his life-partner a bleak smile. He was a blue-eyed, hard-faced man in middle life, with more of the athlete's slouch than the scholar's stoop about his shoulders. He was a hefty bloke, very hefty. His hands and wrists were hairy, he had the jowl of a prize-fighter and his thigh muscles bulged beneath his narrow black trousers. He looked out of the window and suddenly bellowed, " Hi ! Hi ! Hi ! " so that I leapt into the air with fright. The window rattled in its worm-eaten frame and his wife also leapt nervously from her chair.

" It's all right, my dear. It's only William at those hens again. The boy's a perfect curse. I shall be glad when the holidays are over, except that I must have him to play for the village against Much Hartley on August Monday. We're a man short, now that Sir William has had Johnstone run in for poaching. Sir William, I really believe, would let a man off for shooting his mother but not for poaching his game. A nuisance. Johnstone could be relied on in the slips and would have made a useful change bowler."

" Never mind about cricket," said Mrs. Coutts. " The thing that worries me about the Bank Holiday is this wretched fête at the Hall."

" The sports, you mean ? " The vicar, having barged her off the subject of his last sermon, became more genial.

" I do not mean the sports, Bedivere, although I am aware that you take interest in nothing else that goes on in the village," she said. The old man let out a groan and decidedly weakened.

" But does anything else go on in the village ? " he

asked. " I mean, of course, apart from the daily round ? "

" If you've no conception of what goes on in the village, Bedivere," said the lady, finding a spot and proceeding to bowl slow twisters, " it isn't my fault. I've attempted to bring it to your notice time and again. And I must say, even at the risk of becoming tedious, that the kind of behaviour which obtained last year at the village fête has got to stop. The village will get itself a name like Sodom and Gomorrah if things are allowed to go on unchecked. It is your clear duty to announce from the pulpit next Sunday, and to repeat the announcement on the following Sunday, that you will publicly proclaim the names of all those who transgress the laws of decency and proper behaviour in Sir William Kingston-Fox's park on August Bank Holiday."

" But, my dear girl," said the batting side, pulling itself together, " apart from the fact that the whole thing would most certainly be regarded by the bishop as a rather cheap stunt to fill the church, how on earth am *I* to know how the village behaves itself in the Hall grounds on August Monday ? You know as well as I do that my activities are confined to assisting to put up the tea tent for the ladies and to running off the sports finals for the children. And I can only manage the sports if our side is batting and my own innings is at an end. In the evening, as you very well know, I come back here, shut all the windows, and turn on the wireless. People don't want a clergyman about when they're enjoying themselves dancing and skylarking."

Mrs. Coutts' lip curled.

"For all you care, Bedivere, the whole village may go to perdition in its own way, mayn't it?" she said bitterly. "Meg Tosstick and all! Oh, and I was refused admittance to her, if you please! Really, the state of the village——"

"Look here, Caroline——" the vicar sat down and leaned forward with his great hairy hands dangling between his knees—"let's face the facts. I know the sort of thing that goes on. I know it as well as you do. And I say it doesn't matter. Does it harm anybody? You know the custom here as well as I do, and it has plenty to recommend it. I've performed the marriage ceremony in such cases dozens of times, and I'll challenge you, or any other moralist, to prove that there is anything fundamentally wicked in the custom. If of course, the youth doesn't marry the girl, that's another matter, but, hang it all, my dear, the village is so small and everybody's affairs are so well known that the poor chap can't escape. As for that poor unfortunate girl at the village inn, I suppose she is too *ill* to see anybody, even *you*! And now, if that's all——"

"But it isn't all." She clasped and unclasped her hands. "It isn't all," she repeated. There was silence except for a fly buzzing on the window pane. Bedivere Coutts, who had then been married nineteen years, waited patiently.

"I've been to visit her, as I said. The baby was born at two o'clock this morning," said Mrs. Coutts at last. Her hands were trembling. Her thin face was pinched into resentment. "Bedivere, not only was I refused admittance to her bedroom, but, according to Mrs. Lowry, who was barely civil to me, Tosstick persists in withholding the name of the father, and she won't allow anybody to see the baby. Nothing will shake her. Of course, everybody suspects the worst. It's perfectly dreadful ! And that Mrs. Lowry encourages the girl ! "

" And what *is* the worst ? " enquired the vicar, suddenly switching his chair round and taking up his pen. Mrs. Coutts passed her tongue over her lips.

" The squire," she said, dropping her voice. I think they must have forgotten me, of course.

" Kingston-Fox ? " said Coutts. " Oh, rubbish, Caroline ! "

He shook a drop of ink from his pen on to his blotting paper.

" Well, at any rate," began Mrs. Coutts, flushing, so that her thin face looked like a withered crab-apple.

The vicar pushed back his chair and turned round again. I was longing to go, but I hardly liked to make a disturbance.

" And not only rubbish, but wicked rubbish, Caroline, do you hear ? Please do not repeat it. Sir William is our friend and my patron. Whoever started such a beastly lie ought to get hard labour for slander. It's damnable ! " He shouted the words at her. His face was red and his eyes were slightly bloodshot as though he had been drinking too much. He breathed hard like a man who has been running, and his great hairy hands gripped the thin wooden arms of his chair. Then he suddenly subsided, and his voice grew quieter.

" I know that even the best of women enjoy a spice of scandal," he said, " but keep Kingston-Fox out of it, Caroline, please ! "

Mrs. Coutts rose and picked up her hat and gloves. Without a word she walked out of the room.

The old man shrugged his shoulders and looked at me.

" Sometimes I feel like cursing the fête," he said. " She's right, Wells, you know, according to general opinion. No doubt of that. The villagers *do* behave disgustingly, according to most people's notions. But I cannot get excited about it. Never could."

It was a funny thing about Mrs. Coutts. After all, she was married, although she had no children of her own, but the fact was—only the old man wouldn't seem to see it—she couldn't stand the thought of the village people having any of that sort of bucolic fun which consists in squirting water down one another's necks at fairs, or the lads lying on the grass with the girls, or coming home down the lanes at evening with their arms round them. It was nothing to do with right and wrong. She simply had the kink that all sexual intercourse was most fearfully unpleasant and wicked. The village was pretty decent, really. Boys and girls used to keep company until there was a child on the way, then they used to come to us to put up the banns. They were a steady, contented lot, on the whole, and their policy, although some people would condemn it, was based on sound common sense. The lads could be saving money all the time they were keeping company, and, if anything did happen and the man was a little slow to do the proper thing, old Coutts and I would urge him, quietly or forcibly, to get to it and marry. Of course, it was queer that Meg Tosstick wouldn't tell the name of her child's father, but I couldn't see

what business it was of Mrs. Coutts. Meg came from
tainted stock, unfortunately. The Moat House, where
the Gattys live now, was once a private lunatic asylum,
and the story goes that one of the inmates escaped one
night and forced several of the women and murdered
three men. Meg was in the direct line of descent from
the escaped madman and a woman called Sarah Par-
sett. One of the barmen, and, incidentally, the chucker-
out at the inn, a chap named Candy, Bob Candy, was
another lineal descendant of the lunatic, and a further
curious fact was that he and Meg were supposed by
all the village to have been sweethearts. But if it was
Candy's baby, one would think he would have admitted
it and married her. I did put it to him, as a matter of
fact, and he hunched his shoulders and spat into the
gutter and scowled, and I gathered that he was not the
father and was pretty well peeved about the whole
affair. I let it go at that, of course. No sense in coming
the heavy parson. Never does any good.

The talk at tea was again in connection with the
August Bank Holiday fête. Sir William lends his park
for it and gives two-thirds of the gross takings to the
Church Fund. A fair turns up from somewhere, and
pays five pounds in cash and loans us a marquee in return for the privilege of collecting the villagers' money
on roundabouts, swing-boats, houp-la, darts, and a
rifle-shooting game. We don't allow them to import
a cocoanut-shy now, because, at my suggestion, old
Lowry, the innkeeper, gets us the cocoanuts by the
hundred from a pal of his at Covent Garden, and
William, Daphne and I carpentered the stands the year
before last, and we use the tennis club's netting to mark

the pitch and protect the bystanders. William and I run the shy at five hundred and fifty per cent. profit on the great day, in the intervals of batting and fielding in the cricket match against Much Hartley which is another Bank Holiday feature. During our compulsory absences, old Lowry looks after it, which is very decent of him, because every year he applies for a licence to sell beer on the ground, and every year the magistrates, directed by Sir William, who is under instructions from Coutts, who is bowing to the inevitable in the guise of Mrs. Coutts, refuse to grant him the licence. He never seems to get shirty about it. Marvellously good-humoured bloke.

At tea on the following Wednesday, Mrs. Coutts said she couldn't see how on earth she was going to seat fifteen of the nobs on nine deck chairs, and directed Daphne to go and see whether Mrs. Gatty had any to lend. Daphne grabbed my hand under the table and squeezed it quickly three times, which is our S.O.S. signal. I knew she was afraid of going to the Moat House alone, as Mrs. Gatty, who is a fat, placid-looking lady with gold-rimmed glasses, has decidedly bats in the belfry. Hoots at one, and compares one with the beasts of the field. Most peculiar, and, of course, instructive, if one is of a philosophical turn of mind. She thinks I'm a goat. Literally, I mean. She once got me by the ankle in a running bowline and tethered me to the leg of an occasional table. Of course, I know her now, and when I go to see her, which I do fairly often, because she's a lonely sort of woman—her husband is a traveller in motors—I sit in one chair and stick my feet up on another. That does her, of course, because she thinks it

Bᴍ

cruel to tether animals by the neck. One comfort about people with a mania is that they are so beautifully consistent. Once you've grasped their point of view there's nothing more to worry about unless they're homicidal, when to grasp the main theme is hardly good enough, unless, again, one happens to be a philosopher !

After tea, then, Daphne and I set off for the Moat House. It lies a little way out of the village, but is on the main road. It is one of those eerie, shrubbery-haunted houses, with high brick walls and big gates. We walked up the drive and rang the front-door bell, and were received by Mrs. Gatty in person, as she kept only two servants, a parlourmaid and a cook, and it was the parlourmaid's evening out. The cook never answered the door, of course, upon principle. She said it wasn't her place. This was unanswerable. Mrs. Gatty used to liken her to a duck, but the cook was from Aylesbury, so she took it for a compliment, which was just as well, as I can't really believe that it was meant for one.

She asked us in, conducted us to her boudoir—it used to be the padded cell when the house was a private asylum—and asked us to sit down. Then she shut the door and tip-toed to her chair, sat down, leaned forward, and said in an excited whisper :

" It's done ! The deed is done ! "

" Oh, splendid," I said, quite at sea, of course.

Daphne goggled a bit and looked nervously at me. I rose to it.

" Er—could you lend us a couple of deck-chairs for the fête, you know, on August Bank Holiday ? " I said, and she replied most amicably.

" I'll lend you three, if you won't tell anybody. It's Jackson, you know. You won't tell, will you? Mr. Burt told me. I think it's simply beautiful. Don't tell ! "

We said we wouldn't, and I said I'd send the Scouts up with their troop-cart to collect the chairs. She was as good as her word, of course, and we netted three splendid chairs. That was the night Daphne kissed me, so it was rather a jolly evening, take it altogether, except for Bill's adventures, although they ended quite happily, too, and acquired for us two new and almost invaluable helpers for the fête.

Old Coutts went out, apparently, while Daphne and I were at the Moat House, and he had not returned when we got back. I went into the study and did a bit of arithmetic in connection with the cocoanuts and refreshments, and Daphne sorted the prize list. Mrs. Coutts was champing about in the kitchen bossing the cook and the supper, William came in but went out again soon, and everything was jolly fine. At ten p.m. the telephone bell rang, and, when I answered, a frightfully hectic voice at the other end of the wire desired old Coutts' immediate presence at the Bungalow, Saltmarsh Stone Quarries. Coutts being unavailable, I slid along, of course, shoving a Prayer Book into my pocket. I concluded, from the agitation indicated by the voice—a woman's, by the way—that one of the queer household up at the stone quarries had tumbled down one of the holes—rottenly badly fenced, those quarries. Fences were broken down by some toughs one year, and have never been repaired, of course, except on the east side, where nobody ever goes !

A chap called Burt lived at the Bungalow—big, hefty bloke. More about him later.

It took me a good forty minutes to do the mile and a half from the vicarage to the Bungalow. It was uphill nearly all the way, and the foulest, rockiest, ruttiest sheep-track of a road imaginable, once one had left the main road. The track mounted a shoulder of the coastal range of hills in the sides of which the quarries were cut, and the slope on the opposite side descended through bracken and gorse and heather to the sea. The cliffs were low and sandy, and there was nothing much to see or to do when one reached the shore except to bathe or to sit on the stretch of sand or to explore Saltmarsh Cove, a smallish, uninteresting little cave. Why on earth anybody in their senses had ever built the Bungalow in its lonely, exposed position was one of the things which I thought I should never under-stand. I did understand it in the end, of course.

There was a light in the hall, and a light in one of the rooms when I arrived. Just as I was about to knock on the door I heard a scraping sound on the roof, but thought it must be the Bungalow cat. Then I banged at the door and was almost shot on to my face by having the knocker suddenly wrenched from my grasp by some muscular blighter tugging the door open with such force that I tumbled over the step and cascaded down the polished linoleum of the passage. Before I could apologise for hurtling in upon the household, the door was slammed behind me, and a voice, male, said, " It's young Wells." A second voice, William Coutts', exclaimed, " It's Noel ! " And a third voice, female, the same which had squealed over the wire at me some forty-two minutes earlier, exclaimed, " Thank goodness, someone's come for you, ducky ! "

I was conducted into the lighted room, and, at intervals during the next hour, some of which was spent at the Bungalow, and some on conducting William back to the vicarage, I heard a somewhat weird story from the boy. William, although in some ways the most placid kid I know, does somehow contrive to get himself mixed up in any excitement that is going on. Even when his prep. school caught fire, William was the only kid out of the whole ninety-odd who had to jump out of an upstair window on to the sheet held out below. Old Coutts had to take him away soon after that, because he was always getting into trouble for scrapping with kids who tried to rub his nose in the dirt for him. Old Coutts admires a scrapper, and wrote a strongish letter to the headmaster for punishing William, and then removed the kid and sent him to Yeominster.

Considering that William had only achieved the distinction of leaping into space because he was in process of regaining admission to the building by night after having been out in the orchard sneaking the head beak's apples, I thought, personally, that old Coutts' letter was a bit thick. Still, it was no business of mine, of course.

CHAPTER II

MAGGOTS AT THE MOAT HOUSE
AND BATS AT THE BUNGALOW

William Coutts' adventures began when the Scouts
took their troop cart up to the Moat House on that
same Wednesday evening to collect Mrs. Gatty's three
deck chairs for the fête. Mrs. Gatty is fond of boys, and
she invited the Scouts into the dining-room and fed
them with cake and home-made ginger-beer and
home-made treacle toffee. Then, while the rest of them
returned with the chairs, William, as Patrol Leader,
politely offered to stay and wash up all the plates and
glasses. Mrs. Gatty was rather bucked with the offer,
because, of course, the maid was out and the cook was
in the middle of dinner. It was about seven o'clock or
perhaps half-past seven, and still daylight, although
the weather, for the end of July, was fearfully un-
seasonable. In fact, I can't remember a wetter or more
depressing summer. Our one hope was that the Bank
Holiday Monday would be fine.

William returned to the vicarage in a state of great
excitement. This was unusual, for, as I say he was one
of those biggish, hefty, good-humoured, practical-
minded kids who are always on good terms with everyone and never get seriously ragged even at school,
except in the incident last recounted, so to speak. That
was an exception. His nature was placid, and he was

inclined to accept things as they came without annoyance, question or perturbation. Thus, when he burst in on Daphne and me with the air of one who has discovered the Gunpowder Plot, I was somewhat astonished. But I couldn't take him seriously. He told me that Mr. Gatty had been murdered. Daphne was scared, so I rose to it.

" Sez you ! " I observed, ruthlessly.

" No," said William. " I had it from Mrs. Gatty herself while we were washing up. She says the deed is done, and that she wanted to tell you and Daphne, only you didn't seem interested in anything but deck-chairs."

I frowned and lent the theme a little concentrated thought. Those were the words she had used to Daphne and myself in connection with her husband, but one takes it for granted that with anyone of Mrs. Gatty's singular mentality a few odd remarks are in character and need not be regarded with the same amount of close attention that they would excite if they were uttered by some more normal person. On the other hand, those particular words, " The deed is done," do sound a trifle sinister, even when uttered by somebody short-circuited in the brain line. I questioned William closely, but could not shake his evidence. He was going to Constable Brown, our village keeper of the peace, he said, to place matters before him. I was struck quite suddenly with a better idea. Anything, of course, to get rid of William, so that we could be on our own, but not, I thought, the Robert, who is unquestionably wooden-headed, although a jolly good chap.

" Listen, William," I said. " There's an old lady called Mrs. Something Bradley, or Mrs. Bradley Something—I forget which—staying with Sir William Kingston-Fox at the Manor House. She's one of those psychology whales. Take her along to see Mrs. Gatty to-morrow morning. She'll turn her inside and out, and find what the trouble is. Believe me, it won't be a case for the police."

I persuaded him to abandon the idea of going to Brown with the story, but he insisted on getting Mrs. Bradley right away. I was in favour of the scheme, for it would relieve us of his company, so I decided to incite him, so to speak.

" They'll be having dinner," I objected.

" Shouldn't think so," said William, who hates to be thwarted. " You see, Noel, Sir William starts it at six-thirty, anyway, and it's now just after eight. Come with me, Noel, there's a good chap."

I refused, of course. No, but honestly, I didn't think the thing could be very serious. So he tooled off by himself.

He was ushered into the presence of Margaret Kingston-Fox in the Manor drawing-room, and Margaret, who is Sir William's daughter, and rather a Juno to look at, introduced him to one of the most frightful-looking old ladies—(according to William, of course)—that he'd ever seen. She was smallish, thin and shrivelled, and she had a yellow face with sharp black eyes, like a witch, and yellow, claw-like hands. She cackled harshly when William was introduced and chucked him under the chin, and then squealed like a macaw that's having its tail pulled. She looked rather like a macaw, too, because her evening dress was of bright blue velvet and she was wearing over it a little coatee (Daphne's word, of course, not mine)— of sulphur and orange. William's first conclusion was that if Mrs. Gatty were bats, this woman was positive vampires in the belfry. She had the evil eye, according to William. Her voice, when she spoke, though, was wonderful. Even William, who has no ear for music although, for the look of the thing, being the vicar's nephew, he has to sing in the church choir when he is on holiday from school—even William could tell that. She and Margaret listened to his story quite gravely, and Mrs. Bradley offered to accompany him to the Moat House and see what was to be seen. Margaret was inclined to favour the idea that Mr. Gatty *had* been murdered, but, pressed for a reason, could only say that he was a horrid little man and that such awful things happened nowadays. So all three of them went to the Gatty residence. Sir William and the men were finishing the port, of course, and did not accompany them. Didn't know they were going, in fact, I suppose.

Mrs. Gatty herself opened the door to them, and Margaret opened the conversation by asking whether Mr. Gatty had indeed met with foul play. Mrs. Gatty did not answer that, but kept looking nervously at Mrs. Bradley and muttering,

" Serpent, or is it crocodile ? Serpent, or is it crocodile ? " Just the sort of remark, in fact, that gave visitors such a bad impression. Luckily, however, Mrs. Bradley, who had been staying at Sir William's house for more than a week, and so, of course, must have heard of

poor Mrs. Gatty and her peculiarity, was not put out
by the quaint old girl's rather remarkable greeting,
and replied courteously,

" Crocodile, I think. I am generally considered to
be definitely saurian in type. Yorkshire people often
are, you know. It is interesting, I think, to note how the
types vary from county to county, and even from
village to village."

This launched Mrs. Gatty on her favourite topic, it
seems, and Mrs. Bradley had some difficulty in switching the conversation back to Jackson Gatty.

" Ah, Jackson," said Mrs. Gatty. " Yes, Jackson, of
course. Well, it's all over, bar the discovery of the body."

" And where is the body ? " asked Mrs. Bradley.

" If you only knew this village as I know it," said
Mrs. Gatty, to William's great disappointment, for,
of course, he wanted to hear details of the murder,
" you would sit here and laugh and laugh and laugh,
just as I do. Oh, it's too funny for words ! Of course,
the vicar's wife is the funniest of the whole lot."

" Look here, Mrs. Gatty," said William, but no one
took any notice of him.

" I call her Mrs. Camel," went on Mrs. Gatty,
" because she squeals and bites on the slightest provo-
cation, and then kneels to pray. And then there's that
creature at the Bungalow. A Kept Woman, my dear
Mrs. Crocodile ! What do you think of that ? "

" Shocking, interesting and anachronistic," replied
Mrs. Bradley. At least, that is what I think William
meant to say ; and Mrs. Gatty, I suppose, spent quite
a couple of minutes digesting this summary of the
world's Babylonian heritage, for William says that she

sat quite still for ages, while he finished dotting down the conversation in his Scout's notebook. At last she nodded in a solemn manner.

" Somebody at the Manor House could say more than that if he chose. And then take this girl Tosstick," she continued. " That whole business is incredible to me, simply incredible from first to last. First, she is not the kind of girl to have an illegitimate child at all ; secondly, she ought to publish the father's name, as all the village girls do, so that we can all make sure she is treated rightly by the young fellow ; thirdly, I suppose the child is deformed as no one is allowed to see it ; and, lastly, there is the singular conduct of the people at the inn."

" In what way is their conduct singular ? " enquired Mrs. Bradley, politely.

" I don't know," replied Mrs. Gatty. " It just strikes me as singular that they should be so charitable. You know, that Lowry even gets a commission on the cocoa-nuts for the village fête, and he never gives the village children more than a farthing on the bottles they bring back. They find them in the roads left by picnicking parties, and he ought to give the poor little dears a halfpenny, as I do when they bring me bottles for my home-made wine. He is certainly dead by now. Jackson, I mean, of course."

William noticed that Mrs. Bradley had also produced a small notebook, and was surreptitiously dotting down—in shorthand, William thinks—all that Mrs. Gatty said. I discovered afterwards that it was none of the recognised methods of writing shorthand, of course.

" Poor Jackson," said Mrs. Bradley.

" Well," said Mrs. Gatty, " if a man *will* be a wolf, he must be caged like a wolf. And the joke of that is, that he is caged in the sheep-fold. That's funny, now, isn't it ? "

" Funny *and* clever," said Mrs. Bradley, noting it down.

" Caged, you know," said Mrs. Gatty. " So funny that he should be caged. What awful weather for the time of year ! "

" And caged in the sheep-fold ! I must remember that ! " said Mrs. Bradley. She gave her awful cackle, William said, and rose to go. When they all got outside the Moat House, and Mrs. Gatty had shut the door, Mrs. Bradley sent Margaret home to the Manor House and was just about to speak to William when Mrs. Gatty came flying down the drive and grasped Mrs. Bradley's arm.

" And do you know what I think ? " she said.

" No," said Mrs. Bradley.

" I think Mrs. Camel believes her reverend husband is the father of Meg Tosstick's baby," said Mrs. Gatty.

(William, in his narrative to me, interpolated here, " What rot, Noel, isn't it ? " I concurred verbally with this view, but inwardly I was far from sure. The woman Coutts is capable of any frightful thought, so far as I can see !)

Mrs. Gatty, having voiced her opinion, turned and darted up the drive again, and Mrs. Bradley said to William :

" Has the church a crypt, child ? "

" Yes," said William. The evening was drawing in.

" Then lead me to it," said Mrs. Bradley. " And let us hasten, for I perceive that it is beginning to rain."

So William escorted her to the church. They passed through the lych-gate and skirted the south door, which is early Norman, of course, and soon reached the flight of stone steps which lead down to the crypt. A heavy iron gate breaks the flight about two-thirds of the way down.

" Do you just want to squint through the railings, or shall we go inside ? " asked William.

" I should like to go into the crypt," replied Mrs. Bradley.

" All right. I'll go home and get the key," said William obligingly. He surveyed his companion. " I suppose you wouldn't like to get down from the inside of the church, would you ? " he asked. " We needn't bother about the key, if you could get down the steps inside. I can put the lights on."

" It would suit me far better," said Mrs. Bradley. " William, I think Mr. Jackson Gatty, either dead or alive, is in the crypt."

" Who said so ? " asked William, thrilled.

" Mrs. Gatty herself, but she doesn't know she did," replied Mrs. Bradley.

" Golly ! " said William, irreverently. He led the way into the church, up the aisle, and into the vestry. Here he stooped and pulled aside a strip of cocoanut matting. A trap-door was disclosed, of course. The vicar's predecessor had it made, I think.

" Now you be careful," said William. " This trap-door is fairly new. They used to bury people in the crypt, and the tale is that some old girl jazzed it down the steps here and bagged a couple of skulls. So the chap who held the living before my uncle got it, had that iron gate put on the outside steps, and this trapdoor built over the inside ones, and, you'll see in a minute, the trapdoor is about two feet away from the top of the steps, so that it's tricky work getting down."

He looked at Mrs. Bradley again.

" I really think you'd better remain at the top, you know," he said, frankly. " I mean, there wouldn't be much sense in breaking your neck, would there ? "

Mrs. Bradley chuckled softly and replied :

" Let us lift the trapdoor. Perhaps neither of us need go down."

They raised the little hatch and peered into the depths. Then Mrs. Bradley called, clearly but not loudly :

" Mr. Gatty ! Mr. Gatty ! "

A dark shape silhouetted itself against the light which streamed in from a grating. (My translation of William's description. Shouldn't think there could have been much light streaming in, of course.)

" Up the steps Mr. Gatty. This way ! This way ! " cried Mrs. Bradley ; and she and William lay flat on their stomachs and hauled a little, thin man into safety.

" Good God ! " said Jackson Gatty. " Good God ! Thank you a thousand times. I'm very, very hungry ! How anxious poor Eliza will be ! "

" And now," said Mrs. Bradley, dusting the little man down in a motherly manner, " what have you to say for yourself, frightening us all like this ? "

Jackson Gatty coughed nervously.

" I really am most frightfully sorry," he said, " and

I know that Eliza will never forgive me." (He smiled, and William tells me that, upon seeing Jackson Gatty's long canine top teeth, he nearly shouted " Wolf!") " I allowed myself to be tempted by a wager. I think I have won it, too."

Mrs. Bradley began to lead the way out of the church.

" Oh, I beg pardon," said Jackson Gatty, flustered. " I should hardly have mentioned such a matter in the sacred edifice."

William says he shut the trapdoor, pulled the matting into place to cover it, and turned out the lights. Then he closed the church door—it was a foible of the vicar never to lock the church, although the vicar's wife insisted that it attracted courting couples, a species of the human kind that never failed to inspire her with fearful loathing, of course—and followed the other two to the lych gate and out on to the road. He was just in time to overhear Jackson's remark :

" Yes, at the invitation of Mr. Burt, I allowed myself to be incarcerated in the crypt. But I certainly thought they would have——"

Here William thinks that Mr. Gatty stopped talking because he heard William behind him. Mrs. Bradley did not prompt the little man to finish his sentence, and William, with a coy :

" Well, good night," was about to step into the night and return home when Mrs. Bradley stepped quickly up to him, and, to his amazement, put a ten-shilling note into his hand and thanked him for his assistance.

At this point I confess that I can't follow William's line of thought. But, of course, boys of fourteen just don't think along the same lines as any other human beings, and that's all there is to it. It seemed to him, he said, that the least he could do in return for the ten bob was to go up to the Bungalow where Mr. Burt lived, and tax him with the fearful crime of incarcerating poor old Gatty in the church crypt. So, in spite of the fact that it was very dark, that a wretched drizzle was falling, that the Bungalow was nearly a mile and a half from his home and that it was situated above the Saltmarsh stone quarries, a lonely and a dangerous, and, according to the villagers, a haunted locality, he set out at Scouts' pace for the Burt residence, as American stories say. As I said, I can't follow the argument, but William seemed clear that he was doing the right thing.

Foster Washington Yorke, the big negro, admitted and announced William. Yorke was Burt's servant, the only one they kept. Burt was seated in a large easy chair and Cora was on his knees, and neither attempted to move when William was announced. They merely smiled at him, and Burt said :

" Hullo, what can we do for you ? "

And Cora, whom William admired immediately, said :

" Take a pew, ducky, and make yourself at home. Like a bit of cake ? Bring some cake, Dirty ! "

Foster Washington Yorke appeared with the cake, and William sat down on the nearest chair, and, as he confessed to me later, he never felt so much at a loss in his life. He had come to accuse Burt of a murderous attempt on Gatty, and yet, when he looked at this great, blond, healthy, jolly fellow, and reflected that he held records for sport, and saw that he held in his arms, as carelessly as an emperor, the most glorious creature on earth, it seemed madness as well as the most frightful side to accuse him of murdering, or wanting to murder, a poor little worm like Gatty. He said at last :

" I expect you wonder why I've come ? "

" Not at all," said Burt. " You're the vicar's son, aren't you ? "

" Nephew," said William, and there was a silence until Cora jumped up, and, opening the door, shouted to Foster Washington Yorke to bring in the supper.

" Oh, I'll—I'll go," said William, hastily finishing his cake. The goddess laughed and pushed him back on to his chair, and kissed his cheek.

" You'll do nothing of the sort," she said. " A nice boy like you can surely eat a bit of grub if it's put in front of you, can't you ? "

William says it was the most frightful moment of his existence, but he managed to blurt out :

" I—we got Mr. Gatty out of the crypt, so you mustn't think we don't know you did it ! "

" Again," said Burt, leaning forward.

" You betted him, you know," said William desperately, " that he wouldn't let you lock him in the crypt. Well, I mean, it seemed awful to leave him down there like that. I mean, it might have been murder, or something, mightn't it ? "

Burt laughed, and said he had not thought of it in that light.

Here Foster Washington Yorke entered and began to lay the table. A cold fowl and choice salads appeared, and a great bowl of stewed fruit and another great bowl of cream, and various cakes, biscuits, cheeses, cold tongue and meat paste.

Cм

So the evening became a merry one, until, at the end of supper, Burt swore, and said he would have to go into the village for a heavy parcel of books which would be waiting at the station. Cora suggested that he should take the coloured man to carry the books, and she suggested that William should stay and keep her company. They would not be gone long, for the station was less than three-quarters of a mile away, and William could while away the time by telling her the tale of Mr. Gatty and the crypt, she said.

There was little that William could add to what she already knew, but, when the supper things had been cleared away and left for Foster to wash up when he returned, she and William drew easy chairs to the fire, and William obligingly recounted the story of the rescue of Jackson Gatty.

" Oh, and you know Mrs. Gatty's funny trick of making out that everybody is like some animal or other ? " said William. " Well, she makes out old Gatty is a wolf. Funny, because he's a fearfully weak blighter. Why, his first words when we got him out were to hope his absence hadn't caused any inconvenience, or something. He was thinking all about Mrs. Gatty, not himself. If Mrs. Gatty is really as dotty as they say, why isn't she in an asylum ? Oh, and talking of asylums, did you read in the paper about those two inmates scrapping ? One's done the other in, and a keeper got frightfully chewed up. Blood and brains and things all over the place ! " That sort of thing is William's idea of social small-talk, of course.

Cora shivered and said :

" I think we'll draw the curtains and light up, ducky.

It isn't very dark yet, but it's somehow creepy in this half-light. I like this bungalow and the peace and quiet and all that, but it *is* lonely, isn't it ? All the moor and the quarries, and only that one little cart track leading up to it from the village ! I get real scared sometimes. I'm glad I don't have to stop here in the winter. I believe I'd go off my head with the nerves ! "

" But not with Mr. Burt here ? " said William.

" David couldn't do much against a ghost, could he, ducky ? That's what I think. Did you know one of those horrible murders was done at the bottom of our back garden ? Well, it was. You know, when that loony got loose from the Moat House ! Of course, it was years ago now, and the bungalow wasn't built then nor anything, but somebody's marked the spot with one of them —those—great boulders and I often sit here of an evening while David does his work, and make meself a set of undies or something, and wonder whether that poor old corpse ever walks. My word ! I wouldn't be Mrs. Gatty and live in that Moat House for anything you could offer me. I wouldn't ! No wonder she's gone funny ! Gawd—— ! "

She broke off with a gulp of deadly terror.

" Listen, ducky ! " she whispered. " Whatever can it be ? "

Something was stealthily moving across the roof above their heads. There was a scraping noise, and then something heavy slipped and scrabbled on the slates. Cora clutched William's bare knee.

William is a plucky boy. He picked up the poker, pushed her hand from his knee, stood up and advanced to the door.

" Oh, ducky, don't ! " cried Cora. She ran to him,

and clung to his arm. " Ducky, don't leave me ! Don't open the door ! " She moaned in terror, as the sounds began again. They were sounds clearly indicative of the fact that somebody was climbing the bungalow roof and slipping as he climbed.

" Let go," said William, who was probably very pale. " It's only somebody fooling about. One of the village kids, I daresay. I'll scare him."

"You're not to go ! " said Cora. " You're not to leave me ! "

She clung to him frantically. William could feel her heart beating heavily against his shoulder, for she was a tall woman. They listened intently, but could hear nothing more. Gradually the tension relaxed. William released himself, and they stood listening, but with re-covered nerves.

" I expect," said William at last, in a whisper, " it was a biggish tom-cat. They're fearfully heavy, some tom-cats. As heavy as dogs. And the kind of noise re-minded me rather of a cat, too."

" Did it, ducky ? " whispered Cora, trying her hardest to believe him. " How I wish David and the blackie would come back, though, all the same."

" So do I, rather," said William, glancing at the clock. " I really ought to be going home."

" Oh, but you can't ! " said Cora, wildly. She clung to his arm with both her big, plump hands. " I'd die of fright, if you was to leave me now ! I'll tell you what ! Let's telephone your uncle. You're on the 'phone, I suppose, aren't you ? "

" We're on the 'phone, yes," said William, giving her the number.

She picked up the receiver and had just concluded that rather breathless message, received, as a matter of fact, by me, when the peculiar scrabbling noises began again. This time, even the pugnacious William did not want to go and investigate. Cora was white with terror. After about two minutes, the noises ceased again.

" Whatever it is, it's still up there," said William. " What ought we to do ? "

" Stay here," said Cora, her teeth chattering.

" You don't think," said William, " that the others are in danger ? "

Cora groaned aloud.

" Ducky, they might be. He might get them as they come in. Oh, my Lawks, whatever shall I do ! I'm so terrified of that there Gatty, revengeful little toad ! "

She picked up the poker.

" I'll have that," said William. " You won't hit hard enough. You have the shovel, and whack them round the chops with it. *I* can't be hanged if I kill anybody, that's another thing. You *can*."

They advanced to the hall door. The light was burning in the hall. Bending double, William tiptoed to the front door. Cora followed. At this moment they heard the quavering voice of Foster Washington Yorke singing a negro spiritual to guard and cheer him and his master on their lonely road home.

" Keep clear of the door, Cora," said William, in whom the fear born of inaction had given place to the thrill of battle. " I'll open it and let them in quick."

He waited until he judged the negro and Burt were almost at the door, then he flung the door open and shouted, " Quick ! Quick ! "

Washington was badly startled, but he responded immediately, and he and his load of books came hurtling into the house like rain, while William slammed the door.

" Fo' de Lawd's sake, Mis' Cora ! " gasped the negro, rolling his eyes rapidly. " What's de mattah ? "

" There's something on the roof," said William. " There it is again ! " They clutched one another wildly. At the same instant a loud knock at the door heralded Burt. They besought him to enter quickly, and William told him the news. Cora, William supposed, was too scared to explain anything.

" Something on the roof ? " said Burt. " Oh, rot ! " Nevertheless, somewhat shaken by their obvious fears, he walked to his desk, took out a revolver and walked to the door. He had a powerful electric torch in his left hand. Cora shrieked and rushing forward, clung to his arm. Burt shook her off.

" Stay where you are," he said. William and the negro had to hold Cora back, while Burt went outside the house. He returned in a moment or two.

" Nothing there," he said curtly.

" Well, there *was*," said Cora, weakly, sitting down.

" Yes," said Burt, slowly and thoughtfully, and William noticed that he did not replace the gun in his desk, but left it lying on the blotting pad, " there has been something up there. You'd better have a couple of aspirins, Cora. There's nothing to worry about now." He looked at her and smiled grimly. (William's words, not mine.)

" I'd better go home," said William.

"Not *alone*," said Cora. "You'll have to take him, Dave."

"And leave *you*?" said William.

"Nothing doing," said Burt. "I couldn't do that. The kid will have to stay here. Nothing else for it."

He smiled nastily again, William said. He supposed Burt was angry with Cora for getting scared.

"His uncle might come," said Cora. "I telephoned."

It was just about then that I rolled up, of course. They admitted me.

"What's the trouble?" I said, gazing at Burt's revolver.

"Come and have a drink," said Burt, "and I'll tell you. All right, Cora, I'm not going outside the house."

I accepted a small whisky.

"The trouble is that some unauthorised person climbed on my roof this evening and loosened a couple of tiles, damn him!" said Burt. "Incidentally, he scared my wife. She thought young Coutts ought not to walk home unaccompanied. I was out when the thing happened."

"Loosened a couple of tiles?" I said. "Are you sure? I mean, rather pointless." Then I told them about the cat I thought I had heard on their roof as I approached the place.

"Come and look for yourself, when you've finished your drink. Of course, I was only using my electric torch, but it's very powerful," said Burt, "and the roof of this bungalow is low. Nobody to be seen now, of course. Want to come and see the damage?"

"Take your word for it," I said, "especially as you promised you would not leave the house. Oh, by the way ! It wasn't young Taylor, I suppose ? " I added. " Bad hat of the village just at the moment. I've had to relieve him of the job of helping us to manage the cocoanut shy at the fête on August Monday."

" I'll take that on, then," said Burt, impelled by the hypnotic pause which followed my last remark. I am rather an artist in hypnotic pauses. You have to be, in our job, of course.

" Good man," I said. " Report at nine-thirty on Saturday night at the Mornington Arms for details, will you ? Sorry it's a pub, but Lowry gets the cocoanuts cheap for us."

" Right you are," said Burt. " I'll come and give you a light as far as the gate."

" Don't bother, thanks," I said, for really the whole thing seemed rather hot air, of course ! " Come on, Bill."

We made our adieux and had just come into the broad path of light which streamed from the study through the thin curtains out on to the gravel, when something whizzed past William's head and crashed to pieces on the path. It was rather startling, and I was sufficiently taken off my guard to seize William's arm and leap into the shadows, dragging the boy with me. At the same instant, the front door was flung open and a pistol cracked twice.

" Missed him. He's off," said Burt's cool voice. " Hurt, either of you ? "

" No," I said. " Who's the maniac, I wonder ? "

" Stay the night," suggested Burt, not, of course, answering my question.

" No. Lend me your torch," I said. I was rattled. I admit it.

" Take the gun," said Burt, putting it into my hand. We were somehow, inside the Bungalow again, although, for the life of me, I can't remember re-entering. That shows what your nerves do for you. I just simply cannot remember re-entering that bungalow. Queer !

" No, thanks," I said, deeming it inconsistent with my profession to carry fire-arms in time of peace. Besides, although the occurrences had startled me, I was still inclined to think that we were being terrorised by some of the young devils in the choir, who had had it in for me since I swiped three of them for scribbling vulgar phrases in the margins of the hymn books.

We started out again, William filling in the blanks of the story as we went, and arrived at the vicarage without adventure. Mrs. Coutts received us in the dining-room, and demanded from William an explanation of his lateness. It was then about twelve o'clock. William, with an economy of the truth which I could not but admire, stated that Mr. Gatty had been found in the church crypt, and he told the story with such convincing detail that his aunt accepted without demur the implied assertion that the releasing of Mr. Gatty had been the last item on William's programme for the day. William referred to it casually and modestly as his good deed for the day, too, and having received a piece of bread and butter and a mug of cocoa, he went to bed, virtue bally well triumphant.

" Mr. Coutts out ? " I said. " Still out, I mean ? " Making conversation with the woman, of course. Couldn't stick her at any price !

" Mr. Coutts is still out," replied Mrs. Coutts. She

closed her thin lips so tightly that I realised she had no more information to give me. I learned later that the vicar was talking with the Lowrys about Meg Tosstick at the Mornington Arms. He was not allowed to see her. I remained up, chatting with Mrs. Coutts, until the vicar returned home, and then, perceiving that there was going to be a domestic typhoon on the subject of Meg Tosstick and her mysterious baby, neither of whom must be seen by any living soul, apparently, I retired to bed. For some time I chewed over the identity of the person or persons who had chucked tiles at us from Burt's roof, and decided to thrash out the matter with the choirboys at the next choir practice. I am choir-master, as the organist is a free-thinker, and Mrs. Coutts doesn't think the lads ought to come under his baleful influence. (She won't have him play for the Women's Meeting, either !) As the lads themselves couldn't very well be more baleful than they are, the argument didn't cut much ice with me. But I bore up, because Daphne used to attend all the choir practices and help with the treble parts, and we had to wait to see everybody off the premises, of course.

CHAPTER III

SIR WILLIAM'S LARGE MAGGOT
AND DAPHNE'S SMALL ONE

Margaret Kingston-Fox passed her father the cucumber sandwiches. We were at tea at the Manor House. The other guests were Bransome Burns, financier, and Mrs. Bradley.

" And that's your seventh, you pig," Margaret said, as Sir William took a sandwich from the plate.

" I'm superstitious about the perfect number," Sir William answered. He lay back in a long armchair and popped the sandwich into his mouth.

" Of course, if that's the way you eat them ! " his daughter continued. " Mrs. Bradley, do have another. Come along, Mr. Burns. Mr. Wells, you're day-dreaming ! "

" Bread and butter for me," said the financier. Like most kings of commerce, he was a slave to his digestion. "Isn't this the day your poacher comes out?" he continued, addressing his host.

" No. Johnstone's got another month. The silly fool bunged a brick at Heath, my head keeper, and laid him out. I hope he never does anything of the kind to me," replied Sir William, selecting a piece of cake.

" Unpleasant to stop a large stone," agreed Burns.

I thought of the tiles which had been thrown at William and me on the previous night, but said nothing.

" Oh, I didn't mean that," said Sir William.

" Father can't control his temper when people knock him about," said Margaret. She laughed, but not happily, and was accompanied in her rather forced mirth by Mrs. Bradley's eldritch screech of laughter. That woman is clever, I suppose, but one gets no repose in her company. I like old women to be soothing.

" It really is no joke," said Sir William, smiling. " One of these days I shall find myself in the dock ! I know it."

He had a brown face, finely wrinkled about the corners of the grey eyes, dark-red close-cropped hair, and very red ears. His nose was short, well-shaped but pugnacious, and his full lips were pleasantly sensuous. His close-clipped dark-red moustache added to the pleasing masculinity of an open and attractive countenance, so to speak, and his teeth were strong and good. He was dressed in reddish-brown tweeds, and his fox-terrier, Jim, lay on the floor at his feet. In all, he was the novelists' ideal of a country landowner, and was amusingly conscious of the fact.

Tea was being taken in the drawing-room instead of on the terrace, for outside the long windows the rain tore down, and every tree in the park dripped heavily and continuously. An electric fire was alight in the drawing-room to combat the raw dampness of the August weather. It was a record-breaking August— the worst for one hundred years, according to the newspapers.

" Well, well," said Burns—I couldn't stand the man,

of course—after he had refused cake and a second cup of tea, " the poaching fellow—what's-his-name ?—will probably escape pneumonia by being in prison this weather."

" He won't escape my shot-gun if I catch him on my land and assaulting my keepers," said Sir William. He took a cake and bit into it so incautiously that a sinuous portion of cream from the interior of the innocent-looking pastry shot on to the leg of his trousers. Sir William gave a yelp of annoyance, and swore, and wiped the mess off his trousers. He lost his temper very easily, as his daughter had indicated to us. Irritating, of course, cream on the trousers.

" Really, father," said Margaret, grinning, " I do think it's time you learned to manage your food better than that."

I noted that she looked less like Juno when she grinned. One can't imagine Juno grinning. I don't know why.

Mrs. Bradley changed the subject. Resting her claw-like hands on the arms of her chair, she smiled by stretching her lips sideways until her yellow countenance resembled that of a chameleon, blinked her bright, beady, little black eyes several times in quick succession, and observed in the voice which always startled strangers by its richness and beauty—it startled me, of course, the first time I heard it :

" What do you consider the most amazing sight on earth, Mr. Wells ? "

There was a silence, while she darted her quick glances from one to another and then back to me. I could feel myself sweating, and I began to realise what birds feel like when snakes watch them. There was something saurian about Mrs. Bradley—about her eyes, about her lips, about the brain behind those eyes and the tongue behind those lips. She passed the tip of a small red tongue over the lips and then pursed them into a little beak, and I remember being rather surprised to note that the tongue was not forked like a serpent's tongue. " So this," I thought to myself, " is a psycho-analyst." Mrs. Bradley apparently read my thoughts.

" Quite so, my dear," she said. " And, moreover, one who is old-fashioned enough to consider Sigmund Freud the high priest of the mysteries of the sect. Kindly refrain from making the obvious and heart-rending pun, for there should be no jesting upon sacred subjects except by Dean Inge."

She concluded the remark with a startling scream of mirth, and, to my acute embarrassment, she pinched my cheek playfully. Margaret laughed. Margaret had very fine brown hair with golden lights in it, was a good tennis player and a remarkably poor performer upon the ukulele. I speak of her as I found her, of course. Mr. Bransome Burns was a suitor for her hand. He was finding the going extremely sticky, and had twice skidded into the ditch ; once when he lost every point after deuce in a game of tennis with Margaret as his partner and another time when he had struck the fox-terrier for leaping up at him. He was afraid of dogs, and, inevitably, I suppose, was violently disposed towards them. His digestion was poor, as I say. Margaret, who was young, did not realise the significance of this. Her father was in favour of the match, I believe, for Burns had money and was not particularly shady, as financiers go. He was not even reckless, and he played a good game of bridge, but not quite as good as Sir William's. It was, of course, a good deal better than mine. Burns' game, I mean. Mrs. Bradley, who had been a schoolfellow and close friend of Lady Kingston-Fox, informed me that she was watching the progress of the affair with mild interest, but was quite determined to prevent the match taking place. Her theory, startlingly borne out by personal observation, was that married happiness was extremely rare in any case, and was almost impossible of achievement when one of the protagonists was forty-seven and had a weak digestion, and the other was twenty and played the ukulele very indifferently. She liked Margaret and treasured Bransome Burns as the possessor of the most completely fossilised intelligence she had ever encountered.

Burns, I believe, considered her a queer old party and wondered whether she would bite at an investment if it were put to her in sufficiently attractive terms. He could not believe that she had ever been married.

" You don't tell me any man not under the influence of dope ever married *her*," he said to me one day when I was there alone with him.

I understood, I replied, that Mrs. Bradley had been married and widowed twice.

" Gosh ! " said Mr. Burns, impressed. " Got *that* amount of money has she ? "

It was a pity, perhaps, that I could not bring myself to repeat this observation to Mrs. Bradley, for I am convinced, from what I know of her, that she would have appreciated it to the full. I often caught the financier's decidedly fish-like eye fixed ruminatingly upon her. He was trying, I fancy, to estimate exactly how much she was worth, and the problem was difficult. Her clothes, although odd, and, in some cases, positively hideous, were manifestly good. On the other hand, she had a gift for repartee and a fund of bonhomie which he could not associate with a woman who possessed a large fortune, unless, of course, as he said, she was a music hall star or a duchess who had floated the ancestral hall as a limited liability company. She was a far better bridge player than either Burns or Sir William, and was an adept at pool and snooker. She was also the most brilliant darts player and knife thrower that I have ever seen. She was also a dead shot with an airgun, and annoyed Burns considerably by winning five pounds from him one miserably wet afternoon by knocking the necks off ten empty wine bottles with ten successive shots. I know she did that, because I saw her do it.

He could not place her. Neither could I. . . . With all her extraordinary pot-house accomplishments, she had an old-fashioned precision of speech and an unfamiliarity with Americanisms or modern slang which puzzled both of us. She was obviously what we both understood by the term " a lady," and yet, on her own showing, she knew the worst aspects of the worst cities in Europe and the United States, and was acquainted with every form of human degradation and vice. Nothing shocked her, but I've seen her make Burt's hair stand on end. Her only light reading was modern poetry, and her limit of personal indulgence seemed to be one glass of sherry taken immediately before dinner. Altogether an extraordinary woman. But not a freak. No, I must dissociate myself from those who consider her a freak.

" The most amazing sight on earth ? " I said, screwing up my eyes as I considered her question. " Oh, I don't know." I laughed. " A bargain sale, I should think."

" I once saw two sharks fighting," said Sir William, coming courteously to my rescue. The telling of the story restored his good-humour. Mrs. Bradley lay back in her chair and listened. Watching her, I was reminded of a deadly serpent basking in the sun or of an alligator smiling gently while birds removed animal irritants from its armoured frame. Margaret waited until her father had concluded his tale, and then she said.

" Cochet playing tennis is the most wonderful sight on earth. I saw him at Wimbledon last year."

She sighed.

" Last summer wasn't brilliant, was it ? " she said. She stood up and went over to the window. " But this year beats everything. Did you ever know such weather? It's the sort of weather to make morbid people commit suicide. I'm glad I have a naturally optimistic temperament."

She turned round.

" Ring the bell, please, Mr. Burns," she said. Burns complied. Then, re-seating himself, he said :

" The most wonderful sight on earth is a woman trying to extort money from her husband. She is capable of as many tricks and artifices as an ape, and as many changes of colour as a chameleon."

DM

We all protested ; Sir William violently, myself weakly, of course, Margaret indignantly and Mrs. Bradley humorously. Burns grinned his fat financier's grin.

" Well, be honest now," he said. There was always, even in his most innocent remarks, an undercurrent of suggestion that his hearers were *not* honest which got my goat rather, " Have any of you ever *heard* a woman trying to get money out of her husband ? Straight, now ! "

Margaret, whose good-humour, like that of most young women of her age, was as quickly restored as it had been disturbed, laughed, and said :

" By accident, yes."

" Oh ? " said her father, his eyes twinkling.

" Yes, the Burts," replied Margaret. " I was not meant to overhear, of course, but Mr. Burt has a voice like a megaphone and Mrs. Burt—Cora McCanley, you know—screeches like the low-class young woman she really is, especially when she gets angry. I had gone up to the Bungalow to collect Burt's subscription for the village lending library—you remember we started it last winter, Mr. Wells ?—and they were arguing, dreadfully loudly, about Burt's meanness and Cora's extravagance. She declared he never gave her any money beyond the bare housekeeping allowance, and he declared that she didn't want fine clothes to wear in a place like Saltmarsh. It was horribly unpleasant. Oh, well, never mind them ! Let's get the tea cleared away, and then, Mr. Burns, you are to find some way of amusing us until it is time to dress for dinner."

Burns smiled, and racked his brains in a truly gallant

attempt to think of some form of entertainment. By
the time the tea-things had disappeared he was ready.

"You stand over here," he began, and trod heavily
upon the dog. The dog sprang up with an anguished
yelp. Burns shouted to Margaret :

"Sorry ! I didn't mean to do that. I was just going
to say——" The dog began barking and Margaret
stooped to caress and soothe him. The dog, a well-
behaved, good-tempered chap, strove to show that
there was no ill-feeling by leaping up, first at Margaret,
and then, very suddenly, at Burns. Burns, obsessed, as
I say, by a nervous dread of dogs which he had con-
tracted, I suppose, as a very small child and had never
been able to conquer nor even thoroughly control,
shouted and struck at the excited animal.

"Down, boy, down ! " said Margaret, laughing. I
made an ineffectual grab at the dog's collar and tripped
and fell flat, thus adding to the confusion.

"Down, sir ! " said Sir William, rising to control the
dog. "Hurt yourself, Wells ? "

I shook my head and apologised for being clumsy.
I had to shout, for the noise was indescribable.

"Quiet ! Quiet ! " bellowed Burns, dashing his
hand wildly down at the animal's eyes, and kicking
him with a heavily-shod foot. The dog gave way with
a yelp, and then flew at the foot, fastened his teeth in
Burn's sock and began to worry his prey frenziedly.
Burns also was frenzied and tried to beat off the dog.
Nearly mad with terror, he seized a cut glass vase from
the mantelpiece and smashed at the dog's head with
it. Margaret cried out ; her father swore horribly ; I
believe I yelled, too. The dog, sensible of anger, let

go and leapt out of harm's way, and the glass vase crashed to the ground. Before anyone could prevent him, Sir William had gripped Burns by the neck and had begun very efficiently to throttle him to death. Burns' eyes bulged. He gurgled. Margaret shouted. Mrs. Bradley leapt from her chair, and, with great presence of mind, seized a vase containing flowers and flung its contents, which, of course, included a fair amount of cold water, abruptly and forcibly into Sir William's face. Sir William loosed his hold. Margaret, shaking at the knees, gripped the dog by the collar and put him outside the door. Mrs. Bradley sat down again and wiped her thin yellow fingers delicately upon a silk handkerchief. The two men glared at one another. Then Sir William, muttering, turned aside and began to wipe his hair, his face and his suit. Altogether it was an embarrassing occasion, and I was glad to take my leave. Margaret seemed anxious to have me stay for dinner, but I had several things to talk over with Daphne about the fête, and, besides, I was not particularly keen on remaining. Mrs. Bradley walked with me to the gate. Suddenly she said :

" So it was the Burts ? "

" Yes," I replied. " At least, Burt denied making the bet with Mr. Gatty, but did not deny incarcerating him in the crypt."

" Yes," said Mrs. Bradley. I had already told Sir William and the others about the person or persons unknown who had bunged loose tiles at William and me from the roof of Burt's bungalow. I had remarked that I suspected some of the choir lads. I repeated this observation.

" Don't say a word about it to them, young man," said Mrs. Bradley ; and she would not allow me to leave her until I had promised.

I found Daphne in what was still called the play-room. It was a big, bare, chilly room at the top of the house, and I was surprised that she had chosen it. It was to get away from her aunt, I suppose. They did not hit it off, of course, Daphne and Mrs. Coutts.

" Sit down somewhere, Noel," she said. " I say, what's all this about people trying to kill William and you last night ? "

I had to tell her, of course, and then I pledged her to secrecy. She said :

" Oh, I shan't tell. But it's all over the village."

" But how ? " I asked. " William ? "

" He says not." Daphne frowned. " It's those beastly boys," she said. I agreed, but told her that I had been compelled to promise not to tackle them on the subject. She said suddenly :

" They say Mrs. Gatty was quite normal before he made her live there. It sounds rather awful, doesn't it ? I suppose that is what the divorce courts call mental cruelty."

She turned her candid, beautiful eyes away from me, but took hold of my hand.

" It's all very queer, anyhow," I said. " By the way, I wonder whether we shall be able to get hold of a small bell tent for the fortune telling on August Monday ? "

" Oh, we can have it. I meant to tell you. I saw Tommy Manley, and he saw William, and William saw the scoutmaster and he says we can borrow it without charge, so I've invited the troop to the fête. William

is very pleased, I think. Comic how I have to approach
him through Tommy, isn't it ? The Scouts are going to
give us a display of camp-craft and gymnastics and I've
put a special Scouts' Hundred Yards Handicap into the
sports programme. I must let uncle know. And I must
get hold of the prize list from him. The Girls' Egg and
Spoon Over Eleven can't have less than three prizes,
because there are fifteen entries, so I must cut down
the Boys' Over-Fourteen Two-Twenty to a first and
second, because there are only seven entries for that,
and even at that I had to bribe Oliver, the gardener's
boy at the Manor House, to go in for it, or there would
have been only five."

" Six, surely ? " I said.

" No. By getting Oliver to enter I also secured the
entry of a boy named Briggs who hates running and
hates Oliver. But he hates Oliver more than he hates
running, and is entering the race in order to hack
Oliver on the ankle as they fight for inside places on
the bend."

I couldn't help laughing, but we had to get on with
the business in hand.

" I am going to enjoy this fête," I said. " What do
you think I ought to wear for the fortune-telling ? "

" I've renovated my old gipsy costume," said
Daphne. " We'll go and try it on you."

" I shall sport a small beard, I think," I said. " The
Bearded Woman. We ought to charge threepence a
time. I suppose my customers will be mostly the village
girls, and they haven't much money."

" I'd thought of sixpence," said Daphne, " so as to
dodge threepenny bits. Besides, you don't want to be

absolutely overrun. I vote we make it sixpence, with an
extra sixpence for advice about their love affairs. You
ought to coin money. We won't tell uncle and the
Adjutant about it though. They might not like the idea
of the curate doing a stunt like that."

" No, don't disclose my identity to anybody," I said,
grinning lovingly at her. " It will be more fun if I am
supposed to be a stranger."

Daphne sighed enviously.

" I expect you will have a screamingly funny time,"
she said. " I should love to be hidden in the tent so that
I could listen to you. And now sit quite still while I read
to you the list in my diary. There's always something
crops up at the last minute. Listen. Deck-chairs, bell-
tent, marquees, refreshments, roundabouts, swings,
houp-la, cocoanut shy, eggs and spoons, hurdles,
potatoes, marking flags, tennis court marker, measuring
tape, bunting, orchestra, fairy lamps, starter, judge,
referee, whistle, handbell, megaphone, officials' badges,
gate stewards, prizes, urns, helpers, course stewards—
I can't think of anything else, but I know there must be
heaps. Oh, yes ! Winning post tape ! Why on earth
didn't I keep last year's list ! "

She drew her legs up on to her hard, springless armchair, and turned over the pages of her diary, reading
to herself the record of the holiday from which she had
returned some weeks before. Then she came to the
entries for the past week, and at once the little pencil
began tapping against her small teeth and a worried
frown gathered upon her brow. I was sitting on the arm
of her chair, of course, and she allowed me to read what
she had written.

Saturday, July 25th : The weather fine for a change.
What a summer ! Taken into Fellonbridge by Sir
William in his car. Nice of him. So glad uncle and he
do not quarrel, as some rectors and squires do. He was
ever so nice ; asked about holiday and date of going to
College. Arrived home at five-ten in time for tea. Poor
old Bill looked glad to see me. Has marked out quoits
pitch. Challenged me to a game before I got my hat
and coat off.

Sunday, July 26th : Uncle preached rather red-hot
sermon on text, " Judge not, that ye be not judged."
The Adjutant very fed up with him, as the sermon
obviously aimed at the critics of Meg T. whose baby
was born last Friday week. As the Adjutant is quite the
leader of the anti-Meg movement, uncle's sermon
rather a slap in the eye. Several of the congregation
waited in the porch to shake his hand. Even the
Lowrys attended Morning Prayer. The two of them
seem to have been the Good Samaritans, which again
puts the Adj. in a false position, as that, of course, is
her rôle in the village. I suppose it is pretty awful to
hate your aunt and disagree violently with nearly
everything she does, says and thinks. But I *do* hate her.
And yet I believe she's much more upright than uncle.
Of course, she isn't my real aunt, only my aunt by
marriage. What a comfort !

Monday, July 27th : This beastly fête ! Nothing else
talked about ! I'm sick of the sight of the village, I've
been into it so many times to-day ! Borrowed ten deck-
chairs, two camp stools, a wicker invalid carriage and

a bath-chair to seat the Specials. Hope they enjoy themselves, rotten, snobbish old cats ! Called at the public house (side door !) to see Meg Tosstick. They wouldn't allow me to see her or the baby. Nobody has seen it they say, except Meg herself and Mrs. Lowry. Mrs. Lowry was a midwife before she helped at the inn, so Meg did not have a doctor. I expect the poor baby is deformed and that is why they are not letting people see it. I didn't like to suggest that to Mrs. Lowry because it isn't my business, anyhow, so I just said I hoped Meg would soon be better. She smiled at that, and said she had offered her a place as maidservant as soon as she was strong enough to take it. I did not tell the Adj. that I had visited the inn. I am supposed to be a high-minded, innocent girl, which is the Adj.'s description for what I should call a priggish, ignorant fool. I told Noel. He went rather red and changed the subject. I suppose he's had to promise not to talk to me about it. Absurd ! I'm eighteen.

Tuesday, July 28th : My darling Margaret came over this morning, with a woman called Bradley, a most fearful and wonderful creature, just like a lizard or something quite scaly and prehistoric, with a way of screeching with laughter which makes you jump. Margaret seems to dote on her quite lavishly, which made me fearfully sick, as the woman really is most frightful in every way. However, she took the Adjutant down a peg by informing her that her " animosity against the young woman Tosstick was really a sign of subconscious jealousy." The Adj. went purple round the gills and said haughtily that she " could conceive of no cause whatever for jealousy in connection with improper young persons of the Tosstick type." Then the Bradley, ignoring the Adj.'s denial, grinned like a man-eating Ganges mugger, and supposed that the Adj. "had passed the age for child-bearing." The Adj. nearly threw a fit, and the Bradley continued to grin widely. The meeting broke up in disorder after that, and while Noel, who was purple with embarrassment, carted off the terrible Mrs. Borgia, Margaret and I foregathered somewhat hysterically in my bedroom and smothered our yelps of joy in the pillows. Margaret tells me that Sir William has had one of his old fits because one of the servants cheeked him, or something. She seems fearfully worried about it. I suppose the ever-present thought that uncle or the Adj. might at any moment kill somebody in a fit of rage would be a bit sobering even to Bill and me. Comforted her by telling her I was certain Sir William would never go to any real lengths, although I'm quite, quite certain in my own mind that he will. But I have adored Margaret ever since she was our Head Girl and I was a frightened rabbit in the Lower Second, and I would tell any lie to buck her up. Mrs. Gatty has told everybody, except Constable Brown, that her husband has been murdered, but Constable Brown got to hear of it, and came round to ask uncle how to spell "felonious" and to give it as his opinion that the poor old lady has bats in the belfry, as Noel says, because, whenever she sees Brown, she will keep telling him that he reminds her of a patient ox, and that he needn't mind being compared to one because, besides being mentioned in the Bible, oxen have large, sad, beautiful eyes and lovely natures.

Poor Brown snorted a bit to uncle and uncle comforted him and told him he was to open the bowling at the Pavilion end against Much Hartley on August Bank Holiday. Uncle is easily the most tactful man I know. I'm sure tact comes before godliness, and as for cleanliness coming after it—well, poor William will never qualify at all, and yet the Adj. would qualify easily, and that *can't* be right.

Wednesday, July 29th : Bill and the Borgia have found Gatty. He was in the church crypt, and it seems that Mr. Burt, the author, put him down there to please Mrs. Gatty. I can't make it out. We all got rather worried because it was past nine o'clock and Bill had not come home. I never worry about him, but the Adj. was getting a bit hectic, as he is supposed to be indoors by a quarter to nine and she says she will not be disobeyed. Noel answered the telephone, and went out. He and Bill came home together.

Thursday, July 30th : This entry ought to be in yesterday's piece. We think somebody intends mischief either to Bill or Noel. It is horrible. I believe it is all a put-up job on the part of those horrible people at the Bungalow, and just for once I agree with the Adj. in forbidding Bill to visit them. I have a very good mind to go up to the Bungalow, and make them tell me the truth, but it is so awkward now that Noel has got them to help with the fête. We always make it a hard-and-fast rule never to be rude to *anybody* who has promised to help with the fête. How thankful I shall be when it is all over ! The Adj. has implored Bill to come home not later than seven o'clock, and Bill (who must be a

bit scared, although he swears he isn't) has promised
faithfully. How I love Margaret and Bill ! I love them
so much that I really believe, if the Adj. were lovable,
I could love her for their sakes, because they make me
so good and happy. But of course she isn't lovable. I
wonder why uncle married her ? Sometimes I think he
is awfully sorry he did. I've thought that ever since I
was fourteen. It would explain so much if they simply
hated one another. However, I suppose they don't.
Noel—I can't bear to write things down about Noel.
Not " real " things, anyway.

Friday, July 31*st :* It's awful, but I'm afraid to be
out alone. I keep finding excuses to take Bill with me.
I even welcomed an offer from the Adj. to accompany
her into Aldbury to see the caterers. I am a miserable
funk. The queer thing is that I don't know what I'm
afraid of. Uncle announces that the supposed attack
on Noel and Bill was some naughty boys, and he has
turned Bob Matters and Joey Baylis out of the choir,
although they deny it and Bill believes them. Noel has
gone to tea at the Manor House, blow him ! I'm scared,
and I——" Here Daphne put her hand over the page,
and laughed and I kissed her, and she threw the diary
on to a small side table.

" I believe the Borgia is as mad as Mrs. Gatty," said
Daphne to me a little later. " I don't understand her
at all. She says such silly things, and then laughs like
a hyena."

" Oh, she's all right," I said, recollections of a certain
rather brilliant piece of deduction coming into my
mind as I reflected upon how Mrs. Bradley had put two

and two together over the discovery that Gatty was in the church crypt.

Saturday passed without incident. Sir William's park presented the usual heart-breaking spectacle of wheel-ruts in the turf, half-unpacked roundabout and swing-boat stuff, and patches of mud where grass should have been. A dozen or so of the village children had managed to sneak in and watch the proceedings. Daphne, Mrs. Coutts and I were everywhere at once ; the cocoanuts were delayed en route, and William Coutts was sent off on his aunt's bicycle to see what had become of them ; Lowry, the innkeeper, applied for, and was refused, even the right to sell mineral waters on the great day ; the vicar helped the local troop to pitch the bell-tent and the fair-people erected their marquees. The fair lent us their big marquee for the refreshments, and paid five pounds for the privilege of attending the fête with roundabouts and swings. They were also under contract not to damage the turf, of course. " Sez you ! " as William succinctly observed. Anyway, we all returned to the vicarage that evening with the feeling of a job well done, I suppose. I know that I did. It had begun to rain. A slight but determined drizzle had commenced, and at seven o'clock, just as our vicarage party was sitting down to a belated and badly-needed tea, the rain was falling steadily.

" We shall have to put Much Hartley in first, uncle," observed William, holding his slice of bread and jam out at arm's length in order to inspect the large semi-circular inroad which his first bite had made. He giggled suddenly.

" Much Hartley," he said, indicating the jam. The

joke lasted him, on and off, for the duration of the meal. His was a simple nature, of course.

" Mr. Gatty is leaving on the tenth and going to Switzerland," said Daphne suddenly.

" What ? " said her aunt. " Who told you that ? "

" Mrs. Bor—Bradley, Aunt. It's part of Mrs. Gatty's cure, but Mrs. Gatty doesn't know he's going."

" You know, that's an extraordinary woman, that Mrs. Gatty," said the vicar. " I don't believe she's mad at all. I believe it's simply a pose to obtain sympathy. It's her husband I'm sorry for."

" You would be," remarked Mrs. Coutts, with bitterness. She was eating nothing, and she poured out for herself another cup of tea.

" A little bread and butter, my dear Caroline," said the vicar. He had shaved early that morning and already the bristles of a new crop of stubble were visible upon his chin. He felt it, unconscious that he was doing so.

" Oh, please keep your hand away from your face, Bedivere," said Mrs. Coutts. She spoke sharply, for she was tired out. Daphne put down her knife and was about to speak when her uncle prevented it by saying to me :

" Come along to the study, Wells, will you, and hear my headings and sub-headings for to-morrow ? "

" I do hope you are going to make an announcement about the fête," said Mrs. Coutts, reverting to a week-old argument. " And I hope you will put it strongly. The behaviour last year made me shudder ! "

" Then all I can say, my dear," retorted Bedivere Coutts, who was also tired, I suppose, " is that some people must be very fond of shuddering. Kindly remember that you are not compelled to stay and shudder. Show a little decency and come home at the proper time on Monday evening. Really, I advise it ! "

He was remorseful, I should imagine, before the sentence was concluded, but he would not admit it. Somehow one never did admit to being in the wrong to Mrs. Coutts. She was a singularly ungracious woman, of course. Instead, the vicar rose from the table, signed to me to accompany him, and left the dining room. I did not follow immediately. It seemed rather frightful to walk out on the woman like that. I hesitated. Mrs. Coutts put her head down and began to cry. William Coutts rose from the table and stood kicking the edge of the fender in miserable and self-conscious embarrassment. He felt, I suppose, that there was something which ought to be said, something which ought to be done. The sight of his aunt's bowed head must have given him the most unpleasant sensations. The kicking of the fender grew unendurable to Mrs. Coutts, I think. Besides, she knew that Daphne and I were still in the room. She raised her head, glared through her tears at her nephew and cried impatiently :

" Oh, go away ! You and your din ! You and your everlasting din ! "

So we went, all three of us. Really, there was nothing else to do. We all felt pretty miserable, I think, even Daphne, who detested her aunt, of course.

CHAPTER IV

MAGGOTS IN THE CHURCH PORCH
AND PUBLIC HOUSE MAGGOTS

Mrs. Coutts concluded Sunday breakfast with a third cup of tea and a final despairing exhortation to the vicar to threaten, from the pulpit, all those who misbehaved at the fête on the following day. The vicar made no answer and went upstairs to put on his boots.

The service went off much as usual, except that a little shrivelled woman, with a yellow skin and beady black eyes, sat in the Gatty pew beside Mrs. Gatty and that little Mr. Gatty, who was a regular attender at Morning Prayer whenever he was home for the week-end, was absent from the service. Both the Burts turned up. Most unusual.

Immediately the Benediction had been pronounced, Mrs. Gatty rose from her knees and walked down the centre aisle to the church door. Mrs. Bradley hastened after her. The rustic congregation, standing while the vicar and I and the choristers passed into the vestry, gaped after them. The greatest surprise was still in store, however, for, as the congregation passed out of the church, Mrs. Gatty, who was standing beside the broken and ancient holy water stoup in the porch, pointed her finger at the squire and announced in clear tones :

" Thou wast once a lion, and wast killed by the jawbone of an ass."

This was so startling a rendering of the fact that Sir William, who had been an army officer, had found himself obliged to send in his papers because of malicious army-society gossip, that he turned very red, glared at Mrs. Gatty, and, almost dragging Margaret, who was holding his arm, hastened towards the lych gate and literally fled away. Mrs. Gatty next turned her attention to the innkeeper, a gross man, hairless and white-faced, with watery, pink-rimmed eyes. Although he got the cocoanuts cheap for us, I never really liked the man, good tempered though I always found him.

" And thou art unclean, pig that thou art," she pronounced. The innkeeper smiled, with admirable self-restraint, I thought.

" That's all right, Mrs. Gatty, ma'am," he said, kindly. The smile gave a pleasanter impression of the man. He walked on.

I was the next to come under Mrs. Gatty's notice. She pointed at me as the vicar and I came out at the vestry door.

" A kid of the goats ! A kid of the goats ! " she said. I blushed, I suppose. Anyway, I know I laughed.

" Oh, hang it, Mrs. Gatty ! " I protested, and I would have gone on talking, but that Mrs. Bradley signalled me to depart. I don't know why everybody obeys that little old woman.

Bransome Burns, the financier, was compared to a shark. He raised his hat in reply, and hastened down the road in pursuit of his host and his host's daughter. He had been called a shark before, I suppose. Several

Em

others received marks of attention from Mrs. Gatty,
and then Mrs. Bradley got her away, but not in time
to save the vicar, who was compared by Mrs. Gatty
to a curly-fronted bull ; his wife was referred to as a
camel and poor Daphne as a high-stepping, super-
cilious giraffe ; an obvious libel, as, at any other time,
I should have pointed out. Daphne took it well, of
course, and giggled readily, and all of us went back to
the vicarage pursued by the shrill comments of the
mistress of the Moat House. Luckily we had scarcely
thirty yards to go.

" I wonder where Mr. Gatty was ? " said Daphne
to me, as she lingered while I hung my hat on the hall
stand. I do not usually wear a hat, except on Sundays.
" Shall I come to the study and hear your headings ? "

I was to preach at Evensong, and, I don't know why,
preaching at Evensong always puts wind up me. I'm
all right in the morning, you know, but there is something about the solemn evening hour that gives me cold
feet. The vicar won't have the sermon read. He says
that a rustic congregation does not like it, and I think
it most likely that he is right. In spite of all the reasons,
however, why it was essential that I should go into the
pulpit well prepared, I rejoice to state that I put them
aside, and closing the study door behind us, I took
Daphne in my arms.

Whether I did rightly or wrongly, my luck held, and,
having taken a deep breath and a last look at Daphne's
face, I plunged into my discourse that evening, and for
nearly thirty-five minutes I held forth on the text,
" They shall run and not be weary ; they shall walk
and not faint."

Even the choirboys listened. I think they thought I was going to give them some tips for the sports on the morrow. So I did, as a matter of fact, for I talked, among other things, of the virtues of abstemiousness of all kinds. In fact, I preached the very sermon, in view of the Bank Holiday fête, that Mrs. Coutts would have given her ears to have the vicar preach. Both of them congratulated me afterwards, and Daphne held the lapels of my coat and told me that it was a lovely sermon, and that I was to ask her uncle, that night, for his consent to our engagement.

" What if he doesn't give it ? " I said. She replied :
" I wouldn't marry you without it, old thing."

This was a blow, as I considered it extremely unlikely that, with Daphne not yet nineteen, the vicar would consent to her binding herself. However, my luck was in. He listened until I had finished and then asked me about my prospects. Well, out of the thirty thousand, my mother and sisters had had twenty, of course, and I had retained the other ten. He seemed satisfied, and told me I was destined for a bishopric.

" You've a worldly outlook," he said. He hesitated a moment, and then added, " Of course, I don't want you two to marry yet. She isn't old enough. But you may have an understanding, if you choose."

I said to Daphne :
" Did you mean it when you said you wouldn't do it without your uncle's consent ? "

" Yes," she said. " So I'm glad he consented, Noel."

So was I, by the end of the next day. There was a row at the Mornington Arms that evening. (The vicar had done his best to get the magistrate to refuse a license to Lowry if he insisted upon opening on Sundays, but as Lowry undertook not to open until eight o'clock, when the service was over, he got his licence.) Curiously enough, the dust-up was between Lowry himself and his barman, Bob Candy. It seems that Candy had tried to get up to see Meg Tosstick and make her name the father of her baby, and had tried to shove Mrs. Lowry out of the way. She called out for Mr. Lowry, and Mr. Lowry came running up and ordered Bob out of the house. Bob thereupon turned round upon both the Lowrys and accused them roundly, in the presence of several witnesses, of terrorising the girl into keeping her mouth shut. The Lowrys were very indignant at this, and both tried to shout Bob Candy down, and five of the customers took him and locked him in the woodshed in case he should get violent. They don't seem to have been at all gentle with him ; probably, as he was the official chucker-out to the pub, they had some old scores to settle. Bob soon seems to have cooled off in the woodshed—owing, probably, to his unfortunate ancestry, he was terrified of the darkness—and he apologised to Mr. Lowry and begged to be set free, and they told him that Meg Tosstick, far from being terrorised at the inn, was being treated like their own daughter, and that the dear good vicar—old Coutts, of course—had asked that she should have every comfort and attention. All this was also said in front of several witnesses. Interesting evening at the Mornington Arms, I should imagine. Still, only one thing happened to mar the day, as far as I was concerned. Upset, I suppose, by the row at the inn, Bob Candy came round last thing at night—that is, at about eleven o'clock—to say that he would not play in the cricket match on the morrow. This was a fearful blow to us. Bob, although no scientist with a bat, was the sort of chap you find in some village teams—a man with a good eye and a gift for perfect timing. On his day you simply couldn't get him out. We always used to put him in first, because he was a highly restive, excitable sort of bloke underneath his bovine, brooding exterior, and would work himself up into a fearful state of nerves while waiting for his knock. So he went in first, and I've known him, not once, but twenty times, carry his bat. And he was no stonewaller, mind you. He would pick out unerringly and smite unmercifully every ball that was hittable. The others he would leave alone or block. He held a straight bat as though by nature. A natural player, in fact, if ever there was one. And as rotten a field as you'd meet in a fortnight's progress through the shires. We used to play him at mid-off, because village batsmen always hit to leg. It's using a scythe does it. Bred in the bone, those leg strokes of a village batsman. Bob had his uses at mid-off, of course. For instance, you could depend upon him to appeal, in a threatening bass, at every doubtful point in the game. Useful that, with an umpire like Sir William, who wants to do his best for the village, but isn't really taking much interest in the match. It guides his decision, so to speak. Unsporting, of course. But then, village cricket always is. That's what makes it so frightfully sporting, if you know what I mean.

Bob, therefore, was a real loss to us. He would give no reason for dropping out at the last minute, except to say that Lowry had given him a holiday until six o'clock and he didn't want to go to the fête, so he was going off by himself. In the end, we had to let it go at that. A cursed nuisance, of course. We argued for about an hour, but it was not a scrap of good. The poor mutt had made up his mind. Apart from this, I went to bed a happy man. I soon fell asleep, and dreamed about Daphne. It was one of those nebulous dreams. Nothing exactly happened, but we were together and I was extraordinarily bucked. William woke me at six-thirty on the following morning to come and bowl to him, and I was so full of beans that I actually arose from a perfectly comfortable bed, and went and did it. Got him second, fifth and seventh balls, too.

CHAPTER V

THE VILLAGE FÊTE

The fête at Saltmarsh was an all-day affair. The villagers paid sixpence to be admitted, and the tickets, printed by Daphne and perforated by me, were in three portions, so that persons who left the grounds to go home to a mid-day meal or to their tea, could be re-admitted without further charge. People from all the outlying villages came to the fête, and occasionally we got a beanfeast party in motor-coaches, or people from the adjacent seaside resort of Wyemouth Harbour. We reckoned upon taking twelve pounds at least in ticket and gate money, five pounds from the fair people, at least twenty pounds for refreshments—(this of course, was *not* all profit, since we had the caterers to pay) and anything from five pounds upwards from the various amusements .which we ourselves had staged. Of these, I may say that the cocoanut-shy was the most profitable, although we had made up our minds this year that the fortune-telling must be made a great success. The fortune-telling was an innovation, of course, and we wanted it to justify itself. It had been impossible to arrange it during the afternoon because of the cricket match, but stumps were to be drawn at six precisely, and it would take me less than half an hour to bathe, change, have my tea and sneak into the fortune-teller's little tent.

The match began at ten-thirty. We had first knock and made one hundred and five, of which I contributed thirty and the vicar a snappy twenty-seven. As at the last moment Bob Candy had refused to play, and, as we simply had not another male in the village who could hold a bat, so to speak, we consulted with the rival captain, a large, red fellow called Mogston, and decided to play Daphne, who added a beautiful twenty-six to the score and then touched a fast one and point held it.

It was turned two o'clock by the time our innings was over, so we adjourned for an hour and left Much Hartley just three hours in which to beat us.

" We *must* get them out," said the vicar. Old Brown, the constable, bowling slows, opened at the pavilion end, and I took the other. We had altered the field a bit to give Daphne the job of wicket-keeper, for she could get old Brown's slows all right, and was thoroughly accustomed to my bowling, of course. We were lucky from the outset—so lucky that I might have known something was going to happen. Their captain, a left-handed bloke, carted old Brown's first ball clean over my head into the road, and his second, curiously enough, into mid-off's hands. Bob Candy at mid-off would have dropped it as sure as eggs, but this mid-off, sometimes called William Coutts, stuck to it and shrieked his appeal. The umpire, Sir William, of course, woke up, started visibly, and gave the man out. The next bloke played out the over very cautiously. Then Daphne, the peach, picked my first ball off the bat, and their second man retired to the pavilion. Suffice it to say that we dismissed Much Hartley for seventy-nine runs in two and three-quarter hours.

Daphne and I made tracks for the vicarage, William made a bee-line for the fête, and the vicar stayed to give the visiting team their tea. The squire sheered off home for his tea, promising to return and help with the sports finals.

"Funny about Bob Candy," said Daphne, as I sat on the edge of my bed while she sewed me into my fortune-teller's skirt in order that no risks might be run of my coming apart in the excitement of the job. "He's so keen on cricket."

I hadn't time to talk about Bob Candy. To tell the truth, now that this fortune-telling stunt had come to fruition, I had the most fearful wind up. Besides, I had been in the open air for more than eight hours, all told, and I was tired and sleepy. However, the ghastly business had to be gone through with, so, putting my coat on over the get-up, and cramming the fortune-teller's beard, hair and hat into a small gladstone, I set out for the fête. I was lucky enough to get into the tent without attracting much notice. William, whose job it was to stand outside the tent and blow his scout's bugle until a crowd collected, was already on the scene. He stuck his head inside the opening of the tent.

"The cocoanut-shy is doing fine, Noel," he said. "Mr. Burt is the very chap for the job, and old Froth-blower is backing him up like a good 'un. How do you feel?"

"Rotten," I replied, getting out the appurtenances and sticking them on. "How do I look?"

"All right. Shall I start playing now?"

" I suppose so," I said. The little tent contained a small table and two chairs. Two candles, which I had lighted before I donned the hair, beard and hat of the fortune-teller, stood in saucers on the table. A skull, made of white calico and stitched on to a piece of black casement cloth, showed up rather eerily just beside me. William set his bugle to his lips and began to blow.

I suppose I put up a pretty good show, really, take it all in all. Of course, I got on better with our own village people than with the strangers, because I knew more about them. For the look of the thing, and so as not to give the show away, Daphne came in and had hers done. She murmured, as I bent over her hand :

" Nearly through, darling ! Stick it ! They are going to start the dancing in a minute. The Adj. has already gone into hiding, I expect. I haven't seen her about lately. I shall go home as soon as you've finished, I think. I'm awfully tired. We've to take William with us. Them's her orders. He won't half be sick, poor kid."

" How's Burt got on ? " I murmured.

" O.K. Also A.1. I like them, Noel. She may be a dreadful woman, though I wouldn't take the Adjutant's word for it, but she's got an awfully kind heart. Did you know uncle has had an awful row with Sir William over the children's sports ? Seems silly, doesn't it, but they say it was awful. All about nothing, too. You know those boys uncle turned out of the choir ? They claimed the right to run in the choirboys' hundred, because they had put their names down before they were chucked out, and Uncle wouldn't have it at

any price. Unfortunately, they had already run in
their heats, while uncle was playing in the cricket
match this morning, and both had qualified for the
final. The rotten part of it was that Sir William upheld
the boys. Uncle was furious, but he kept his temper.
Sir William lost his, and called uncle a something
parson in front of all the village people, so uncle
punched him in the eye and there was the most frightful schemozzle. Uncle stuck to his point, though, and
the whole race was abandoned. Sir William has gone
off in the most terrible rage, and his eye is swelling up
already. Isn't it a rotten, beastly thing to have happened ? "

I agreed, and was about to enter into the thing more
deeply when the flap of the tent was pushed aside and
young William came butting in.

" Noel ! Noel ! " he said, " Aunt Caroline's here and
she wants you at once. Uncle hasn't been home yet, and
it's nearly ten o'clock, and she's heard about the row
he had with Sir William, and she says you know what
Sir William's temper is, and she's worried to death.
I say, she *is* in a stew, so do buck up, there's a good
chap ! "

I did know what the Squire's temper was. Hadn't
I seen him trying to throttle the financier, Burns, merely
for treading on the dog ? What would he not do in
return for a punch in the eye in front of all the
village ! I pulled off hat, hair and beard, put on my
overcoat, blew out the candles, and, followed by
Daphne, I tore out of the tent, and, together with
William, we hastened to the vicarage.

Mrs. Coutts was not having hysterics, of course. She

was not the type for that. But she did look fearfully white and groggy. I volunteered to go and find Sir William and see what he could tell us of the vicar's movements after he had left the fête. Daphne volunteered to come too, but, much as I would have liked her company, I thought somebody ought to stay with Mrs. Coutts. I wouldn't have William, either, because I knew that his aunt would worry all the time he was out. Off I went, alone, therefore, to the Manor House, to see what was what. They were all in bed except Mrs. Bradley. The servants were all at the fête, so she came to the front door and let me in. From the park, through which I had just walked, came the sound of the brass band playing for the dancing. I entered the Manor House and followed Mrs. Bradley to the library, where there was a small but cheerful fire. She invited me to sit down and then she asked whether she had to cross my palm with silver. It says something for my state of mind that I had completely forgotten my gipsy costume. My overcoat had fallen away and disclosed a bright red skirt to her somewhat hawk-like gaze. I frowned and shook my head.

" No. I've come with rather serious news," I said. " The vicar can't be found. Er—we believe he had some sort of a dust-up with Sir William late in the afternoon, and it struck us, perhaps——"

" That the poor man may be lying at the bottom of the stone quarries with a broken neck," said the frightful little old woman.

" I'm not joking, you know," I said stiffly. Her remark seemed to me in poorish taste, of course.

" Neither am I, young man," she said, poking me in

the ribs with a forefinger like the end of an iron bolt. " So come along at once, in case he isn't dead."

" But is Sir William at home ? " I asked.

" Yes," she said. " And in any case I don't believe he would do the vicar any harm, but we'll go and see."

" But not the stone quarries ? " I said.

" Why not ? I've often thought them a perfect gift to a simple-minded murderer who could retain sufficient gumption to push his victim over the edge and then leave the thing alone, and keep his mouth shut and his nerves in working order."

" Footprints ? " I said.

" Grandmothers ! " retorted Mrs. Bradley with, I am bound to confess, a certain tartness in her tone which jarred upon me. I mean, I am one of those men who have simple faith in woman being the gentler sex and all that. Anyhow, the next thing I knew was that we were walking through the park, dodging the crowds. We called at Constable Brown's house and took him and his two lodgers, a couple of second year undergraduates named Miller and Bond who had been spending a few weeks in Saltmarsh to do some quiet reading, along to the vicarage to find out whether the vicar had turned up. He had not, so, shutting our ears to William's entreaties to be allowed to accompany us, we set out for the quarries. Mrs. Bradley had a powerful torch, Brown had his policeman's lamp and the two undergraduates carried a bicycle and a car lamp respectively. I walked with Mrs. Bradley, and, as we mounted the uneven track which led uphill to the quarries, an idea occurred to me which I communicated to Brown.

" Mr. Burt," I said, " who lives just over yonder at the Bungalow, would help in the search, I'm sure. Shall I go and knock him up ? "

Brown, who seemed oppressed with a sense of personal responsibility for the vicar's uncanny disappearance, assented, and we all took the road to the Bungalow. Two rooms were lighted up. I knocked at the door, but nobody came. Queer, of course. I knocked again, and waited, but there was no answer. Apparently Burt and Cora were still at the fête, so we proceeded with our search.

Even by day the stone quarries give me the hump. By night I found them quite alarming. I kept thinking of all the holes that weren't fenced, and tried to remember the paths where they were. We picked our way carefully along narrow paths made partly by men's feet and partly by sheep and ponies. We shouted as we went along, and queer echoes came back at us. We travelled in Indian file for a time, until Mrs. Bradley said :

" I think we ought to separate at the next junction of the paths."

Having no light, I decided to follow her. Miller came with us, and Bond and the constable bore away from us to the left. For two hours, I should think, we called and listened. It was useless to descend the quarries, of course, as well as extremely dangerous. We could check the position of the other party by the lights they were carrying. At last, as though by mutual consent, although nothing had been said, we foregathered and decided to return to the village. I think the constable still wondered what on earth induced us to come to the stone quarries, and I myself was beginning to think ridiculous my idea that the squire had done the vicar some mortal injury as a result of their quarrel.

" He's probably at home by now, cursing me for keeping him out of bed," I said to Mrs. Bradley.

" I am sure I hope so, young man," said the little old woman. I offered to escort her home, but she would not hear of it. However, I hope I know my duty to the sex, so I followed behind, and, in Indian file, we crossed the park, whence all the revellers had departed, and gained the front door. Sir William himself opened it. He was in pyjamas.

" Ah," said Mrs. Bradley, " and where did you leave the vicar, Sir William ? "

" The vicar ? " said Sir William. " On the sports field, damn his eyes ! The interfering, muddle-headed, self-opinionated damned ass ! Yes, and you can tell him so from me, Wells ! " he continued, suddenly spotting me behind Mrs. Bradley.

" Then you haven't made away with him ? " I said idiotically.

" I'd like to," said Sir William, savagely, " Are you coming in, or going out ? One or the other, only make up your mind quickly, because I'm going to shut this damned door."

" Good night. Good night, Mrs. Bradley," I said, as curtly as I could. Then I ran back to the vicarage. Brown and the undergraduates were there, but Mrs. Coutts was not. She came in about ten minutes later, sat down at the table with a face like chalk, and her fingers went drumming, drumming, on the cloth. She said that she had searched Sir William's shrubberies from end to end. Old Brown had his helmet off and was scratching his head in the intervals of assuring us all that there was nothing more to be done until the morning. William was standing by his aunt and looking washed out and scared stiff. My poor little Daphne was crying, and the two undergraduates were trying to stifle their yawns and betray their concern at one and the same time. Of course, it was after twelve midnight by this time, and we were all just about all in.

I was able to assure them that I felt certain the squire had done Mr. Coutts no bodily injury. This had its effect. Brown and the undergraduates made a move towards the door. Daphne sat up and dried her eyes. Two spots of colour came into Mrs. Coutts' cheeks. Suddenly young William hooted :

" I say ! Mrs. Gatty's locked him up, I bet ! Like she did Mr. Gatty in the crypt ! *You* know ! "

There was a sensation. Dash it, it seemed quite feasible. The poor woman was bats enough for anything. So off I went with Brown to the Moat House, leaving Bond and Miller to hold the fort at the vicarage.

The Gattys were in bed, and were not too pleased at being disturbed. Old Gatty was distinctly querulous, in fact, and wanted to know what the hell, and a lot of things like that when we hiked him out of bed to answer a few leading questions. He is one of those weird birds who wear night shirts. Most embarrassing !

When he heard the news, however, he calmed down and was most obliging. He went into the bedroom—we were interviewing him just outside his bedroom door with two startled maidservants goggling at us over the banisters of the landing above—and dug Mrs. Gatty out of bed. She appeared in curling rags and a dressing-gown and with her gold-rimmed pince-nez stuck firmly on her nose. I suppose she slept in them, or didn't feel dressed without them, or something.

" The vicar ? " she said.

" Yes," we said.

" Dear me ! "

" Yes."

" Missing ? "

" Yes."

" You know," said Mrs. Gatty, in the voice of one who sees a great light, " he must have fallen down the stone quarries. Most dangerous, those workings. I've always said so."

You know, she really sounded quite sane, and old Gatty looked at us as one who should say :

" All done by kindness, mesdames and messieurs ! "

We took our leave, and Brown returned to his home and I to the vicarage. We sent William to bed, and, in the end, I persuaded the others to go, too. Mrs. Coutts, I expect, lay awake all night, but having left the door unbolted, so that, if the vicar should return, he could let himself into the house with his key, I rolled into my bed and was soon asleep. I was pretty well tired out, you know, what with one thing and another.

CHAPTER VI

A STUDENT OF DICKENS

At about five-thirty next morning I was awakened by William Coutts. His shining face, wet with perspiration and beaming with unholy joy and fierce excitement, loomed over me as I opened my eyes.

" I say, Noel ! Oh, do wake up, you fool ! Listen ! I say ! Noel ! Noel ! "

He thumped me vigorously and blew into my right ear, which was uppermost. My first thought was that I was back at school, so I sat up in bed with the idea of getting some rotter's head in chancery and jolly well giving him beans. Then the identity of my assailant dawned on me, and so I merely rubbed my eyes and prepared to curse him.

" Get up ! " commanded young William, before I could produce the book of words germane to the situation. " I've found him ! "

" What ! " I said, wide awake, of course. " Where ? "

" In the pound," said William, " and I can't get him out. He's chained up."

Without stopping to reflect upon the peculiar nature of the tidings, I put on my shirt and trousers, thrust my feet into my boots, tied the laces, of course, and in about twenty seconds I was tearing after William down the stairs.

We had an ancient pound in the village. It was upon

the village green. It was practically a historical monument, of course. Never used. Anyway, the vicar was in it. A huge stake had been driven into the ground, and the vicar, gagged with a leather driving glove and an army puttee—(can you have it in the singular? I suppose you can ! It was only one, anyway, of course) —was tethered to it by a collar and chain. His arms were bound, and he looked the wildest, filthiest, angriest, most disreputable person in creation. The collar was padlocked on him, but I managed to detach the end of the chain from the stake and to remove the gag.

" Don't attempt to talk, sir," I said. " Good thing William found you so early in the morning."

He'd been pretty well knocked about. His mouth was pretty badly bruised and the knuckles of both hands were cut almost to the bone.

" Yes," he said, looking at his hands with what the books call gloomy satisfaction, " if my assailants were local people, it won't be hard to pick 'em out. I *think*— I *ra*-ther think !—I've left my mark on them."

This was after he'd had a rest and some bread and milk. I shot a stiffish dose of brandy into the pig-food before he started on it. Mrs. Coutts remonstrated, but, for once in our lives, we ignored the woman. I'm all for temperance, of course, but if ever a man needed— *needed*, mind you !—a drop of the amber adder, it was poor old Coutts. He was pretty far gone, take him one way and another. I think it was only his frightful annoyance that kept him up at all. His tale was a curious one, and when we had heard it, I said immediately :

" Mrs. Bradley is the person to get to the bottom of all this."

Briefly, the yarn was as follows :

After having had the row with Sir William Kingston-Fox over the final of the choirboys' hundred yards, old Coutts, in accordance with custom, returned to the vicarage, got himself a glass of lemonade and some bread and cheese and a handful of raisins, and settled down, with the wireless, to have a pleasant evening. However, what with the row he had had with Sir William getting thoroughly on his nerves, and the beastly wireless clicking a foreign station that *would* butt in and ruin the concert he was listening to, he got thoroughly fed, and decided to go out for a walk as far from the fête as he could.

He had been tinkering with the radio set for some time, trying to cut out the interference, and had taken a bit of time to get his meal and eat it, and so forth, so that it must have been, he thinks, round about nine o'clock when he left the vicarage, but it might have been later. With the idea of getting clear away from the fête, the raucous music of the roundabouts and all that, he walked up towards the stone quarries and down to the beach by Saltmarsh Cove. He walked fast, and was pretty tired when he reached the cove, so he sat on a bit of rock and gazed at the sea and decided it was a good chance for a swim. Bit of a Spartan, old Coutts, of course. It was getting dark by that time. (You can't reach the cove in less than an hour and a half from the vicarage, even going all out.) He stripped off his flannels—he had been playing cricket during the day, of course, against Much Hartley—and pushed them just into the entrance to the Cove, as the tide was almost out. He had his swim—a lazy one, he admits—and was rubbing himself as dry as he could on a hand-kerchief—ever tried it ?—when he was surprised to see a lantern swung rhythmically three times out at sea, apparently from the rail of a ship. He was interested, because there was no reason that he could think of for a ship to anchor out there. She must be taking a risk, he thought, to do so. She must be lying off an unin-habited island called Skall Rock, but the channel between the island and some totally submerged rocks was known to very few people indeed, and those strictly local men. No big ships could make the passage, and even small ones ran considerable risk in attempting it. Besides, there was no point in attempting it, as the way into Wyemouth Harbour was clearly charted, and was marked, where necessary, by buoys. He screwed up his eyes and thought he could just make her out. Sud-denly, as he was thinking all this out, a beam from the ship's searchlight fell clear upon him, and was im-mediately withdrawn. At the same time a lantern was swung three times again, this time from higher up—from the bridge—he thinks it must have been from the bridge—it looked high off the water anyway. It was all a bit queer, but he was getting chilly, so he ran about a bit to finish drying, put on his clothes and was about to reach for his straw hat when somebody behind him, who must have come up like a cat, gave him a terrific shove in the back, and down he went. Before he knew what was happening, some great bloke fell on him. He put up a good show, he said, and, if his knuckles were anything to go by, I should say he did ! However,

another fellow came up and they got him gagged at
last, blindfolded him, tied him up and carted him along,
by devious ways, to the pound. Weird ! They must have
spotted our torches and dodged us—Brown, Mrs.
Bradley, the two students and myself,—while we were
searching for him. Or he must have been in the pound
by then. Everybody else was still at the fête, or else in
bed. They didn't meet a soul, anyway, Coutts thinks.
Well, I mean, they couldn't have done ! What a neck,
though ! Both his captors had blackened faces, he
thought. An old poachers' trick, that, to avoid being
recognised. And neither spoke a word. They communicated with one another in series of grunts. Well, I mean,
it's jolly difficult to recognise a chap by his grunt, as
witness those frightful parlour games we all have played
at times. One is called " Mum " and the other, I believe
is known to the trade as " Squeak, Piggy, Squeak."
Anyway, they grunted their intentions to one another,
and one drove the stake into the middle of the pound
and they both chained him up as I've already described.
They left him gagged, but took the bandage off his eyes.
We tried to get him to make a guess at the fellows'
identity, but he couldn't hazard a single one. It was
very dark, of course. He hadn't seen them clearly at all.
We had to look out, he said, for two big fellows, one
of whom had a face that looked as though it had been
hit by the front of an express train.

" I know I didn't mark one of 'em, the bigger one,"
he said, " because he kept out of my reach. But the
other must look like the outside page of a kids' comic
paper. So if they're local men——"

He seemed not so keen on the idea of lugging Mrs.

Bradley into it, but I put the point so forcefully that he agreed. Daphne and I went off to Sir William's house, and I, for one, had a certain interest in seeing Sir William himself. He was biggish. True, I couldn't quite imagine him blacking his face in order to escape recognition ; neither could I see him calling in assistance, in the form of another black-faced desperado, to settle a private quarrel. Still, they had had a fearful row, he and the vicar, so really the whole thing was a bit of a coincidence. The Squire had the very devil of a temper, and the vicar's peculiar code would probably forbid him to name the squire as his assailant even if he had recognised him....

I was in the midst of decanting these theories to Daphne when we arrived at the lodge gates of Sir William's park and, entering, began to cross the park to the house.

Talk about the morning after the night before, or the abomination of desolation ! The park was in a simply fearful state. The turf was torn, worn, wheel-rutted and strewn with bits of paper, banana and orange peel, broken bottles, confetti, a hat, three odd gloves at least—(I speak of what we could see as we walked along !)—empty chocolate boxes, bits of cocoanut ; the father and mother of a horrible, disgraceful mess. I'm a member of an anti-litter society, and so I know what the many-headed can do when it chooses, but, upon my word, I've never seen anything to equal the state of Sir William Kingston-Fox's park on that August morning. It had not rained a bit during the night, which probably made matters a bit better than they might have been. And yet, I don't know ! It was awful !

Sir William's face was as usual. Not marked at all, I mean, except for the rather puffy eye he had received from the vicar at the sports. He heard our story, as did Mrs. Bradley, Bransome Burns, the financier, Margaret Kingston-Fox, and Storey, who was waiting at table. He coughed—Storey, I mean—as an indication that he had something to say.

" If you please, Sir William——"

" Well ? "

" It sounds as though the smugglers had begun their games again."

" Oh, rubbish ! Rubbish ! This is not America, Storey."

" No, Sir William. It just occurred to me, that's all. Saltmarsh Cove was a regular smugglers' hole in my great-grandfather's time, sir, and there's an underground passage to the inn, sir, or so I've heard tell, although I believe it is blocked up now."

" Ah, very likely. Wells," he said, suddenly turning to me, " this is serious, you know. As a magistrate, I say that it is very serious indeed ! The vicar of Saltmarsh to be assaulted in his own parish ! Upon my word, it's really monstrous ! He marked the men, you say ? "

" One of them, Sir William," I replied, trying to keep my face straight. Hang it all, *he* would have been the first person to assault the vicar in his own parish, had not the vicar assaulted him first ! Daphne said :

" Yes ; his poor hands ! "

" Ah," said Sir William. " Then all we have to do is to find the fellow the vicar marked so severely, and get from him the name of his accomplice, and get the couple of them a spell of hard labour, the damned scoundrels ! "

He looked round after tenderly feeling his eye. Margaret said :

" They are probably not local people, Daddy."

Mrs. Bradley said :

" In the pound, you say ? "

" Yes," I replied.

" Curious," said the little old woman. " It was only on Sunday that Mrs. Gatty was calling him a bull. The bull strayed on to someone else's land and was put in the pound."

She fixed her black eyes on me.

" Do you read the Pickwick Papers, young man ? "

" I have read them, yes," I replied. As a matter of fact I'm fond of the book.

"Aha !" said Mrs. Bradley. "A little of Dickens and a little of Gatty, and what a curious situation arises !"

She chortled in a way that made one's blood run cold, and then helped herself to kidneys and bacon from the sideboard. Did I say we had arrived at breakfast time ?

" Oh, how do you mean, Mrs. Bradley ? " I asked. She wagged her fork at me and grinned fiendishly.

" What happened when Captain Boldwig found Mr. Pickwick asleep in the barrow ? " she asked. I racked my brain.

" After the shooting ? " I said.

" Yes, and after the lunch :

Complete with cold punch," said Mrs. Bradley,

positively hooting with mirth at her own absurd rhyme.

" Why, the captain ordered his servant to wheel Mr. Pickwick to the pound," said I, " He was trespassing on his land, or something, wasn't he ? But then, Mr. Coutts wasn't trespassing. He was——"

" Obviously he was where he wasn't wanted," said Mrs. Bradley.

" By Jove ! " I said, struck by an idea. " I'll get one or two men to help me, and we'll go along there to-night, and see what happens. Surely five or six of us should be a match for a couple of roughnecks, shouldn't we ? "

" Don't go, Noel," said Daphne.

" Let him go," said Mrs. Bradley. " Nothing on earth will happen, child."

" How do you know ? " said the squire. " I myself will come with you, Wells, and, by the powers, I'll bring along half a dozen of my own men, fellows I can thoroughly trust. Meet you outside Burt's bungalow at nine o'clock to-night."

In its way it was quite a bit of excitement, of course, and I found myself swanking along the village street as though I were the chief of the Chicago police planning to clean up the city. But, as things turned out, when we did go to patrol the sea-shore, we were not only on the track of the men who had attacked the vicar but, as we thought, on the track of the man who killed Meg Tosstick. As though there were not mystery enough surrounding that poor girl, the next thing we heard was that she had been strangled at some time between nine o'clock and ten-thirty on the night of the Bank

Holiday, and that there was no sign anywhere of the baby. People must actually have been dancing, or I myself may even have been concluding the fortune-telling, while that poor girl was being done to death. It was the most shocking and dreadful news I think any of us had ever had. Brown, the village constable, panting and exhausted, came to the vicarage soon after Daphne and I had returned from Sir William's house, and told us what had happened. Then the vicar had to tell his story, for he bore too many marks of the fray to be able to hush the thing up. Old Brown shook his head.

" Mark my words, Mr. Coutts, sir," he stated solemnly, " it's the same gang. I wonder what their game is ? "

" How was she killed ? " asked Mrs. Coutts.

" With a gent's 'and-knitted silk tie, ma'am," replied Brown. " It had been put round her neck, tied in a bow in front, like as if someone had been having a little friendly joke with her, and then a wooden clothes peg had been used to make what the First Aid books calls a tourniquet. Oh, she's not a nice sight, ma'am. She isn't really, poor young gal. Got a nasty lump on 'er 'ead, too, but strangling was the cause of death, the doctor says."

Well, that was the way in which we received the news. Brown had been called on to the scene by Lowry after Mrs. Lowry, going to take the poor girl her break-fast in bed—for she still was accustomed to remain in bed for the greater part of the day—made the dread-ful discovery of her death. Brown had called in Doctor Fosse, and then had rung up the police station at Wyemouth Harbour, our nearest town, and they had promised to send down an inspecter. Brown was easily the most important man in the village that day, I should think, although the Lowrys ran him close in reflected glory and personal popularity. A small crowd of villagers was outside the inn every time I passed that way, and knots of boys followed Brown wherever he went.

Of course, look at it as you please, it was a most inexplicable thing. One hears of girls being murdered when a baby is going to be born and the show, so to speak, is going to be given away thereby. There have been classic instances, followed usually by mutilation of the body, decapitation to avoid identification, and games of that sort. But the plain facts of our Saltmarsh affair were, first, that the baby had been in the world for eleven whole days before its mother was murdered ; secondly, that there was no reason why anybody should have wanted the poor girl out of the way, apart from the baby business, and (see above, so to speak), if the father, whoever he was, didn't want to acknowledge paternity, why should he ? Did he think the girl would give him away ? What was the mystery ?

Struck by a sudden thought, I said to Mrs. Coutts : " I suppose the poor girl did *have* a baby ? "

She said :

" Whatever do you mean ? There was no doubt at all that when she left my service she was pregnant."

" Ah, well, that's that, then," I said. " It had just struck me that, as no one seems to have seen this baby, and as it has completely disappeared since the murder, it might never have existed."

A bright and thoughtful opinion, I considered.

"You need not worry," said the woman, viciously. "That baby has been moved, with the connivance of the Lowrys, to some home approved of by its natural father. Nobody was allowed to see that baby, my dear Noel, for a very good and sufficient reason. You mark my words ! That baby *resembled* somebody too closely for its father's comfort. That's the reason for all this mystery surrounding the baby."

She snapped out the words as though they had been said on a typewriter.

"So you think the father killed the mother, in case she should give him away ? " I suggested, going on with what seemed to me the logical sequence of the story. "That is the police theory, too, I believe." I was wrong about that, of course.

Mrs. Coutts suddenly swayed, and pitched forward. I had never seen anybody faint before. She went dead off. I was fearfully alarmed. It was the merest luck, or sheer instinct, or something, which prompted me to freeze on to her before she struck her head. Dicky heart, of course. She had looked very groggy since she had reported old Coutts' absence on the night of the fête. Very groggy.

The police from Wyemouth Harbour and an inspector and the Chief Constable of the County all came down during the course of the day, and the village positively hummed. We got a fair crop of reporters, too, all seething with enthusiasm, and hosts of amateur detectives (holiday-makers from Wyemouth Harbour, chiefly), hunting for clues—or rather, souvenirs of the murder. Frightfully ghoulish, the many-headed, of course.

William Coutts went snooping, too, and apparently walked into a hornets' nest up at the Bungalow. He had spent a hot and dirty couple of hours in and about the Cove and the quarries, and then decided to call at the Bungalow to pick up any fresh trail, he said, but I concluded that he meant to see whether he would be asked to stay to lunch. The front door was open, as usual, so he walked in, and was just going to barge into the dining-room, whence he could hear voices, when it was borne in on him that Burt and Cora were having the most frightful row. He didn't stay, of course. He heard the words :

" —get a damned good hiding if I hear any more of it ! Yes, and that Tired Business Man ! Blast his eyes ! "

" —beastly old hole, enough to make a pig home-sick ! "

" —pig is what I said ! And now get on ! You'll miss that train."

Then he came away. I imagine that Cora and Burt quarrelled a good deal. They were both hot-headed, I had decided, and as I said before, it couldn't have been much of a life for a gay-living high-spirited young woman of Cora's type and mentality.

But all minor excitements paled before the great blaze of terror and thrills that followed the discovery of the murder.

William, I know, slept with his heaviest catapult under his pillow, and I shrewdly suspect that Mrs. Coutts used to put the kitchen poker on the chair beside her bed. I took care to accompany Daphne even into the garden to pick gooseberries and garden peas. At night I made a point of tapping upon her bedroom door and enquiring whether she was all right. She always was, of course.

On the Tuesday afternoon and evening the men of the village, headed by the squire and the vicar, who had sunk their private differences in this terrible affair of the murder, and supported strongly by William Coutts and the local Boy Scouts, determined to track down the beast who had killed the poor girl. I dug out Burt, who, with his brains and physique certainly would have been a match for any murderer. He agreed willingly to help us, the more so as he was feeling a bit at a loose end, for Cora McCanley had received an offer by telegram that same morning to appear in a piece called *Home Birds* which was touring the provinces, and he supposed he would not see her again until after Christmas. Not that he seemed to care much. The row, I suppose.

Our first task was to patrol the shore by the Cove, but, although we kept it up from seven in the evening until nearly one in the morning, nothing happened at all. Personally, I could not believe that there had been no connection between the attack on the vicar and the murder of the girl. We were harbouring Thugs in the village. When we arrived home, Mrs. Coutts, William and Daphne were all in bed. The vicar went into his wife's room, and the next moment I heard him calling me.

"Get some sal volatile from Daphne," he said. It was rather nice to see Daphne asleep, but I was compelled to wake her for the stuff.

It appeared that Mrs. Coutts had been out to look for us when it got dark, had missed her way and nearly fallen down one of the unfenced quarries. She was rather bad.

And, blow me, if, on the Wednesday, another beastly mysterious affair didn't occur which put the most fearful wind up Daphne and myself.

As Mrs. Coutts was so very groggy, and complained of her heart and a bad headache and shock to the system, Daphne had to go down to the church and play the organ for the Women's Weekly Prayer Meeting and Devotional.

This was Mrs. Coutts' job really, so Daphne, who was rather taken on the hop, thought she had better go along at about half-past six that evening and practise the hymns. Although I say it that love her, Daphne is not at her best on the organ unless she's had considerable practice first. So we arranged to put in an hour from six-thirty to seven-thirty when the meeting was billed to begin.

I say " we," because, since the attack on William and myself outside the Bungalow, Daphne had been exceedingly nervous, and so I had fallen into the habit of " standing by." We kept this pretty little fact to ourselves, because Mrs. Coutts would not have approved.

So I accompanied Daphne to the church and worked the beastly bellows for her. She was in the middle of " Lead, Kindly Light," and doing well, when I heard the music stop.

" Gee up ! " I said loudly and encouragingly. There was no answer, so I slid round, to see what was what.

" Oh, Noel ! " said Daphne. She threw her arms round me, clutching me tightly.

" Somebody put their hands on my neck ! Somebody put their hands on my neck ! " she said.

It was about five past seven then, and the verger came and lit up, and the earliest arrivals began to trickle in. I thought, to be quite honest, that Daphne was suffering from nerves. Nobody had come into the church unless they had come in from the vestry, and that was always kept locked. We ourselves had come in by the west door so as not to bother old Coutts for the keys.

" I shrieked your name as soon as I felt the hands on me," said Daphne, when the meeting was over and we were on our way home. Old Coutts had stayed behind to talk to some of the congregation, of course. Although the incident had given me quite a jolt, I would not discuss the subject with Daphne. I was certain really she had been imagining things. But I promised to stand by more closely than ever, and advised her to lock her door at night as an antidote to nerves. We were all suffering from nerves, more or less, that week, I think.

I told Mrs. Bradley about it, of course. She looked more grave than I expected.

" Don't let her go about alone, Noel," she said. " After all, no arrest has been made yet for the murder of Meg Tosstick. It may take place to-day. But keep close to little Daphne. They may not arrest the right person, you know ! "

She gave her ghoulish chuckle and patted me on the shoulder.

CHAPTER VII

EDWY DAVID BURT—HIS MAGGOT

The police arrested Bob Candy, of course. It seems that in these murder cases the police are always looking out for two things ; motive and opportunity. Well, it appeared that poor Bob headed the list of possible suspects very easily on both counts. In fact, I mean, if one didn't know Bob Candy, it looked a clear thing. Nobody denied that he had walked out with the girl ; everybody denied that it was his baby. If it had been, he would have married Meg Tosstick, according to the local custom, and there would have been an end of the matter, except for the nine or ten children that the two of them would produce, and the two or three out of those nine or ten that would eventually live to become adult, and, in their turn, to procreate others. Bob denied paternity of the baby, and everybody, even the police, believed him, because the police took the view that jealousy was the motive for the murder. As for opportunity, well, the two of them were living under the same roof and it would have been the simplest thing in the world for Candy to have sneaked into Meg's room at night and strangled her as she lay in bed. As far as the method of doing the girl to death was concerned, there was no doubt at all but that she had been strangled with the man's knitted silk tie which was still round her neck when her dead body was discovered by

Mrs. Lowry next morning. The tie was proved to have been given to Bob on his birthday by the dead girl, who had knitted it, as her weeping old devil of a father bore witness, " with her own hands for him." In reply to this, Bob was understood to state that the tie was his, but that, thoroughly upset by the birth of the baby, he had cast it aside and had sworn never to wear it any more. Pressed, he said that he could not remember exactly where he had put it. He thought he had thrown it away, and then again, he might have thrust it into a drawer, carelessly, but, on the other hand, he had a vague recollection of having used it as a lead for a lurcher he had had to bring to the public-house from the railway station the Saturday before Bank Holiday. He admitted, sadly, that it was a wonderfully strong tie. It was, of course.

Sir William undertook to pay for the man's defence, and he took some trouble to broadcast his belief in Candy's innocence. Curiously enough, our own Constable Brown also refused to credit Candy with the murder. It was the inspector from Wyemouth who ordered the arrest after the adjourned inquest. Poor old Brown was quite upset about it.

" It's like this, Mr. Wells," he said to me. " These town chaps is all right in their way, but it isn't like *knowing* a chap. Now, I've knowed Bob Candy since he were seven or eight years of age, and I *know* he never done this 'ere murder. I tells the inspector so. ' Proof,' he says, ' proof ! ' I scratches my head, at that, Mr. Wells, because, things being how they are, it looks black again him. No doubt of that. So they arrests him. Well, I look at it this way. Somebody done it, didn't un ?

And that somebody weren't Bob. So what we got to do is to find out who that somebody were before this 'ere old trial of Bob's come along, and make an end of poor young chap."

Right on the meat, of course. But there was the beastly motive. After all, who on earth, except Bob Candy, had any motive for killing the girl? I put this to old Brown. He took off his helmet and wiped the inside of it with his handkerchief.

" Don't you think, Mr. Wells," he said, " that the father of the baby might have done it? "

" Yes, perhaps," I said. " On the other hand, the baby was born about a fortnight before the murder, and the cat was well and truly out of the bag, so to speak. I mean, in the classic cases, the murder is to prevent the birth of the child, isn't it? "

" Is it? " said old Brown. " Anyway," he added, stoutly, " I'm going to keep my ears and eyes open, Mr. Wells. There's been some very funny things happening, and poor old Bob can't be held responsible for all of them. He hasn't got the head on him, for one thing, and he hasn't got no accomplices, for another. What about the parson being put in that there old pound? "

Well, of course, as soon as you got on to the subject of poor Bob's brains, where were you? It was another point against him that there was that unfortunate affair of the escaped lunatic in the middle of his family tree. I mean, it seems as though this game of strangling young females is a proper lunatic's trick, and Bob Candy's ancestry told against him somewhat heavily.

I was returning from visiting rounds in the parish one

afternoon during the second week in August when I encountered Mrs. Bradley. She was walking along with her eyes fixed on the ground and did not see me until I said, " Good afternoon."

" Ah, here you are," she said. Quite brisk and businesslike. I gazed round for assistance but there was none available. " I want you," she said, fixing me with the most frightfully basilisk eye, " to introduce me into the bosoms of certain families in this village. Dear little Edwy David Burt for example. Are you really friendly with him ? "

Well, I was at the time, of course. Burt had upheld the cocoanut shy nobly during my enforced absences on August Bank Holiday, and I had indicated as much to him. A stout fellow, Burt.

" What about him ? " I said cautiously.

" I'm on the track of the person who murdered that girl," said Mrs. Bradley, " and I want to clear a few things out of the way."

" Including Burt ? " I asked, with an attempt at facetiousness.

" Including funny little Burt," said Mrs. Bradley, gravely. She grasped my sleeve. " You and Constable Brown and I are going to bring a murderer to justice," she said, with the most frightful leer.

" You mean——" I burbled.

" I want your help," she said. " I require your invaluable assistance, child. Who so respectable as the earnest young curate ? Who so universally adored as the handsome, untidy, almost illiterate young man who has not had occasion yet to quarrel with his bishop ? "

She yelled with laughter, let go of my sleeve and dug me in the ribs.

" Do you believe Bob Candy did it ? " she said.

" No," I replied truthfully, " I am sure he did not." I moved out of the reach of her claw-like hand.

" Then up with the bonnets of bonny Dundee," said Mrs. Bradley, taking my arm. " To Burt's bungalow— boot, saddle, to horse and away ! "

Burt was out, of course. This did nothing to deter my frightfully energetic companion.

" Never mind," she said, " let us go and see Mr. and Mrs. Gatty. There are one or two questions that I am simply bursting to put to that delicious pair ! "

Mr. and Mrs. Gatty were at home. He was snipping off the dead roses and she was mowing the lawn. Both stopped working when they saw us and came to greet us.

" We've come about the murder," said Mrs. Bradley. " I suppose you two dear people will sign a petition for poor Bob Candy ? "

" But he hasn't been convicted yet," objected little Gatty.

" We want to be prepared," said Mrs. Bradley solemnly. " Do come indoors and sign. It won't take a minute. Come along, Mr. Wells. You will have to witness his signature. Mrs. Coutts is getting up the petition, of course," she explained to old Gatty, who had put down his scissors and gardening gloves on the wheelbarrow and was meekly accompanying us into the house. He gazed with distaste at the entrance hall of his gloomy residence.

" I do wish I could persuade Eliza to move," he

said. " I do hate and fear this beastly house, but she's quite attached to it."

I must confess that this remark by Gatty nearly flabbergasted me. It was generally understood in the village that Mrs. Gatty was in a terribly nervous state owing to the influence of the ex-lunatic asylum upon her system. Now, to hear Gatty seriously asserting that he was the nervous one and that his wife was the one who was determined to stay on at the house, was rather a jolt. I was about to enter into an argument with him about it when Mrs. Bradley forestalled me by saying :

" I thought your wife disliked the house ? "

" Far from it," replied Gatty. " Where's this petition you want me to sign ? "

He grinned. Well, he *was* rather like a wolf, of course. A sudden thought struck me.

" I suppose it wasn't you on the roof of Burt's bungalow that night ? " I said.

He looked a bit flummoxed, but answered up like a shot.

" It was, Mr. Wells."

" Well, but, well, I mean to say ! " I said.

" What do you mean to say ? " asked Mrs. Bradley, turning a none too cordial glance on me. At least, it looked a bit frosty when I met it, which I did, squarely, of course. I believe the woman thought she was going to intimidate me !

" Well, I mean to say, he might have murdered somebody," I stuttered, anxious in a way to placate the old lady, who was now looking too fierce for my comfort. Besides, I was anxious too, very anxious, of course, to know what he meant by bunging slates at me that night. " What's the idea ? " I continued, severely to Gatty. Gatty wilted a bit. I stand five feet eleven in my socks.

" It was Burt's fault," said Gatty, getting a bit red round the ears. " He shouldn't have locked me in that horrible crypt. I had no idea that he would play me such a prank."

I was about to exclaim when Mrs. Bradley accidentally knocked Gatty's fountain pen out of his hand, and we all bent and groped for it. It took us so long to find it—(my private belief is that Mrs. Bradley had had it in her hand for several minutes, for she was the one who eventually handed it back to him)—that my remark faded. Mrs. Bradley had a large sheet of paper on which were several signatures, and Gatty wrote his name under the rest, and we prepared to take our leave. We waved to Mrs. Gatty, who was at the further end of the garden, and regained the road.

" Some time," said Mrs. Bradley, thoughtfully. " I must go into the question of lying much more thoroughly. I wonder why Mrs. Gatty lies ? Is it for fear, compensation or wantonness, I wonder ? "

" But *does* she lie ? " I asked.

" Certainly," said Mrs. Bradley. " And, by the way, young man, if you are to be of any real assistance to me in this enquiry, you must not ask direct questions of the people I am interviewing. You'll spoil everything if you do. Tell me some more about the roof of Burt's bungalow," she added.

" About Gatty, do you mean ? " I asked.

" About Gatty. So nice to know it wasn't a thug,"

said Mrs. Bradley, nodding her head. " All the details, please."

So I told her the tale all over again.

" I must go back to the Moat House," she said, when I had finished. " There is just one thing I must get clear. You stay here, dear child."

" Not much," I said. She seemed such a little old woman, and I didn't like those wolf-teeth that Gatty showed when he smiled. Gatty and his wife had changed jobs. He was mowing the lawn now, and she was attending to the roses.

" Here are Mrs. Crocodile and Mr. Goat," she called to her husband. He let go the mowing machine and came toward us. I could not but admire Mrs. Bradley's forthright methods. She said at once :

" How did you say you got down into the crypt ? "

" I was thrust down there by Burt and his negro," said Gatty. I gasped. He had distinctly told me that he went there as the result of a bet. Apparently he had forgotten that. So both the Gattys were liars, it seemed !

" Why ? " asked Mrs. Bradley. " Had you annoyed him in any way ? "

" I don't think so. I believe he has some secret and that I was within an ace of finding it out. It was the night my car broke down outside Wyemouth and I had to walk home by way of the Cove and the stone quarries. I was just poking about when they seized me and carried me to the church. I can't think why we didn't meet anybody. When you had set me free, I decided to go to Burt's bungalow and find out what I could, by way of revenge. Just fancy, I was in that dreadful place for about thirty-six hours ! So I climbed on to the roof of Burt's bungalow that night when I had had food and some rest, and tried to see down the sky-light into his loft. I couldn't see anything. It was much too dark. So I scrabbled about a bit and was unlucky enough to loosen two tiles. They slipped as Mr. Wells here and the lad Coutts came out on to the path. I was terribly alarmed. I thought at first the tiles had struck them. I was hiding behind the chimney stack out of reach of Burt's horrible gun when they slipped from my hand. I still believe Burt's got some game on, and I still mean to find out what it is ! "

" Good for you," said Mrs. Bradley, cordially. " Good luck to your mowing."

He looked at her as though she was mad, sighed, and pushed the mowing machine forward. Mrs. Bradley turned to find Mrs. Gatty standing at her elbow.

" Darling Croc," said Mrs. Gatty, "why do you talk with the wolf ? "

" Dearest Cassowary," retorted Mrs. Bradley, " who told you the wolf was in the crypt ? "

" Nobody told me," said Mrs. Gatty, beaming at us both through her gold-rimmed glasses like any com-fortable woman of fifty. " I saw him down there. Oh, that's wrong. Mr. Burt told me. He thought I should go and let him out, I think ! "

She began to giggle at the recollection.

" And didn't you try to get him out ? " I asked. Mrs. Bradley suddenly prodded me in the ribs. I had forgotten her commands, of course. I muttered an apology, but the mischief, whatever it was, was done. Mrs. Gatty grew grave, and answered :

" No, I didn't try to get him out. It was so *right*, you
see. It was so satisfying. I peeped at him—he didn't see
or hear me—and then I came home and thought about
him, and then, when I knew he was asleep, I went and
spoke to him."

I looked appealingly at Mrs. Bradley. In that in-
stinctive way which women have, she seemed to understand me. Almost imperceptibly she nodded her head.
Emboldened, I asked Mrs. Gatty what she had said to
her husband while he was asleep in the crypt.

" I said, ' Bogey ! Bogey ! ' " replied Mrs. Gatty
solemnly. I shouted with laughter. Mrs. Bradley laughed.
Mrs. Gatty laughed, and up came little Gatty to
know what we were laughing at. I pointed a shaking
finger at his wife and feebly stuttered :

" She said, ' Bogey ! Bogey ! ' " Then I went off into
fresh howls of mirth. I controlled myself at last and
wiped my eyes. Old Gatty's face was a study.

" How interesting it all is," said Mrs. Bradley, when
we had taken leave of the Gattys once more. " Child,
it's going to rain again. How provoking ! You will have
to take me into the vicarage for shelter, won't you ? "

Considering that we had to pass the gates of the
Manor House to reach the vicarage, I thought this
suggestion was a bit thick.

" With pleasure," I said my heart sinking. She and
the vicar's wife were good for three hours if once they
started gossiping. I believe the Bradley is going to put
the Coutts into a book or something. There's a sinister
licking of the lips about her facial expression after she's
managed to get Mrs. Coutts to spread herself on her
favourite topic. It makes my blood run positively cold

to witness it. She's a ghoul, not a woman. Mrs. Coutts' favourite topic, of course, is Immorality, under which heading, since the dreadful death of Meg Tosstick and the removal of Cora McCanley, whom she hates, she has taken to including Daphne and me. She found me outside Daphne's door on the night after Meg Tosstick's murder, and promptly blew her cork out. I explained that I was only asking Daphne if she were all right and not scared, of course, but the woman insisted upon believing the worst. The next night she found me *in* the room, of course. I'm not going to be dictated to by a person with her frightful mentality, even if she *is* Daphne's aunt.

Upon finding me seated upon Daphne's bed she decided that the worst had happened. (It hadn't, of course.)

" You're enough to *make* it happen, aunt," said Daphne, in tears at the nasty things which were being said. "Here, Noel, darling ! " And she handed me the ring. I received it dumbly and dropped it into my pocket. Then we kissed with histrionic effect, and I stood aside to let Mrs. Coutts pass out. She didn't budge, so I didn't. I wasn't going to leave Daphne to be chewed up after I had gone. In the end she went, and I followed her out. I gave the ring back to Daphne next day, of course, and she explained that she had only returned it to save her bally aunt throwing a fit. Mrs. Coutts' nerves and temper had been steadily deteriorating since the murder of Meg Tosstick. She chivvied her husband, who had been like a goaded bull since the village pound business, and also had practically said in so many words that he might think himself lucky he got off as well as he did. She muttered something about seducers and the cloth which sounded to me rather hotter even than her usual diatribes. The remark was equally divided between the Reverend and myself, of course. I believed the woman was mad. Really I did ! I would have married Daphne on the morrow if it could have been managed, to get her out of it all, for it was beginning to tell upon the poor kid, but, apart from the fact that a curate can't very well get married at a registrar's office, I had passed my word to old Coutts to hold off until Daphne was older.

Well, I had to usher the Bradley into the vicarage, for the rain began to come down pretty heavily, and we both got pretty wet, walking from the Moat House. Nothing would satisfy Mrs. Coutts, who had taken a violent fancy to Mrs. Bradley, than to rig her up in dry clothes, shoes and stockings and have a fire lighted. Daphne grabbed me in the hall when the two of them had gone upstairs, and said :

" Oh, Noel ! Uncle's been talking to the inspector who's in charge of the case, and he says there's sure to be a local crime wave for a bit. He says these crimes get imitated—these sort of crimes. I think it's horrible."

The talk at tea was about the murder, of course. Mrs. Coutts spread herself on Immorality, as usual, and Mrs. Bradley listened, and prompted her when she seemed like drying up. I was pretty well fed with the conversation, and so was Daphne.

At six the Bradley tore herself away and beckoned me to follow her. I went, of course. I really don't know why. She saps my will power, that woman. I had intended to stay with Daphne and discuss the Harvest

Festival, but I followed Mrs. Bradley as meekly as a dog and we took the road which leads towards the stone quarries and then stops abruptly half way up the slope. She said, as we journeyed onward, shouting against the wind :

" I know Mr. Burt's little game. Are you afraid of him ? "

" Of course I am," I yelled.

" Yes, yes, I know," she bellowed. " Why don't you like me, Mr. Wells ? "

I couldn't think of anything to say, so I just went pretty hot and stammered a bit, of course. She mouthed at me :

" I want your help. It would be easier if you could overcome your prejudice." She paused and, added, fortissimo, " I could overcome the vicar's, if you liked, you know."

" What is his ? " I shrieked.

" You want to marry his niece," she screamed. The wretched women seemed to be wise to everything. " And I know a few bishops and things," she added at the top of her voice. I halted and looked down at her. I hope my face was grim.

" You are trying to bribe me, Mrs. Bradley," I ejaculated.

" Yes, yes, of course, dear child," she hallooed into my left ear. Horribly moistly, of course.

" It's a bargain. Come shake hands."

She took my hand in her skinny, yellow claw. Heavens ! What a grip she had ! Harder even than Mrs. Coutts', with her pianist's wrists and fingers.

" Stay here," she shouted. " If I don't emerge from

you will have to promise me that your fortune-hunting is over. No more cargo must be landed at Wyemouth Cove and brought to this house. You understand, don't you? And—er—about your quarrels with your wife——"

She spoke gently, but her terrifying, black, witch's eyes never left Burt's angry face. I was horribly alarmed to see Burt's furious expression. The odds were too frightfully unequal. Unostentatiously I bent and picked up the poker. It was a nicely balanced, fairly weighty weapon, and swung prettily between the fingers. I dangled it, getting the feel and the balance of it. Mrs. Bradley was grinning with a kind of fiendish blandness at Burt, whose neck was beginning to swell.

" You wouldn't commit a murder, Edwy, would you? " asked the terrible little old woman.

" *I—don't—know!* " said Burt, taking a stride towards her. " I *might*—if I were *hard pressed* ! "

" Tut ! tut ! " observed Mrs. Bradley. She pointed a yellow talon at him. " Naughty boy ! Sit down ! "

Burt sat down. He even grinned, sheepishly, of course. I replaced the poker, as unostentatiously, I trust, as I had taken it up. He glared at me.

" Damn your eyes, you poodle pup ! " he said. I smiled, weakly, of course. Mrs. Bradley said :

" Why were you so rough with the vicar, Edwy? "

" He put up such a fight," said Burt. " He knocked poor old Foster about. If Foster weren't a black, he'd have had a face like a rainbow."

All sorts of things began to emerge from the back of my mind, and take shape, and slip into place. The vicar had mentioned two men with blackened faces. Why on

HM

earth hadn't it dawned upon me that one of them might have been a real negro? Mrs. Bradley had started from that point, probably, and argued the whole matter from Foster Washington Yorke to Burt. The Bungalow was much the nearest dwelling house to the cove, of course, and smuggling was much the most obvious thing to connect with the appearance of the ship which Coutts had seen, although Sir William had scouted the notion when his butler had put it forward.

" I suppose the whole thing connects up with Lowry, the landlord of the Mornington Arms," I said to Mrs. Bradley, as the boisterous wind nearly blew us off our feet and into the village below. I believe Mrs. Bradley was going to dismiss this idea as absurd, when suddenly she prodded me in the ribs in an ecstasy of joy.

" My dearest, dearest child ! " she observed, cackling like a hen with an egg. " What a sweet idea ! No, just fancy ! I should never have thought of connecting Landlord Lowry with the smuggling ! "

I was not as surprised as she seemed to be. My experience of the sex, consisting, as it does, of a knowledge of the vagaries of such different ornaments of womankind as Mrs. Coutts, Mrs. Gatty, my mother, my sisters and Daphne, has led me to the inevitable conclusion that, outside certain well-defined and exceedingly narrow avenues of knowledge, women are singularly ill-informed. Mrs. Bradley might have deduced that Burt was a smuggler, but apparently the fact that wines and spirits were the smuggled articles had completely escaped her. I dare say she was not even aware that such imports are dutiable. I gave her a short, but I trust, informative discourse, upon the subject of import duties. We were almost running down the hill, and the wind was tearing and shouting behind us. My talk was a summary of the first of my winter lectures to the Boys' Club, of course, a series of talks entitled, " Great Englishmen." The first lecture was to be the life of Sir Robert Walpole. She seemed interested, I thought, and certainly thanked me warmly when we arrived at the Manor House. I was relieved when she had gone. Daphne and I talked about the Harvest Festival and other matters until supper time. After supper, to my surprise, I received a summons from Sir William to go at once to the Manor House, as Mrs. Bradley wished to see me. Had the message come from Mrs. Bradley herself, I am strongly disposed to believe that I should have ignored it, or, at any rate, sent an apology in lieu of going to see her. But a message from Sir William was a different matter. I begged the vicar not to sit up for me, took my hat and waterproof, for the night had set in wet once the great wind had dropped, and was soon on my way to the Manor House.

I could not help thinking about the murder as I walked at a good brisk pace along the main road, away from the village. There are no cottages near the Manor, except for the dwelling of Constable Brown. It heartened me to remember that this ignorant but staunch keeper of the village peace was convinced of poor Bob Candy's innocence. It struck me, as I came abreast of his cottage, that it would be a good plan to stop there for a moment on my way to the Manor House and find out how far the Wyemouth inspector had gone in his investigations of the crime. Brown, I decided, would probably know all that there was to know, as he went everywhere with the inspector and took copious, albeit laborious, notes of all that his superior said and did. The inspector, I suppose, was flattered by this proceeding, and suffered the constable gladly, fool though he considered him, I expect. He wasn't, of course. Not at all a fool. Brown, I mean.

I knocked at the door and it was opened by Mrs. Brown. She invited me in and showed me into the parlour, which was immediately inside the street door, of course. There I found Constable Henry Brown and his two lodgers. I had thought a good deal about those lodgers. After all, I argued, surely it was more sensible to suppose that a stranger had murdered Meg Tosstick rather than that one of our own villagers had done such a dastardly thing ! I observed the young men narrowly, but could not conscientiously admit that either of them showed symptoms of abnormal depravity. Neither had they the nervous, hunted look that I associate with unconvicted murderers. Not that I had ever seen any, of course, at that time.

Brown had no real news to give me. The inspector, he said, had now finished interviewing everybody in the village who could possibly be expected to know anything at all about the murder, and it had advanced the case against Bob Candy no further. That was the most optimistic thing he could find to say, and it was not particularly cheering. Brown ventured the opinion that the prosecution would have an easy job of it at the trial.

" You see, Mr. Wells," said the good fellow, " the police have got their case all mapped out, like. They don't really want no more evidence to hang poor young Bob with. They've been getting their witnesses ready, that's all. Who to call, and who not, as you might say, sir. The inspector don't want to find anything now as'll put him in a muddle, don't you see."

" Do you mean, Brown," I said, rather horrified, of course, " that the police don't want to get at the *truth* ? "

" Oh, they want the truth all right, as you might say," Brown replied, waving his pipe, " but, you see, sir, they think they've got it. No doubt at all but, to their way of thinking, poor Bob done it. No, what the inspector has been going round for is to find something to *bolster up* the truth a bit. If he can't find anything, he can't, and no great harm done. The lawyers must do the best they can with what they've got already, that's all. But, on the other hand, he don't want to hit a snag, sir, do he ? I mean, that 'udn't be human nature, saving your presence, Mr. Wells. As it stands, it's a very nice case ! You wouldn't expect 'em to go out of their way to queer it."

I nodded gloomily. So did the two young men. The point was well put, of course.

" I'll be going, then," I said. " Thanks, Brown."

" I'd heard tell that the little old party from London was a rare wonder at finding out things," said Brown, escorting me to the door, " but I expect she doesn't take much interest in us country folks, sir."

" Oh, I don't know so much," I said, wagging my head a bit. I didn't think I ought to tell him that she had discovered that Burt was a smuggler, so, looking pretty mysterious, of course, I pushed on to the Manor House, and was soon telling the assembled company, which consisted of Sir William, Margaret, Bransome Burns and Mrs. Bradley, everything which Constable

Brown had said. I concluded by saying that matters looked utterly hopeless for Candy.

" Anyway, Brown seemed inclined to take your name in vain," I said to Mrs. Bradley, " so I upheld your reputation as best I could."

" I don't think you need have troubled yourself, Mr. Wells," said Margaret, rather cuttingly. I perceived, of course, that I had dropped a bit of a brick, so I hastened to gather up the fragments.

" Oh, no, no ! Of course, rather not," I said, in my heartiest mothers'-meeting voice. " Of course not. Certainly."

" I hope," said Mrs. Bradley, " that you didn't mention Burt ? "

" Not a syllable, on my word," I replied eagerly, frightfully thankful, of course, that I had put that particular temptation behind me. " I didn't think it would be wise. Fancy his smuggling liquor, though," I added, with an amused but tolerant smile.

" He doesn't ! " said Mrs. Bradley. Her usually mellifluous voice was so sharp, and her scowl so particularly ferocious that I merely said :

" Oh, doesn't he ? " And left the rest to fate. Mrs. Bradley changed the subject so abruptly that my suspicion that she was side-tracking the truth became amplified. However, I judged it wiser to lie low for a bit.

Sir William said :

" What evidence do they offer against Candy, besides the motive ? "

" Opportunity," said Mrs. Bradley, " He was at the inn when the murder was committed. There is an odd fifteen minutes of his time that he can't account for satisfactorily."

"It's simply horrible," said Margaret. "He *couldn't* have committed a murder ! Why he used to be in my Lads' Bible Class."

"He isn't capable of it," exclaimed Sir William. I was glad to hear them championing the man so warmly and I glanced from face to face to see whether they all agreed. I was surprised at the peculiar expression on Bransome Burns' unprepossessing countenance. His lips were drawn back from his ugly teeth in a malicious smile.

"Good heavens !" I thought. "He believes Sir William did it !"

Almost as though I had spoken the words aloud, Mrs. Bradley observed :

"Of course, there is this point to be considered. *You* do not believe that Candy was capable of murder. *I* believe he was."

"But——" thundered Sir William. At least, he would have thundered the sentence had he been permitted to conclude it, I think. But Mrs. Bradley interrupted him.

"I am not convinced of Candy's innocence. I believe that Candy was capable of murder, but I also know "—she looked at each of us in turn—" that there are *others* in this village who are potential murderers. Take Sir William, for example."

Sir William got a bit purple at that, of course, and was obviously working himself up into one of his terrible rages, when Mrs. Bradley checked him.

"Don't show off, dear host," she said. "Mr. Bransome Burns will bear me out."

Bransome Burns—I rejoice to think that Mrs. Gatty called him a shark—he was a blue-nosed shark if ever I saw one—I never have seen one of course—stuck his forefinger behind his collar stud and made polite, deprecating noises. All the same, there was a cold gleam in his nasty, fishy eye. He had not forgotten the day he kicked the dog. I could read the man's mind like a book.

" Then," said Mrs. Bradley, turning suddenly on me and leering with a kind of fearful joy, " there is our young friend, Mr. Wells."

" I a murderer ? " I ejaculated. It was laughable ! I *had* picked up the poker at Burt's bungalow, of course. And (I should admit it if pressed) I had picked it up with the idea of swiping Burt a meaty, fruity slosh over the head if he kicked up rough or turned in any way nasty. But the Bradley was biting the hand that would have defended her. I could hardly say so, of course.

" Then there is Mr. Burt," said Mrs. Bradley. I could agree to that. I myself had heard Burt confess to her that he would kill if he were forced by pressure of circumstances so to do.

" Then there is Mrs. Coutts," said Mrs. Bradley, " although I confess up to the present I have no proof except psychological proof (which is incontrovertible, but not acceptable yet to the lay nor the legal mind)— that Mrs. Coutts is a potential murderess. And then," she added, grinning at us, " there is myself. I actually have a murder to my credit. I was tried for it and acquitted, but I did it, boys and girls, I did it."

She shook her head sadly, and then turned to me.

" Do you really believe that Candy was incapable of murder ? " she asked.

" I have not heard you prove anything which persuades me that he murdered Meg Tosstick," I said.

" You will at least allow that he *could* have murdered her," she said. " Why, child, he had the virus in his blood ! "

" Well, Lowry knew of that fact, and yet risked employing him as barman and as chucker-out," I said.

" Yes, so he did," admitted Mrs. Bradley. I forbore to press the point, except to add :

" The moral is obvious to me."

" Oh, yes, so it is to me," said Mrs. Bradley hastily. Anxious apparently, to change the subject, she remarked :

" About Burt's smuggling, Sir William. You are here in your private capacity, and not as a Justice of the Peace ? That is understood ? "

" Well, not exactly. Perhaps I'd better go," Sir William said. Huffy, of course, at being called a murderer. Margaret followed him out, but Bransome Burns stayed with us.

" What made you think of liquor ? " enquired Mrs. Bradley of me. She seemed amused.

" Obvious," I said.

" Yes," she retorted swiftly. " Obvious that it couldn't have been liquor. If it had been, do you not think that every soul in this village, man, woman and child, would have been aware of the fact, and would have got his pickings out of it ? But nobody knew. Nobody was interested. And why ? Because Burt smuggled books,

not liquor. Banned books, dear child. Nasty, porno-
graphic literature, dirt and offal, dear child, and did
not even make a fortune out of them, so his conduct
really was inexcusable!"

She hooted with outrageous laughter. Bransome
Burns said nervously,

" How beastly. What's happened to his wife, by the
way? I used to talk to her down at the post office
sometimes, but I haven't seen her since the murder."

" No, you wouldn't," Mrs. Bradley answered, before
I had a chance to do so. " She is absent from the Bungalow."

" Oh, really? " said Burns. " Nice-looking girl.
Pity she married that rotten fellow."

So we talked about the Burts until I took my leave.

CHAPTER VIII

BOB CANDY'S BANK HOLIDAY

I was not as much surprised as I might have been. Burt was exactly the opposite of my conception of a distributor of indecent literature, it is true ; on the other hand, his language was of that revolting type which revels in causing embarrassment to those that hear it. I frowned judicially and stared in dignified displeasure at the carpet. I did not really know what to say, of course. Luckily, Mrs. Bradley was at no loss for words. She continued, after giving me sufficient time to digest the tidings.

" Of course, he won't be able to carry on the good work."

" Certainly not," I agreed. " I say ! I bet Lowry was in on the game, whether it was books or beer ! He's a proper old miser, you know, and not one to let good money slip past him—well, bad money, I mean, of course ! "

I laughed at my own joke, but Mrs. Bradley did not seem frightfully amused. I take it, from my fairly close observation of the sex, that women have not a very keen sense of humour. I played my trump card, however, and caused the old lady to sit up a bit, I fancy.

" You see," I said, " he must have used Lowry's secret passage sometimes to escape detection, and he could hardly do that without Lowry's connivance, could he ? "

I don't know why it is, but the mention of a secret passage always interests people. It interested Mrs. Bradley, and she asked me a lot of questions about it. I could not tell her much more than the fact that there was such a smugglers' passage leading from Lowry's cellars to the Cove, that it had been blocked up, but that I did not see why it shouldn't have been unblocked by Lowry and Burt.

" Why choose the Cove, if not for the secret passage ? " I asked, triumphantly. Mrs. Bradley still looked interested.

" A baby could have seen through that lonely bungalow business," she said, at last. " If ever the situation of a house shrieked that something illegal was going on, the situation of that one did so. Add to that an occupant, who, far from observing the most elementary precautions, goes out of his way to waylay and half-murder the local vicar, and plays a silly and cruel trick on a little jackal like Gatty, and places himself, as you say (I hadn't, of course !) in the hands of a fox like Lowry, and something is bound to go wrong. If *I* hadn't put two and two together, someone else would have done so, and then——"

" Yes, all for the best. After all I do think that the public morals——" I began, but Mrs. Bradley cut me short.

" I never did, and I never shall, believe that vile things affect the minds of any but the vile," she said, firmly. " Besides, evil and filth are the most incomparably dull, boring, surfeiting things in the world.

See the published works of George Bernard Shaw."
She hooted. " Corruption, as he indicates, is not only
nauseating to the senses, but it palls upon the imagination. Evil is the devil's worst advocate. Refer again
to the above-mentioned sources. Why, child, you, as
a priest, should know that it is the little insidious vices,
treachery, malice, envy, jealousy and greed, covetous-
ness, slandering, sentimentality and self-deception that
enslave mankind, not filthy postcards and erotic literature, Mrs. Grundy, my dear."

She spoilt it all, of course, by howling like a hyena and
poking me in the ribs until I was forced to remove myself out of reach of her terrible yellow talons.

" ' Honi soit qui mal y pense,' you mean ? " I suggested, by way of finishing the conversation. But she
only shrieked louder than ever. A most extraordinary
woman. Sincere, in her way, of course.

" Then I suppose that even murder——" I began,
when the air was still again. I had not the slightest
idea of how I was going to finish the sentence. My
object was to change the subject of conversation.
I never like people to know that they have worsted me
in an argument. I feel that I owe it to the cloth to keep
my end up and the Anglican flag flying.

" Oh, murder ! " said Mrs. Bradley, fastening on to
the word with grim relish. She wagged her head at me.
" Murder is a queer crime, young man. If it *is* a
crime."

" Of course it's a crime," I said. " It's a sin, too,"
I added, buttoning the black jacket and composing the
countenance into ecclesiastical lines.

" Rubbish, child," retorted the Bradley, with spirit.

" Murder is a general heading for a whole list of actions, most of which ought to be judged merely as misdemeanours. The second division ought to be the special preserve of murderers."

" It would be, wouldn't it ? " I said. She waved aside the shaft of wit.

" Look at Crippen," she said. As I have always looked upon the little thug as one of the hottest exhibits in the Chamber of Horrors, this suggestion fell flat so far as I was concerned.

" What about him ? " I said. " The victim of an illicit passion, that's all."

" The victim of an inferiority complex," returned Mrs. Bradley. I chewed the thought.

" Hm ! " I said. These psychologists frighten me. I don't talk their argot, of course, and that puts one at a disadvantage.

" Besides," said Mrs. Bradley, warming to it, " most murderers are insane at the time of committing the murder. Take Patrick Mahon."

" Oh, but that was frightfully nasty," I said.

" You are confusing the two acts of the unfortunate man when you say so," responded Mrs. Bradley.

" But he dismembered the body ! " I protested. I mean, hang it all !

" Yes, that's what I am saying," she said. I blinked.

" If a man laid an entirely false trail for the police, misled them, hoodwinked them, drew red herrings across the track and dived and doubled in order to escape them, you wouldn't say that he was any more of a villain than if he took no steps to secure himself from arrest, would you ? " she asked. I thought it over, and replied, cautiously, in the negative.

" Well, a man who dismembers a body and hides the head is only trying to secure himself against arrest," said Mrs. Bradley. " You should try to think clearly, child."

" But murderers who are found to be insane are lodged in Broadmoor," I said, adroitly side-stepping once more.

" Ah, Broadmoor," said Mrs. Bradley. " What a waste of public money ! A painless death would be far the better method. There's a great deal of rubbish talked about death, young man. Mind you, there must be none of that dreadful period of waiting for the execution morning that obtains under our present in-human and disgraceful system. I do not say abolish the death penalty, but, instead of a penalty, let it be a re-lease. We must always have the moral courage to release from life those who are not fitted to bear life's burdens. Social morality, consisting, as it so largely does, in refraining from action, is to some minds an unachievable ideal, and to others simply nonsense."

" Ah, but the duty of the church——" I interrupted. Then I stopped short, because, of course, the church is not primarily concerned with morals. At least, it ought not to be, for morals are not even the A.B.C. of re-ligion. I doubt whether, at most, they are more than the pothooks and hangers of our spiritual life.

" Priests are but men," I said, lamely, of course.

" Not always," retorted the Bradley, with her fright-ful cackle. My trouble is that I never know when the woman is serious, but I found myself thinking of Mrs.

Coutts with her murky mind. Beside her, this queer little reptilian was like a rainbow or an iridescent shell of pearl. Mind you, you couldn't exactly guarantee what you would find underneath the shell, but I felt that while it would be possible to imagine the Archangel Gabriel blowing his trumpet in Mrs. Bradley's ear, it would be impossible for Mrs. Coutts even to recognise the Archangel and the sound of his trumpet on the last great day. There was something about the Bradley. I should be the last person to deny it. One felt, in the words of the rather Nonconformist hymn, that she was on the Lord's side. Curious.

She clapped me on the shoulder. It was quite a welcome change, of course, to being poked in the ribs.

" And now, to the question of the hour," she said. " Talking about murderers, let us include our own." She paused a moment, and then added, " Oh, by the way, do you know which train is best from Wyemouth Harbour if one wishes to arrive in London in time for dinner and a theatre ? "

" Oh, yes. The 3.30 is easily the best," I said. " For one thing, it doesn't stop anywhere until it gets into Waterloo, and for another, it has a restaurant car."

" Ah, thank you, my dear," she said. " The 3.30." She wrote it down.

" And now, dear child," she said, " this murder of the girl Tosstick. A queer affair, you know." And, arguing, I suppose, from the general to the particular, she began to talk about Bob Candy, which was what I had been trying to urge her to do.

" I want you to go and see Bob," she said. " And

I want you to ask him some questions about what happened on August Bank Holiday."

" But his lawyers," I began, " are surely the people——"

" Yes, yes," said the little old woman. She began to stroke the sleeve of her orange and black dinner frock as she talked. " But I want *you* to go. He always liked you, didn't he ? "

" Oh, averagely," I said.

" Yes, well, you get at his alibi, young man. And, if he hasn't an alibi, find out the truth. I don't think he has told the police the truth, and, if my deductions are correct, that's because the truth would be one more weapon in the hands of the prosecution. I have thought a good deal about Bob while I've been clearing up the little mysteries in connection with Mr. Burt, and I have come to the conclusion that Bob *was* with Meg Tosstick some time during the afternoon or evening of August Bank Holiday, and that, instead of having thrown the tie away, he was actually wearing it on that day. You must admit that he did not come out very strongly on the subject of that tie."

I admitted it, of course. Anybody could have seen that the poor fellow had been lying about the wretched knitted silk tie with which Meg Tosstick had been strangled.

" Tell me about Bob," said Mrs. Bradley.

" Oh, well," I said, " he was a big, sturdy fellow. You saw that for yourself, of course. He never showed any signs of abnormality except a tendency to glower and brood over fancied wrongs. His gifts as chucker-out were seldom in requisition, because the village is

Im

orderly and we seldom have men drunk. It's easy enough to get rid of the guests at closing time, I am sure. Bob was simply a barman, really. He fell in love with the poor unfortunate girl Tosstick, and they were both saving up to get married, I know, because they tried to get the vicar to mind their money. Of course, Coutts pointed out that the Post Office would pay two and a half per cent. interest, which he was not in a position to do, and persuaded them to start a Savings Bank account. It was all in the girl's name, because Bob said it was to be. Coutts wanted them to have separate accounts, but Bob wouldn't hear of it."

" Well, you've put several points which are in the young man's favour," said Mrs. Bradley. She frowned. " Not at all the sort of young man who ought to be hanged," she said.

" You see that Bob did not gain financially by Meg Tosstick's death ? " I said, eagerly. " Constable Brown put that to the Wyemouth inspector, but he chose to ignore it, I suppose."

Mrs. Bradley nodded.

" And you have also shown that Bob had no particular enemies," she said.

" Oh, the chucking-out business ? No, I'm sure he hadn't. He got handled a bit roughly on that Sunday evening, but he's quite popular really."

" Yes. You, as his advocate, must find every possible point in the lad's favour. A number of quite small points might be sufficient just to tip the scale towards an acquittal, if you really want him to be acquitted."

" You've no hope, then, of discovering the real murderer ? " I asked. I was disappointed. The woman had managed to convey the distinct impression that she had something up her sleeve.

" Oh, I tell you that I can very well guess who the murderer is," said Mrs. Bradley. " But the trouble will be to get *some* people to believe it. You surprise me, you know. You still seem certain that Bob Candy was not capable of committing murder. And that is absurd."

She had put the point before ; this time, without giving me a chance to say anything, she proceeded to enlarge upon it.

" A young man must be very much attached to a young girl to trust her with all his savings," she said. " Don't you think that it was an extraordinary thing that everybody in the village was so astonished at the news that the girl was going to have a child ? Upon your own and Mrs. Coutts' showing, I take it that conception before marriage is not an uncommon thing in the village."

" It's the custom," I said, prepared to stick up for it of course. After all, our people are essentially moral. You can't call that sort of thing immorality, although Mrs. Coutts does, of course. It's simply local colour. One has to be broadminded. Mrs. Bradley was prepared to accept the facts without criticising them, it seemed, for she merely nodded and said :

" Assuming, as you are determined to assume, that Candy is innocent, here is a workable hypothesis to go on. Let us say that Meg Tosstick, begged by several interested persons, including the Lowrys, to disclose to them the name of her seducer, refused to comply with the request. We do not know her reason for withholding the father's name, but apparently she did withhold it. Now—a remarkable point, this—nobody seems to have encountered the proverbial little bird. Meg's secret is still a secret—even to me—so that I have no way of putting my convictions to the test, and they remain merely convictions for the present, and are not established facts. Now, I imagine that she kept the secret for one of two reasons. Either she was being terrorised by the baby's father, or else she knew that her lover would commit murder if the secret came out. A girl of Meg Tosstick's type might easily be terrorised by a stronger personality. This stronger personality, however, was not strong enough to dare Bob Candy's vengeance if the secret leaked out. The girl, in a weakly hysterical state, poor thing, after all that she had suffered both mentally and physically, was in just the frame of mind to blurt out with tears and self-reproaches the whole pitiful, shameful story. The wretch whose lust had victimised her was terrified at the thought of the consequences to himself if she did that, and so he planned to murder her to close her mouth for good and all. Immediately the murder was accomplished, poor, innocent Candy was arrested, as the murderer foresaw that he would be. How's that ? " And she laughed heartily.

" Then we have only to find the father ! " I exclaimed. " Oh, but you have a conviction, you say, that you know him. Can't we frighten the truth out of him ? "

Mrs. Bradley cackled.

" I think you would find that he was more afraid of the gallows than of your threats, child," she said.

" Besides, we can't do very much without proof, and in any case, what I have just told you is not necessarily the truth, remember. It is merely a working hypothesis which covers all the facts that we know. Now when you've visited poor Bob, and have found out exactly what he did and where he went on August Bank Holiday, let me know. Persuade him that to tell the whole truth is his best plan. By the way, I have briefed Ferdinand Lestrange for the defence."

" What, *Sir* Ferdinand ? " I gasped, thinking, of course, of the fees.

" Yes. My son by my first husband," said this re-markable woman. " A clever boy. Nearly as clever as his mother, and quite as unscrupulous as his father, who cornered wheat on Wall Street and then slipped up and all the wheat fell on him ! "

She screamed with Satanic mirth and poked me in the ribs until I fled the room. Her laughter pursued me to the front door, where I grabbed my hat from the footman and bolted down the drive. I managed to get a short talk with Daphne as soon as I arrived at the vicarage. The other inmates of the vicarage were in bed. She had been to bed, also, but, upon hearing my latch-key in the door, she had sneaked downstairs to the dining room. She sat on my knee while I told her all that I had heard—well, most of it, of course. She squeezed my arm.

" I bet she means Lowry, horrid, fat old pig ! " declared my beloved. " He looks just that sort of man."

" I plump for Burt," I said. " A noted atheist and a nasty-minded fellow if ever there was one. Burt would make nothing of twisting girls' necks. He used to beat Cora, you know. I don't wonder they had a dust-up."

" He doesn't gave you the shudders, anyway, as Lowry does," said Daphne, " and girls like Cora don't mind being whacked. They like their husbands to be rough with them."

Personally, I have always considered this Ethel M. Dell stuff to be a myth, but Daphne did not give me time to argue. She lowered her voice, and looked hastily over her shoulder. Then she said in my ear— it tickled me a bit, of course :—

" You know the Adj. thinks it was either Uncle or Sir William, don't you ? The baby business, I mean. She thinks Meg and the Lowrys wouldn't show it because of the resemblance."

" Your aunt is mad," I said, softly but with considerable heartiness. " I say, Daphne, come over to Clyton with me when I go to see Candy. You could wait in the public library for me, couldn't you ? We could have tea together in a little teashop I know of, and anyway there would be the journey both ways. It takes about an hour and three quarters because the connections are so frightfully bad, so we'd get at least four hours together, one way and another."

We fixed it up and then went up to our separate beds. I was longing for my marriage. I wondered how long I would have to wait.

Three days later I got permission to visit Candy and we set off. I left Daphne in the magazine and periodicals department of the public library and went to the prison by tram. The prison lay about a mile and a half outside the town. Candy seemed quite pleased to see me,

but shut up like a clam as soon as I began trying to
talk business. He looked a bit pale, but quite well, I
thought, and talked hopefully about the trial.

" They'll have to let me off," he kept saying, twisting his hands together, " because I never done it, see ?
They can't hang me if I never done it ! That aren't
the law, Mr. Wells, that aren't."

" But look here, Candy, old fellow," I said, desperately anxious not to put the wind up the poor chap,
of course, but just as keen not to let Mrs. Bradley down,
" they may think you did do it. And, look here, Candy,
there are some very rich and clever people interested
in you, and they're going to get you off, but they can't
do it unless you tell *everything* you know."

He sat there as dumb as the Mona Lisa, and looking
about as soft, and the way he kept twisting his fingers
got on my nerves. He wouldn't say a word, so, at last,
knowing that time was passing, I determined to try
a bold shot. I leaned forward and said in my sternest
rebuke-of-the-old-Adam tone, which, in a priest, of
course, amounts to about the same thing as an army
officer's parade voice :

" Why don't you confess that you spent the evening
with the murdered girl ? "

He jumped so suddenly that I jumped too.

" You —— ! " he said. " It weren't the evening,
damn you, it were only the afternoon ! "

" Everybody knows about it, Bob," I said, gently,
hoping that the lie would be forgiven me. " So why
don't you make a clean breast of it ? It was in the *evening* that you saw Meg Tosstick." Sheer bluff of course,
and I was ashamed of it.

" I didn't do it, I tell you ! I didn't do it ! " he said.

" I know you didn't, you fool!" I said, trying a little savaging. " But what chance do you give anybody, if you won't tell the truth ? "

He licked his lips. A muscle at the side of his jaw twitched and twitched.

" Here you are, then," he said sullenly. " I didn't have no heart to go to the fête, and I knew we wouldn't be busy at the Arms until the evening, so I get Mr. Lowry to give me the morning and afternoon off, and I promise to be back by six. Well, we open at half-past six, see, and they chaps at the fête be getting thirsty by then. I get away to Little Hartley, because I told the vicar I didn't want to play in that there old cricket match against Much Hartley, and I wander about the woods and the common, and have a bit of dinner I brought along, and in the afternoon I sneak back to Saltmarsh to see Meg, and have a few things out with her. I have no chance before to talk to the poor maid because Mrs. Lowry was always for keeping me away. Afeared I'd do her a cruel turn, I do suppose," added Bob, his face darkening.

" Did she say that ? " I asked. He shook his head.

" No. Her would always say maid was too bad, or too tired, or was asleep, or was suckling, or some excuse, to keep me from her."

" Then you didn't see Meg to speak to from the time the child was born until August Bank Holiday ? " I asked.

" That's in the way of it," he answered. " Anyway, I knowed the master and missus and all the gals and men 'ud be at the fête in the afternoon, so, with them thinking

I was away to a day's holiday on my own, I could see it were my chance to get speech with Meg. I wasn't going to frit the poor maid ; only ask she, pleasant-like, who was her fancy chap, and did she prefer him to I, and suchlike. But not rancorious, Mr. Wells...."
He looked at me pleadingly, but I said nothing at all, so at last he continued :

" Well, Meg looked proper frit when I walked in. Her was white and looked weary. Couldn't see nothing of babby. Her had it too close and all covered up not to have its looks give nawthen away, I reckon.

" ' Why, Bob,' her says in a whisper, ' How be ? '

" ' I be fine,' I says, ' How be you ? '

" ' I be all right,' her says, ' Oh, Bob, have ee come to upbraid me ? Don't ee upbraid me, Bob, nor yet miscall me, my dear,' her says, ' for I can't abide no hard words, I be that weak. And don't ee ask Babby's surname, neither,' her says. So we set and talk, and at last her says :

" ' I do know I lost ee for good and all, Bob,' her says, ' but do ee lay thy face down on pillow beside me, and give me a bit of comfort, my dear.'

" So I lays down my head on pillow, ah, and body, too, on top of quilt, and puts arm over she, having took off collar and tie for comfort first."

" The—the knitted silk tie ? " I gasped. He nodded, and then smiled sardonically, and said,

" Ah. Funny bit, that there, weren't it ? Well, like silly chap, happen I fall asleep, what with the quiet and the warmth and such, and first thing I know, Meg shaking I and telling I to get up and go away. Sure enough, when I look at clock, five past six her say, so

I hop up in a hurry, part my hair with Meg's comb, put on collar and can't see tie. Meg say she'll find un and hide un, but I must go. Poor maid seem so set on it, and so frit to think somebody might see me there, that I pack up and go. I get another tie from my own bed-room, put on my barman's overall, and step down into the bar. Mr. and Mrs. Lowry wasn't back from fête, but the gals and Charlie Peachey, the other barman with me, soon come in, and we open as usual. But master and missus never come in until goodness knows when that night, for Charlie and I close the house at half-past ten, and he go back to the fête for the dancing, and the gals with him, and I go upstairs. I tap at Meg's door, but get no answer, so I twist the handle, but the door was locked, so I go along to my bed."

" At what time, exactly, would you say you got to your own room ? " I asked. Candy considered the question.

" Not before a quarter to eleven and not after eleven o'clock," he said. " But, of course, it's that there quarter of an hour I were down the cellar they've got against me."

I spoke a few reassuring words to him, but I knew that that quarter of an hour was the snag. At last I took my leave, for my time was up.

" So you see," I said to Daphne, as we sat at tea, " the poor girl must have been murdered before Candy went up to bed that night. The medical evidence at the inquest put the time of death between nine o'clock and ten-thirty."

" Just the time," said Daphne, " when Candy would be kept busy, and could not interfere."

"Just the time," I said bitterly, "when the damn fool decided to go down the cellar and bring up some more beer for the jug and bottle department, presided over by Mrs. Lowry."

"Well, I suppose she asked him to go down the cellar!" retorted Daphne.

"How could she? She wasn't in the house at all," I replied. "Bob told me that both the Lowrys were out, and that he doesn't know when they came home. Mrs. Lowry simply left word that some time during the evening the job was to be done."

"Hm. It looks beastly suspicious to me," said Daphne.

"My dear girl, do be reasonable," I said.

"Well, Noel, it's rather funny that just at the time when they're out of the house and no suspicion can attach to either of them, poor Meg gets murdered, isn't it? Not to mention the fact that it was also the very first time Mrs. Lowry had left her to herself!"

"But, Daphne," I said—laughing, I must confess, at her simplicity—"naturally the murderer would prefer to attack somebody in the Lowrys' house while they were not there. It's only common sense to suppose that the murderer has some gumption, isn't it?"

"Anyway, I hate those Lowrys," said Daphne. "I'm sure there was something fishy when they took Meg to live with them in the first place."

"But your uncle, I understood, paid for her board and lodging," I said weakly.

"Oh, *did* he?" said Daphne. Nor could I persuade her to add anything to the rather moot point suggested by the question.

" Well, anyway, while Bob's story is fresh in my mind," I said, " I think I'll dot it down in shorthand, so that I can tell it to Mrs. Bradley in his own words, as nearly as I can remember them."

I have rather a remarkable verbal memory, and I am a fairly accomplished shorthand writer. I can do my hundred and forty, of course. So, armed with Bob's depositions, we returned to Saltmarsh, and I went immediately to the Manor House to see Mrs. Bradley.

" The first person to interview," said she, after I had read Bob's yarn to her, " is the girl who was taking Mrs. Lowry's place in the jug and bottle department that evening. By the way, isn't it rather unusual to have the host's wife serving in that particular department ? "

" It's to cater for motorists," I said. " It's more like an off-licence department, really, only they stick to the old name so as to be able to keep it open on Sundays."

" Ah, yes, that would be so, I dare say," said Mrs. Bradley.

She cackled, as startlingly as usual, and we sallied forth to the Mornington Arms.

" You don't know which maid was serving in the off-licence—I mean jug-and-bottle department on August Monday evening," she said, as we walked along the road, " and so we had better have speech with Barman Charlie Peachey, I think. What kind of a man is Charlie ? "

" Oh, all right, I suppose," I said cautiously. " He doesn't come to church. He's a Roman Catholic."

" Oh, well, he's the less likely to be a murderer," said Mrs. Bradley. I was still pondering this queer axiom when we arrived in front of the public house.

The Mornington Arms is no longer the small, white-washed, flat-fronted village inn that it used to be. It is set back from the road in its own tea-gardens, and was rebuilt, about three years before the murder, in the form of an Elizabethan half-timbered house. It can garage twelve cars and has ten bedrooms. The Lowrys were making a very good thing out of it, I believe. They catered solely for summer tourists and visitors, of course. During the winter months they did nothing beyond supplying the village with beer.

" You go in," said Mrs. Bradley to me, " and have something to drink, and get Charlie to tell you the girl's name. I'll wait in the Post Office."

I went in and ordered a gin and ginger, and tackled Peachey squarely. He was a thin, sandy-haired young man whom I hardly knew because of his Roman opinions.

" Who was in charge in the jug and bottle on Bank Holiday evening ? " I asked.

" Mabel," said Peachey. " Want to see her, Mr. Wells ? "

" She couldn't make some excuse to slip down to the Post Office, could she ? " I asked. " I could talk to her better there."

" Sure she can," said Peachey. " She's not doing anything, and madam's making herself pleasant to a shooting party from London, and the boss is out, I know."

There was no-one else in the bar, so I leaned towards Peachey and asked quietly :

" What's been going on here, Peachey ? Was there ever a baby or not ? "

He wiped a few spots of beer off the counter and then said :

" It's rum, ain't it, Mr. Wells ? There was a babby all right, because we all heard un cry. Ah, but what's happened to that babby is a rare mystery."

" Well, look here," I said, feeling somewhat Sherlock Holmesian, of course, and beginning to pant like a bally bloodhound when it sees land in sight, " what do you yourself think ? Hang it, man," I said, " you knew Bob. Presumably you knew something of the dead girl. What was it all about ? Who *did* kill Meg Tosstick, eh ? And where's the baby ? "

Peachey said, doubtfully :

" I don't know as I ought to talk. You ain't the police, Mr. Wells. Still, if you won't let it go no further——"

I promised, but said that I should like to talk things over with my friends. However, if he wanted me not to, I wouldn't.

" The little sharp party from the Manor ? " he said. I assented.

" Oh, all right then. Mind, I don't *know* nawthen. 'Tis only what I thinks. You understand that ? "

" Oh, quite," I said.

" Well, then, I reckon it's that there Mr. Burt. And what's more, I reckon he had a rare facer when poor young Bob got taken up. He meant to fix it on the boss."

I gave the man a shilling for his trouble, as he was not of our own flock, and sauntered out as soon as I had finished my drink. Sure enough, by the time I had strolled to the Post Office and helped Mrs. Bradley choose a couple of picture postcards, along came Mabel Pusey, the barmaid, looking extremely scared. She asked for a three-halfpenny stamp, stuck it on the letter she was holding and we all walked out of the shop. We had taken no notice of Mabel, of course, while we were inside the Post Office, but as soon as she had posted her letter, we foregathered. Mabel was certainly in a pitiable state.

" Oh, ma'am," she said to Mrs. Bradley immediately, " I know it's going to get poor Bobby hanged, but how was I to know ? How was I to know ? Mrs. Lowry said before she went as we might need some more pale ale and perhaps a dozen of stout up, and how was I to know ? I'd have bitten out my tongue before I'd have told the police Bob was down there for a quarter of an hour, and after nine o'clock, too, but how was I to know they'd twist it into the time he murdered her ? "

" Listen, Mabel," said Mrs. Bradley, kindly, in her wonderful voice. " You want to help Candy, don't you ? "

" Oh, I do, I do ! " said the girl. " Why before Meg Tosstick had him——" She stopped, but it was easy to finish the sentence. The poor girl was in love with Candy, and she felt that words of hers were sentencing him to death. Decidedly an unpleasant thought, of course. We nodded sympathetically. Mrs. Bradley said :

" And how many bottles did he bring up out of the cellar that night ? "

Mabel answered :

" About three dozen. Certainly not less."

" Where is the cellar, Mabel ? "

" It's under the garages now, where the old house stood before we was rebuilt. To get down the cellar we have to cross the bit of yard and go in the first lock-up, and the trap door to the cellar is in the far right-hand corner. You switch on the electric light on the wall of the lock-up over the trap door, and that lights up in the cellar and down you go. It's where that old passage used to end."

" And ought it to have taken Bob Candy fifteen minutes to bring up three dozen bottles, Mabel, do you think ? "

" Well," said Mabel, hesitating in order to consider the question, " in court I'd say it would, perjury or no perjury, I would, and of course, the knife and boots, little tyke, wasn't there, so you can't hardly say, what with one thing and another."

" What difference would the knife and boots boy make, Mabel ? " asked Mrs. Bradley.

" The knife and boots had ought to be there at the top of the steps to take the bottles from Bob and de- posit 'em in a little soap-box on wheels Bob made, and wheel 'em into the jug and bottle," replied Mabel, " but the knife and boots was at the fête. Said the missus had given him the whole day, and he wasn't coming home till morning. And he never, neither, the little runt." She spoke with honest indignation. " He didn't half get a flea in his ear, neither. They was just locking up for the night when he come tearing in. It was nearly one o'clock then. ' Boys will be boys,' says the master, but madam, I thought she'd have fetched him a clout side the head."

" What did Bob do when he first heard that Meg was

going to have a baby ? " asked Mrs. Bradley. Mabel
shrugged.

"He cursed a bit and got drunk, but got over it after
a bit, you know," she said. She sighed. " Chaps aren't
like us maids, ma'am. Oh, Bob got over it all right, I'd
say, and *shall* do if asked in court."

CHAPTER IX

THE VILLAGE SPEAKS ITS MIND

"That last remark Mabel made is important, don't you think?" asked Mrs. Bradley, as we walked on together. I considered it.

"Why, especially?" I asked, feeling fogged, of course.

"Bob had got over his resentment long before the murder," said Mrs. Bradley. "It rather knocks the motive on the head, doesn't it?"

"One moment," I said. "This Mabel Thingummy herself. Could she have done it, do you think?"

Mrs. Bradley pursed her thin lips into a kind of little beak, and then shook her head.

"You need strong hands, and a lot of nerve, and even then it must be a very unpleasant way of killing anybody," she said. "You are arguing from the point of view that Mabel is in love with Bob and might have wished Meg Tosstick out of the way. I don't think there is much in it. Mabel doesn't strike me as the jealous, vindictive, possessive type of lover. Besides, if she were fond of Bob and had committed the murder herself, she would confess in order to save him, wouldn't she? Still, we could keep her in mind. It's a point, certainly, that Bob was not the only person who had a motive for putting the girl out of the way."

"Thank you," I said, quite bucked, of course, that

she had not turned the idea down flat. " Pray sum up will you ? Shall I take down ? "

" It would be nice of you," said Mrs. Bradley. We had been walking towards the Manor House, and as she spoke, we entered its gates. In a few moments we were in the library.

" First," said Mrs. Bradley. " I believe if Candy could give the story of that Bank Holiday afternoon to the Court as he gave it to you, any jury in the land would acquit him. It was very affecting, and very possibly true. Secondly, it is obvious that if he could provide himself with an alibi for that quarter of an hour in the beer cellar, the case against him would fall flat. Personally, I think the police acted very hastily and ill-advisedly in arresting the young man so soon, even on the strength of that quarter of an hour. It was exceedingly unlucky for Candy that the knife and boot boy should not have been there to perform his usual duties, wasn't it ? "

" The trouble is," I said, " that everybody was at the fête, of course. And, because of that fact, everybody in the village will have much the same alibi. Even if their friends can't vouch for them——"

" Everybody in the village will *not* have the same alibi," said Mrs. Bradley, interrupting me. " Incidentally, you noted the fact that Candy didn't get sight of the baby, I suppose ? "

" Yes," I replied. " Poor little thing. It must be deformed, mustn't it ? Or do you think he did see it, and was lying for some reason ? "

" There are so many kinds of deformity," said Mrs. Bradley, seriously. I waited to hear what more she had to say, but apparently her remarks for the day were concluded. She did not even bother to answer my last question, but, just as I was about to take myself off, she looked me in the eye and said :

" You really do still believe in Candy's innocence, I suppose ? "

" I'd pledge my soul ! " I exclaimed.

" Rash Faustus," retorted the little old woman, and her evil cackling pursued me down the drive. As I walked back through the twilight from the Manor House to the vicarage, I found myself still wondering what had become of the baby. Nobody seemed interested in the fact that apparently it had disappeared since the murder. I called at Constable Brown's cottage and put the point.

" It's funny you should ask that," he said. " See here, Mr. Wells, what do you make of this, like ? "

He produced from a drawer a visiting card. It had Gatty's name on the one side and on the other, in roughly printed capitals, the words :

" Where is Meg Tosstick's baby ? "

" Who did this ? " I asked.

" Ah," said the constable, scratching his chin with the edge of the small rectangle of pasteboard, " there, sir, you do me ; proper you do me. I don't know. It weren't given to me, of course. May be you're thinking it was. Oh, no, sir. Mrs. Coutts brought me this here, about two o'clock this afternoon. ' Here, Brown,' she says, holding it like it would have a nip of her hand if she didn't look to it, ' what's all this ? '

" ' All this, mum,' I says, like I might say it to you now. ' All this, mum,' I says, sort of silly like. ' Why, I don't know,' I says. ' What *is* it, mum, if I may ask.'

" ' I've brought it to you to find out,' she snaps. Well, beg your pardon, Mr. Wells, but she do snap. Snaps like my brindled whippet bitch used to. You remember her, I daresay. Master William wanted one of her last litter, but his aunt put the cash in a missionary box. Well, I looks it over and I can't make nought out on it except what it says. ' I'll look into it, mam,' I says. ' Wants investigating carefully, this do.'

" Course, I haven't done nothing about it, Mr. Wells, because, to tell you the truth, I don't know where I are. One thing is quite certain, how I look at it. It isn't a Gatty job."

" A Gatty job ? " I said.

" A Gatty job," repeated the constable. He turned the card over and showed me the name and address.

" Don't mean to tell me, Mr. Wells," he said, " as Mr. or Mrs. Gatty sent this, when they could have come along themselves to the vicarage and said it. If they wanted it kept secret who they were, why send a visiting card ? It aren't sensible, Mr. Wells."

I agreed. Curiously enough, Mrs. Coutts met me at the front door of the vicarage with a similar bit of pasteboard in her hand.

" What ? What ? " I said.

" I know it can't be the Gattys," said the woman, pushing the visiting card at me, " but do just run along to the Moat House and see."

I groaned, but went, of course. The Gattys were in, and denied all knowledge of the printing on the back of the card. They handled it pretty freely, but then, so had I, and so had Mrs. Coutts and the rest of them.

Fingerprints, I mean. No good for fingerprints. I clawed the card away from them and went back to the vicarage.

" Another one has come," said Mrs. Coutts. Old Coutts had gone up to bed with neuralgia, and Daphne and William were playing quoits tennis out of sight of the front door.

The next day happened to be Sunday. On Sundays we breakfast at eight o'clock, on weekdays at eight-thirty. I have never discovered the reason for this unless it is to get the vicar out of bed soon enough for him to have a last glance over his sermon for Morning Prayer. I usually have to be wakened, therefore, on Sundays, but on this particular Sunday morning something roused me with a start. I sat up in bed, and observed a large squelchy object stuck on the outside of the bedroom window. It had all the appearance of an over-ripe, flattened-out tomato. I arose and inspected it. It *was* an over-ripe, flattened-out tomato. Blinking, as much to clear the brain as the eyeballs, I took another goggle at the frightful fruit. Beyond it I could see the vicarage hedge, and beyond the hedge a collection of the lads of the village. They were engaged, apparently, in plastering over-ripe fruit, bad eggs, and chunks of horse and cow manure over every window of the vicar's residence. I opened the window, rashly, as it turned out, and began to shout at them. Just at that moment the window beside mine was flung up and young William's boyish, excited bleat announced :

" If you don't cheese it, you ugly stiffs——"

A chunk of horse-dung took him over the eyebrow. At the same instant a last season's egg got me in the left ear. We both shut our windows, shot out on the landing and made for the bathroom. William was seriously annoyed. He didn't know many expletives, but those he knew he made full use of. I couldn't very well follow suit, of course, but I listened sympathetically.

" But what's it for ? " enquired William, scrubbing his now shining face upon the towel. " What's the giddy idea ? That's what I want to know."

I charged out to dig up the old man, closely followed by William. Daphne came out on to the landing. She had her blue dressing gown on—rather jolly. Her hair was rumpled, of course. Small kid sort of effect. I managed a hasty but quite charmingly satisfactory salute. She rubbed it off, absentmindedly, of course, and told us gratuitously, of course, about the mob of sans culottes at the front. Mrs. Coutts, up and dressed and not a hair unbrushed, joined us, and we all goggled out of the landing window. The populace had stopped chucking the soft fruit and other bouquets, and were beginning on the chunks of soil and the stones course. The dining room windows seemed to be copping it rather badly, and a chunk of rock about the size of a large grapefruit crashed through my bedroom window and broke a picture called Nymphs at Play which used to hang over the head of my bed. I didn't like the picture, but it served to annoy Mrs. Coutts, and she used to push in every morning, to my certain knowledge, and turn it face to the wall, before the maid came to make the bed.

The general din brought old Coutts out. He had arrived at the shirt and trouser stage and had not shaved. Nothing would satisfy him, when he had had a look at the ancient society of rock-chuckers, but to harangue them.

" Useless to do so from the open window of a bed-room," he said, surveying the two-foot hole in my casement. " I will go into the garden and enquire into this disgraceful demonstration."

Even Mrs. Coutts, who usually represents the Church Militant in times of stress, thought this a damn-fool idea, and I am compelled to state that I upheld her. At least, I upheld her until I caught Daphne's eye. When I did, I said that if he went, I would go with him. He didn't even stop to put his coat and waistcoat on, but marched out at the front door and began by booming at them. His voice, on this occasion, was the voice he keeps for weekdays when we have the school-children *en masse* in church, and they hoof the fronts of the pews and surreptitiously play football with the hassocks, and whack each other's shins with the edges of the hymnbooks, and cough aggressively after the first six minutes of the address until the pronouncement of the Benediction.

" Good people," megaphoned old Coutts, " what is the meaning of this ? "

A dozen voices answered him in a kind of chant :

" Where be Meg Tosstick's babby ? Where be Meg Tosstick's babby? Us ask the landlord ! *He* don't know ! Us ask his missus ! *Her* don't know ! Where be Meg Tosstick's babby ? "

After that, it sounded like the new setting we had to the Te Deum last September, or a dog fight at the Battersea Kennels, and the air was filled with stones.

Suddenly there was a sharp report, and somebody on the outskirts of the crowd yelled :

" Duck your heads, lads ! They'm shooting at us ! "

Sure enough, young William's airgun spoke the second time, and there was a decidedly anguished yelp from the ranks of the besiegers. The vicar swung round.

" William ! " he yelled. " Stop that ! Do you hear ! "

" All right ! " screamed William. " But I've got another slug ready for whoever bungs the first brick. You howling cads ! " he continued, addressing the villagers. " If my aunt and sister weren't holding the seat of my bags, I'd come down and make you sit up ! "

The vicar took advantage of the diversion created by his nephew to announce that he would receive a deputation after Morning Prayer if they had a grievance. They were so used, I suppose, to cheesing their conversation when the old lad spoke, that they listened fairly quietly while he laid down the law about damage to property and unprovoked assault, and, at the end of his decidedly spirited address—delivered on an empty stomach, too, of course—they melted away without much backchat, and the vicar and I returned to the fortress and assessed the damage.

" I shall pay for the window out of the Bible Class Social Fund Box," said old Coutts, sucking his finger which he had advanced too near the jagged edge of what was left of the pane.

" And in the meantime, Noel will have to sleep with William," interpolated the woman.

" Not on your life ! " I hastily, but, of course, ill-advisedly remarked. Mrs. Coutts spent breakfast time in recriminatory remarks directed chiefly at me. The village, I gathered, thought *I* had sneaked the baby. I let her run on. Really, it's the only way.

I must confess that I felt a bit like the first missionaries must have felt as we walked into church behind the choir that Sunday morning, but the service was allowed to run its usual course, and although the tougher element of the village sat at the back and chewed gum, there was no disorder and no interruption. After the Benediction had been pronounced, the vicar stood on the steps of the chancel, cleared his throat, looked all round the church, and said :

" I am ready to meet in the vestry any person or persons with a grievance against me or against any of my household."

He was not belligerent, but he sounded dangerous. However, two youths and an older man were at the vestry door when we were ready to go back to the vicarage for lunch. The older chap, a respectable bloke, but an atheist and a postman, was the spokesman. He took off his cap when old Coutts invited him into the vestry, and spoke quite respectfully, but there was no mincing of words. He said bluntly :

" I wasn't at your house throwing they stones. I don't hold with misdirected violence nor 'timidation. But us wants to know what you and your good lady done with that poor girl's babby, Mr. Coutts. Us knows you be the father, but where be little un ? "

Old Coutts went most frightfully red.

" My good man," he said, in a kind of choking gargle, " you are being profoundly, utterly and ludicrously slanderous. Your remarks are actionable. Be careful what you say."

He paused and scowled at the postman fiercely, snorting somewhat.

The man stuck to his point.

" Beg pardon, Mr. Coutts," he said, " but that poor girl was living under your roof when it happened, wasn't she ? "

" She was," said the vicar, grimly.

" Unless it were Mr. Wells," said the frightful fellow, suddenly turning on me.

" I deny it," I said feebly.

" I'll let the lads know, then," said the postman, " but I doubt whether they'll be satisfied with plain denials. It's facts we're after, Mr. Coutts."

" Then you can go to hell to get them," said old Coutts, irascibly, forgetting, of course, where we were.

So the bird slouched off, taking the two youths with him.

" I'm going to get Burt and his negro and Sir William to put out anybody who causes a disturbance at Evensong," said the old boy, grimly. He'd been a missionary at some period in a probably purple past, and seemed well on to the psychology of the thing, for a disturbance at Evensong there certainly was. In fact, a bally riot would perhaps convey a more correct and enlightening impression.

Whether the second lesson was an unfortunate choice, or whether the time for the hurling of the first hymn-book had been pre-arranged, we shall never know ;— any more, I suppose, than we shall know the same thing about the stool chucked by the old Scotswoman at Archbishop Laud's backer in the year sixteen-thirty or forty something. Anyway, it came whizzing along, and only just missed me. I was reading the lesson, of course. I didn't know what to do, but the vicar's voice behind me said :

" Carry on, Wells," and I was aware that he was standing beside me at the lectern. Suddenly the air was full of hymnbooks, and amid the frightful din— I stopped reading, of course—I had to—I could hear Mrs. Gatty's voice declaiming :

" Cuckoo ! Cuckoo ! "

Most inapposite, of course.

CHAPTER X

SUNDRY ALIBIS, AND A REGULAR FACER

By the time I had struggled out of my surplice and coat, the riot was nearly over. The last stalwarts among the attacking party were being thrown out among the tombstones by Burt (who seemed to be enjoying himself), the vicar (who was trying not to seem to be enjoying himself), and Foster Washington Yorke, who, to the strains of " I got wings " was doing his bit with zealous fervour and Christian impartiality. Coming in at the death, so to speak, I put my boot behind a youth named Scoggin, whom I had been longing to kick for nearly eighteen months, and we barred the church door and continued the service. The vicar cut the sermon down to thirteen minutes by my watch, and, at the conclusion of the service, instead of going out into the vestry, he marched straight down the aisle to the West door, and, unbarring it, strode into the porch. I followed him, of course. There were the attackers lining the path, waiting for us. Our appearance immediately at the conclusion of the service was unlooked for, however, and it was obvious that we had taken them by surprise. The vicar gave them no time to recover, but, raising his arm and pointing first at those on the right and then at those on the left, he said :

" You have committed sacrilege. You have also

disturbed the peace. I shall lay an information with the constable, and you will be called upon very shortly to give an account of yourselves. You may go."

Of course, I don't like old Coutts, but one can't help admiring him. The lads looked at each other and licked their lips. Then they began to shamble off. There were fifteen of them. Some were not from our parish, but from the neighbouring village of Stadhemington.

" Interesting, of course," said Mrs. Bradley, when she heard about it.

" Well, it shows what the villagers think," I said.

" Yes," said the little old woman. She grinned.

" And why do they think it ? " she asked.

I shook my head and murmured something about smoke and fire, also about throwing mud and it sticking. Mrs. Bradley pursed her little beak and shook her head.

" Mrs. Coutts," she said. " The camel bites and squeals. Anonymously, dear child."

" You mean the Gatty visiting cards ? " I said.

" Certainly," said Mrs. Bradley. " Those cards came *to* the vicarage *from* the vicarage. What do you say to that, young man ? Is the vicar innocent ? Is he mad ? "

" Oh, come," I protested. She grinned again.

" Take your choice, my dear," she said. " Do you believe he is the father of Meg Tosstick's child ? His wife believes it. That has been her trouble all along."

" Never ! " I exclaimed, hypocritically, of course. I knew quite well that Mrs. Coutts had believed it from the beginning. A most frightful woman ! Most frightful !

" The point is," continued Mrs. Bradley, " upon what, I wonder, does she base her opinion ? Does she base it upon Certain Knowledge, as a friend of mine would say ? Does she deduce it from information in her possession ? Does she suspect it, and is attempting to prove it by driving her husband to confide in her ? Or what ? Especially the last named."

As I had not the faintest inkling of what she meant, I grunted and tried my best to look intelligent.

" If the vicar were the father, that would let Bob out," I said, after a moment's pause.

" Why so ? " enquired Mrs. Bradley.

" Well——" I recalled the show put up by old Coutts against Burt and the negro before they got him chained up in the pound—his knuckles couldn't have looked worse if he'd knocked out a tree—and the way he had shot those roughnecks out of the church on the Sunday. Squeezing a girl's neck would be a mere nothing to a man like that. I propounded this theory to Mrs. Bradley. She merely grinned.

" Well, you must admit that if he's the father, he had a good enough motive for shutting the girl's mouth," I said doggedly.

" Yes," said Mrs. Bradley, " but why wait until the baby had been in the world over a fortnight ? It's of no use, Noel, my dear boy. If you are going to pin that murder on to the baby's father, you've got to explain why he waited so long."

" Well, the vicar paid for Meg's keep at the inn, I understood," said I.

" You understood ? Don't you know ? "

" No. I was given to understand that he did," I replied. After all, I reflected, Daphne had not actually denied this.

"Not good enough," said Mrs. Bradley, firmly. "Ask yourself whether it is."

"I could ask the Lowrys, I suppose, to make quite sure," I said, "or Coutts himself, of course."

"I imagine that Mrs. Coutts did that at the time the child was born," said Mrs. Bradley, drily. "I think, too, that all three persons concerned returned an evasive answer."

"On which she based her suspicions?" I asked.

"Oh, no. I expect she had had her suspicions from the first," replied Mrs. Bradley. "If she had not, why did she dismiss the girl from her service? A woman of Mrs. Coutts' mentality could have had an exceedingly interesting time torturing the girl with the dreadful instruments of charity and forgiveness. Cruel people don't let their victims escape them unless there is a good reason for it."

Well, the old lady scored there, of course. Lifting the fallen (with inquisitorial accompaniment) was Mrs. Coutts' great stunt.

"Well, what do we do?" I asked. "Hang it all, it was you who suggested that Meg's seducer was also her murderer."

Mrs. Bradley grinned fiendishly, and, picking up one of those little pieces of paper which the packers place between layers of cigarettes, she printed on it:

"If you persist in this foolish policy, your husband will be hanged."

She placed the slip in an envelope, printed Mrs. Coutts' name and address on the outside, and stamped the envelope.

"I'm going to be anonymous, too," she said. "Come

along. We'll go and post it. And now about these alibis."

" What alibis ? " I asked, accompanying her to the front door and down the drive. " Oh, you mean Coutts and the murder ! " I laughed. " He wasn't the murderer, of course," I said, " but still he was O.K. until the row with Sir William about the Sports finals. After that, there was the attack by Burt, but we haven't any very clear idea of the time the attack took place. So that leaves him unaccounted for from the time he left the fête until the time he was attacked by Burt and Yorke."

I glanced at her. She nodded. Her black eyes were gazing straight ahead, down the gravel drive. There was a gentle, appreciative smile on her lips. At least, I hope it was appreciative.

" According to Coutts' own story," I continued, " he went for a walk over the stone quarries towards the sea. He thinks he left the house at about nine o'clock, or perhaps later— By Jove ! " I said. Mrs. Bradley's eyes opened. She grinned again.

"Exactly," she said. " Suppose he did not go for his walk towards the Cove until after the murder ! Suppose he *knew* that at the Cove he would be attacked by Burt ! Suppose Meg Tosstick did die by the vicar's hand, after all ! What a score for Mrs. Coutts' maggot ! And how awful for Mrs. Coutts ! "

I shook my head, although I myself had voiced the theory, but a little while earlier, in the Manor Library.

" He wouldn't kill anyone," I said. Suddenly, in spite of my own previous arguments, I felt convinced of this.

" Facts are facts," said Mrs. Bradley, " and the fact
Lm

that emerges clearly from our consideration of the
vicar's movements on the night of the murder is that
he had the time and the opportunity to murder Meg
Tosstick before he was set upon by Burt and the negro.
Added to that, if his wife is right, and the villagers are
right, and he is the father of Meg Tosstick's child, he
had a bigger motive than Candy for wanting the girl
out of the way. But we have discussed that before.
His question all the time would be : ' How long will
the girl keep my secret ? ' Nasty, unpleasant situation
for the shepherd of Saltmarsh souls ! "

I was somewhat appalled, of course. Not, as I say,
that I believed in the vicar's guilt. I don't believe I
ever had, except intellectually, so to speak. The case,
as put, however, certainly did hang together. I mean,
apart from everything else, there was the point that,
while, upon all the evidence, even that of the police
who had arrested Candy, poor Bob had had a bare
fifteen minutes in which to commit the murder and
bring three dozen bottles of assorted beers out of the
public house cellar, the vicar had had a possible hour
to an hour and a half. I thought I wouldn't put this
point to Mrs. Bradley. She wasn't safe !

" I'll see Burt," I said, "and find out exactly at what
time the vicar was attacked."

" Splendid," said Mrs. Bradley. " I'll come with
you. You don't mind going the longer way, via the
post office, do you ? I really must post this letter."

Burt was up in his loft. He came down rather obligingly, gave us drinks, and started laughing and talking about the riot in the church.

" Look here, Burt," I said, " you know the night of

August Bank Holiday, when you tied the vicar up in the pound——"

" Oh, dash it ! " said Burt, " Let bygones be bygones, can't you ? After the stout work I put in on his behalf yesterday evening at the kirk—look here ! "

He pulled up his trousers and showed us two badly-hacked shins. We sympathised, and I thanked him for what he had done.

" I only wanted to ask you the time when the vicar was first set upon at the Cove," I said. " We want some sort of defence for Candy when his trial comes on."

Burt put it at twenty-past ten or perhaps half-past. Curiously enough, he didn't seem sufficiently interested in the murder to ask how the attack on the vicar would assist Candy.

" Not earlier ? " I asked, my heart beginning to thump rather horribly.

" Oh, couldn't have been earlier," said Burt. " I left the fête as soon as it got round about six o'clock, came back here and had tea, and then went down to the Cove and helped the ' Sans Baisers ' to land the tomes. My beautifully exact translation of ' Les Soeurs de Matabilles,' dear boy." He patted my knee. " Eighteen and six a copy in England, Mrs. Bradley," —he had the hardihood to wink at her—" and sold strictly sub rosa and under the 'snow' laws, but dirt cheap at the price. Do you still read Browning ? Wouldn't you like to 'grovel hand and foot in Belial's gripe' ? But anyway, it's too late, laddie. A gent's word is his bleeding bond. Besides, the lady opposite would jug me if I so much as touched the dust-jacket of the ' Soeurs ' now, wouldn't you, Mrs. Bradley ? "

I returned to the Manor with my worst fears confirmed. The vicar could have had ample time to commit the murder at the inn and get over to the Cove by twenty minutes past ten.

" Never mind," said Mrs. Bradley. " That is only one. Come along. Let us check Sir William's movements."

" But he came straight back here after the quarrel with the vicar, didn't he ? " I asked.

" He did," said Mrs. Bradley.

" Then that must be that," I said, surprised that she had brought his name forward.

" Yes, that must be that," Mrs. Bradley agreed. I gazed at her rather hard, but could make nothing whatever of her amused smirk. After a moment she said :

" Very well. Let us try Edwy David Burt. Mark this, child. If the vicar had no alibi, neither had Burt."

" Nor Yorke," I interpolated, cheering up. " We ought to get hold of Yorke. He's simple and will tell us about Burt, I should think, because he won't see what we're getting at."

" An excellent idea," said Mrs. Bradley. " Lead on, MacDuff."

" What, now ? " I asked.

" Why not ? " asked Mrs. Bradley. So off we trailed again, up the hill and past the quarries and in at the front gate of the Bungalow. Instead of snooping round the back and taking cover behind the water-butt as preliminaries to our seeing Foster Washington Yorke without Burt seeing us again, Mrs. Bradley led the way to the front door and rang the bell. Burt himself opened the door. His hair was rumpled and his eye was wild,

and he had a fountain pen in his hand. He stumped
down the passage and flung the door open and scowled
at us. He looked positively murderous. Not at all the
genial host of an hour earlier.

" Go to hell ! I'm busy ! " he said, and banged the
door in our faces.

" That being that," said Mrs. Bradley, with her
unnerving yelp of laughter, " we will now concentrate
upon our objective."

She led the way to the back regions, and we found
the negro chopping wood.

" Did you know Burt wouldn't want to see us ? "
I asked the old lady.

" Of course. He always writes at this time of the day,"
she answered. " Surely this is a much nicer way of
interviewing our friend with the axe than if we had
darted from currant bush to currant bush to avoid
being seen by the master of the house ? "

She hooted, and dug me in the ribs. Yorke grinned.
He seemed pleased to see us, and, guided, of course,
by Mrs. Bradley's questions, he gave us a very clear
account of the manner in which he and Burt had spent
August Bank Holiday. Mrs. Bradley skilfully steered
him past the uninformative hours of nine a.m. to nine
p.m. but after that his story was interesting—at least,
I thought so. It dove-tailed so beautifully with Burt's
that I was fascinated. Burt *had* left the fête at about
six o'clock, it seemed, and had returned to the Bungalow for tea. After tea, he and Yorke had taken advantage of the fact that all the village would be at the fête,
to receive the copies of the scrofulous book from the
ship which, later, was seen by the vicar. The volumes,

which were German-printed copies, in English, of Burt's translation of a French book, were landed in packing cases marked " Hefferton Carlisle School, Bootle : Social History." The ship's boats brought the packing cases to land. Apparently the job was always done openly, boldly, and at dusk. Burt trusted that if one of the packing cases were opened by a customs official or by order of the county police, the fact that it contained copies of a book which had not even been officially banned in England would be sufficiently uninteresting to prevent any further notice being taken. The Customs, said Burt, had no soul for literature.

" Hm ! " said Mrs. Bradley to me later on. " If I had to classify Edwy David, I should place his name under the heading of Criminal Optimist. I suppose it never occurred to him that anyone might *open* the book ! "

The phrase " Criminal Optimist," stuck in my mind. Burt was big enough, ruthless enough, lawless enough, amoral enough to commit even such a beastly crime as the strangling of that poor girl. . . . I allowed my mind to dwell on the idea. I was rather attracted by it. The only flaw seemed to be that Burt had not once been separated from Yorke during that hour and a half during which the murder had taken place. They provided each other with a perfectly watertight alibi. Suddenly I switched my mind on to Yorke the negro. The more I thought of Yorke the more likely it appeared to me that he was the murderer, and that Burt was covering him. Burt would, of course. After all, strangling a girl like Meg Tosstick was so un-English a crime that it was much more probable that Yorke rather than Burt had committed it. I thought of Yorke's pink-palmed sooty-backed hands with their beautiful, long, thin, fingers. I remembered the way they were curled round the handle of the axe, and I could imagine them curled round a girl's thin throat. She had had a throat like a child. I could remember the swallowing motion she had made with it when Mrs. Coutts dismissed her. Very pathetic and trying, of course. But what a perfect nuisance that their stories coincided so completely ! To me it had all the appearance of being a put-up job. And still one had to take one's choice. Yorke or Burt ? Burt or Yorke ? Either ? Neither ? Both ? Stymied, I thought, disgustedly. I was distressed, too, since everything still pointed to Coutts.

" No hope that it was either Burt or the negro," I said to Daphne that same evening. I didn't mention her uncle to her, of course.

" What's collusion ? " asked Daphne, suddenly. I didn't explain, of course. I don't care to discuss with Daphne the vocabulary of the divorce courts ; but the question gave my own idea more weight, so I hastened to the Manor House immediately after tea, to lay my argument before Mrs. Bradley. She scoffed, of course. I had thought she might. What motive would Burt and Yorke have had, she wanted to know, for making up a tale ? When did I think the books had been landed, if not before they set upon the vicar and impounded him ?

" Burt might be the father of the child," I said, " and want it kept a secret from Cora."

" You mean that Burt is the murderer ? " said Mrs. Bradley, " and that Yorke knows it ? "

" There's no reason against it, except the ridiculous

alibi supplied by Yorke," I exclaimed. " And you must realise as well as I do that Burt's morals would allow of anything—adultery, seduction, murder—anything. A man who translates that kind of filth into the English language——"

I found myself almost hysterical upon the subject of Burt's morals.

" I am glad that you enjoyed the book," said Mrs. Bradley, calmly. " Of course," she added, before I could say anything, " as you say, Yorke could have been the murderer, except for this ridiculous alibi supplied by Burt. And Yorke's morals, for the reason that he is not even a white man—— ! "

She began to cackle, softly at first and then louder, until she was screeching with hideous merriment. I felt very uncomfortable. Sometimes I could not rid myself of the terrible suspicion that the woman was as mad as a hatter, madder than a March hare, and almost as mad as Mrs. Gatty ; and of a second terrible suspicion that sometimes she might be laughing at me.

" However," she said at last, reassuringly, " I dare say we shall manage to get Candy off. I'm sure I hope so. I hate these hangings. They are barbarous anachronisms, are they not ? "

" It isn't a case of getting Candy off," I declared with a certain amount of vehemence. " It is a case of proving his innocence to the hilt."

" Ah, that's another matter," said Mrs. Bradley, calmly. " do you understand the Einstein theory of relativity, dear child ? "

I hastened to assure that I did not. I also attempted to convey the impression that I didn't want to.

" Ah, well," she said, " if your mind were capable of grasping that theory, there might be some possibility of proving Candy's innocence."

A frightful thought struck me. Not, of course, for the first time.

" I say," I said. " In spite of all you've said, you do believe that Candy *is* innocent, don't you ? "

Mrs. Bradley sighed.

" If only I could prove who fathered the baby ! " she said. " If only I could prove it."

" I suppose you believe poor Bob Candy was guilty of that, too ! " I said, hotly. The old woman gazed gravely at me.

" Why, no. I thought we were agreed that in that case there would have been no murder," she said.

" You mean they would have married, and that would have been that," I replied, grasping the salient point in the social ethics of the village.

" Exactly," said Mrs. Bradley. But her answer, for some reason, did not satisfy me. Somewhere in our conversation, I felt sure, some vital point had been left untouched on. I racked my brains, but I could think of nothing. At last, more to continue the conversation than for any other reason, I said lamely :

"Funny where the baby can have gone. Do you think the father, whoever he is, can have it in his keeping? "

" Yes and no," said Mrs. Bradley. She grinned. " The villagers thought it was at the vicarage, didn't they ? " she said. She nodded, slowly, rhythmically and continuously, like those absurd mechanical dolls they use for advertising purposes.

" The prosecution will probably accuse Candy of

murdering both mother and child," she said. " I hope they will, anyway."

I spent the night in trying to work things out, but couldn't manage it, of course. Also, I could not get my mind off Burt. He was just the sort of loose-living, foul-tongued man to have illegitimate children, and commit murders, and get drunk, and fake alibis, and engage in criminal conspiracies with his serving-man, I thought. My mind passed on to Lowry and Mrs. Lowry. Unfortunate that they should have been out just when the murder was committed at their place. Well, fortunate in a way, for them, of course. Suddenly I stiffened. My feet curled with excitement. What of Lowry ? What of that gross and hairless man ? What of the pig, as Mrs. Gatty had called him ? Why had he given Meg Tosstick shelter, food and care ? Why had he promised her a job as soon as she was well enough to take it ? The thing was crystal-clear. He was the father of Meg Tosstick's child ! Then why, I asked myself, rising on my elbow in the bed to ask the question, why had he killed the girl ? Pat came the answer. He was afraid she would betray him to her lover. He feared Bob Candy's vengeance. And Bob, the dupe, the wronged, the innocent—Bob was being held on the capital charge, while this arch-egg, hairless, gross, bestial and poisonous, got away with two murders, those of the poor deluded girl and her innocent new-born child !

I remember grinding my teeth. I suppose I lay down and slept after that. In the morning, as I ate my breakfast, and allowed the usual early-morning, eight forty-five-edition of Coutts v. Coutts to go in at one ear and out at the other, I made up my mind to go myself to Lowry and confront him with the truth. One thing only prevented my carrying out this resolve. One person, rather. Mrs. Bradley. I was afraid of the old lady. I admit it, frankly. The idea of doing anything in the case without her full approbation and consent became repugnant to me. After breakfast, on pretence (a subterfuge which I had been obliged to shelter behind some half-dozen times before to cloak my frequent visits to the Manor House) of visiting the sick, who were, of course, much better off without me, I went to lay my new suspicions before Mrs. Bradley. She immediately damped my ardour.

" I'm sorry for your sake, dear child," she said, " but I took the liberty immediately I heard that the murder had been committed, of checking Lowry's alibi by making discreet but very searching enquiries round the village, and it seems that not one minute of the day was he alone, or even in the sole company of Mrs. Lowry. I learn that he collected a large party of friends and treated them to all the fun of the fair. Part of the time he was seen minding the cocoanut shy, or watching your fortune-telling tent, Noel, my dear child, wittily inviting all and sundry to enter. He danced with sixteen maids and matrons, including Cora McCanley, and it was nearly twelve o'clock when he returned to the Mornington Arms. His alibi is hole-proof, fool-proof, and destruction-proof. And, of course," said Mrs. Bradley, at the end of this unusually energetic outburst, " there is no reason to suspect that so perfect an alibi conceals more than it reveals, dear child. I believe the landlord of the Mornington Arms is a very popular man. He certainly is a very good-humoured one."

I grinned. " Yes, I can't see that we can do much with Lowry, after all," I said. " He couldn't have committed the murder by proxy, could he ? "

I smiled weakly at my own joke, and then suddenly stiffened. The word proxy always leads me to think about Queen Mary Tudor, and from Queen Mary Tudor it is an easy transition to Mrs. Coutts.

" What about Mrs. Coutts ? " I said, excitedly. " Motive enough there, and heaps of opportunity ! Look here ! After dusk she began her usual snooping about the park in search of courting couples, so you can jolly well bet that nobody spotted her or can swear definitely to her having been at any particular place at any particular moment. She can take cover like a Red Indian ! What was to prevent her slinking off to the inn, murdering the poor girl while the barmen and Mabel Thingummy were busy serving in the pub, and going home to the vicarage and raising that hue and cry ! Why, hang it all ! " I exclaimed, getting all hectic, " That hue and cry might only have been a blind ! She may have waited and waited for the evening of the fête to afford her the opportunity for the murder ! How's that ? "

" Very creditable indeed," said Mrs. Bradley. " I see Bob Candy being carried shoulder-high out of the court ! Oh," she broke off, " it's not Bob I'm worrying about. I firmly believe that we can get him off. Ferdinand will eat the prosecution. The police arrested the lad too soon."

" How do you mean—you are not worried about Bob ? " I asked. " Do you mean that something else is worrying you ? "

" Yes," replied Mrs. Bradley. " The second murder—the murder that nobody has mentioned, the murder without a corpse—is worrying me to death, because I don't know what to do about it."

" Whatever can you mean ? " I gasped.

" The murder of Cora McCanley," replied the little old woman astoundingly.

" But she isn't murdered," I said. " She's on tour with a show called—called——"

" *Home Birds*," said Mrs. Bradley. " But she isn't, you know. That's just my trouble. But I can't get hold of any definite information."

" She had a telegram," I said. " She went off suddenly. Caught the 3.30 train or something. That's all definite enough, I should think."

" Yes," said Mrs. Bradley, mechanically, as though her thoughts were far away. " Who told you about the train ? " she asked, waking up a bit.

" Burt," I replied. " He told us both. Oh, no, he didn't mention the train ! Still, it's the only possible train of the day, isn't it ? I say," I went on, rather aghast, of course, " that row she had with Burt ! " I had just remembered it.

" Yes," said Mrs. Bradley. She did not speak mechanically this time. " That row she had with Burt, dear child, is both interesting and important. And so are all the other rows she had with Burt."

" What other rows ? " I asked.

" About money matters," Mrs. Bradley replied.

" I thought that was just one long continuous row," I said.

CHAPTER XI

REAPPEARANCE OF CORA

Our village hall, just before the commencement of one of our annual concerts, is as good a place as I know for the exchange of confidences. I had been up to see Burt about Cora. After what Mrs. Bradley had suggested, I was resolved upon making a few guarded enquiries. He gave me beer and answered my questions with what I could only regard as suspicious readiness. I made the village concert the excuse for introducing the subject. As a matter of fact, I pretended not to know that Cora McCanley was to be absent for any length of time from the Bungalow, and represented myself as an agent from Mrs. Coutts with the request that Cora would do us a song and dance item if she returned from her tour in time. Of course, had Burt known Mrs. C. as I do, he would never have swallowed this. Anything less like Cora McCanley's idea of a song and dance show than the average item in the average village concert in Saltmarsh can scarcely be imagined. Mrs. Coutts exercises a rigid censorship over the concert programme and would be about as agreeable to the Folies Bergère taking part as to anyone of Cora's reputation doing so. Burt, however, was not wise to this, and he answered, quite civilly, that Cora was off to God-knows-where in some bleeding high-kicking revue, and would only return when the boss bunked with the gross takings. His expressions, of course, not mine.

" Oh," I said, affecting to be considerably dashed. " Then you don't think she will be back by to-morrow week ? "

" I don't know anything about it. I haven't even the faintest idea where she is. I don't even know the name of the people who are running the show, and, except that she is supposed to be touring the North-Eastern counties with the soul-destroying, hick and hayseed, damnation stuff, I couldn't put a finger on Cora for the next few weeks for any money you offered me."

I went away, a sadder, and, of course, a wiser man. Horrible suspicions nestled like adders in my mind.

" And when she does come back," said Burt, as he saw me off the premises, " she'll get what's coming to her. That's how."

" What do you mean ? " I asked. He explained. Cora was " going gay " as I believe the saying is. A man, and so on. His remarks were expressive, but not edifying. A bit of a brute, I should say. And yet, of course, if he really thought she was coming back, he couldn't possibly have murdered her. And yet, again, if he wished to disprove any wild rumours of her death—I went straight to Mrs. Bradley and confided to her my doubts and fears. For or against Burt, so to speak. She shook her head.

She said, " Please don't say anything to him about my suspicions of Cora McCanley's death. I don't want the poor boy going round with a hatchet."

" Poor boy ! " I snorted. At least it was intended for

a snort. They are not easy words to snort, of course.
" Do you know he used to beat her ? "

" Well, I don't suppose she minded that," said
Mrs. Bradley, noting it down. As Daphne had said
practically the same thing, I couldn't very well call the
old woman a fool. Besides, she did not give me the
opportunity to do so, for she continued, almost without
a pause, but with her frightful grin :

" Sadist plus masochist equals happy marriage."
I blinked, and very slowly translated the idiom into
reasonable English.

" Oh, cave-man stuff ? " I said.

" I beg your pardon ? " said Mrs. Bradley. She
cackled. I am prepared to wager that, if there was any
cave-man stuff in either of *her* marriages, it was on the
distaff side, so to speak.

" Let it pass," I said, quoting from my favourite
author. " But about poor Cora McCanley. We ought
to inform the police."

" I have done so," replied Mrs. Bradley. " I informed them while you were up at the Bungalow this
afternoon."

" What did they say ? "

" They said," replied Mrs. Bradley, " that they
would make enquiries. They thought——" she em-
phasised the word very slightly, " that I was suffering
from murder-phobia."

" From what ? " I asked, trying vainly this time to
cope with the patois.

" That isn't a scientific term," explained Mrs.
Bradley. " I mean that the police are accustomed to
receive scaremongers' tales in any district where a

murder has been committed. They will go up to the Bungalow, interview Burt, get this story, check it as far as Wyemouth Harbour main line railway station, and, if it checks with Cora's movements on the day she was murdered, they will let it go at that unless I can give them some further proof that my assertions are the truth."

" And can't you ? "

" Plenty, speaking psychologically. None, speaking in the language of the police."

For some time after this conversation, we were both busy over Bob, and on account of the concert, and we did not meet again until the evening of the entertainment. Mrs. Bradley had been up to London twice, I knew, to talk matters over with her son, Sir Ferdinand Lestrange, the defending counsel, and I had visited Bob Candy, of course, two or three times, and tried to cheer him up, for, as the time of the trial grew nearer, he seemed to be sinking into a morbid condition of the utmost melancholy and depression, and talked of pleading guilty and so getting the trial over more quickly.

" Oh, you can't do that, Bob ! " I exclaimed. " Think how unfair it would be to all the people who believe in you ! "

He promised that he would drop the idea, but I wondered whether Mrs. Bradley were right, of course, and the poor fellow, in a mood of desperation, had done the deed of which he was accused. She had not *said* she believed Bob was guilty, but her manner indicated it. Commonsense asserted itself, however, in my own case. Why had Bob waited until eleven days after the

Mm

birth of the baby, when he must have known for nearly six months that Meg was to be the mother of a child ? My three years in London slums had taught me that in cases of this kind the jealous lover invariably tries to take his revenge before the birth of the child, and, as I saw the thing, Bob was in the position of jealous lover. And what had become of the baby ? Killed, I supposed, and not by Bob. Ah, but then, I did not believe that Bob had killed Meg either.

At the concert, which was held in the village hall, of course, I was seated in the front row at the far left-hand side, and Mrs. Bradley sat next to me. On her right was little Gatty. Mrs. Gatty's name was on the programme in a one-act sketch. I was surprised. We had never dreamed of asking Mrs. Gatty to take part in the concerts before. I pointed out the name to Mrs. Bradley.

" This is your doing," I said accusingly. She nodded and grinned.

" The completion of my cure. I think you will find that Mrs. Gatty's maggot has been destroyed for good and all," she said.

" No ! " I exclaimed. It was so, of course. But I anticipate the sequence of events.

" You were asking me about Cora McCanley," said Mrs. Bradley, suddenly. " The police have done little more than I said they would, especially as Burt received a letter from her three days ago."

" Genuine ? " I asked. She nodded.

" Cora had written it, certainly," she said. " It was dated for the day previous to that on which Burt received it, and was postmarked at Leeds."

"Leeds is a big city," I remarked, idiotically.

"Quite. That fact, however, did not prevent the police trying to find out whether a show called *Home Birds* was put on during the past few weeks."

"And it wasn't ! " I exclaimed. " Good heavens ! "

"Of course it was," Mrs. Bradley retorted. "The person who murdered Cora McCanley and Meg Tosstick isn't a fool, young man."

"But Cora——" I began.

"Had changed her stage name, according to Edwy David Burt, but he doesn't know what the new one was. Flossie Something, he thinks. Oh,"—she cackled wildly—" and the naughty boy told me that he had tunnelled a cross-passage from the foundations of the Bungalow to meet the old smugglers' passage from the inn. He used to get the books along that way when for any reason the overland route was dangerous or the weather was very bad. So Lowry did not come into the smuggling business after all, you see. Never mind ! It was a very good idea of yours, dear child."

She poked me in the ribs and laughed again, very heartily. I shrugged my shoulders and returned to the real subject of our conversation.

"And the show possessed no Flossie ? " I asked, keenly.

"On the contrary, it possessed two Flossies," Mrs. Bradley replied. "Flossie P. Kennedy, and Flossie Moran. Take your choice."

"You mean that neither of them is Cora ? "

"Of course neither of them is Cora. Burt and the police both think that Cora went off with a lover, and never had any intention of joining the show. We shall hear next, I firmly believe, that Cora never received any telegram inviting her to join the show. What happened, I think, was that Cora and her lover, between them, worked that letter. In the reprehensible speech of the day, a stunt like that is old stuff. The lover got Cora McCanley to write it and send it to a friend in the company, with instructions that it was to be forwarded to Burt when the company arrived in Leeds. Probably the letter was written and sent off on the very day the poor girl was murdered. Are you getting hold of any salient point, child ? "

" You mean that Cora did have a lover just as the police say, and that he murdered her just as they were planning to do a bunk together ? The letter was to cover their tracks," I suggested.

" Quite good. Go on."

" Well, I mean, it's the murder part that I don't see —why shouldn't the police and Burt be right in supposing that Cora has merely gone off with another man ? That type always does, you know."

" Yes, but why was Meg Tosstick murdered ? " demanded Mrs. Bradley.

" But, good heavens, you don't think that *Bob* murdered Cora, do you ? " I asked. She shook her head.

" Of course I don't," she replied. Then she added, " I am giving the police about five days in which to discover that all of Cora's old or new associates can be accounted for. And you will note, my friend, that nobody has left the village of Saltmarsh since Cora's disappearance. Therefore, presuming that her lover is still in Saltmarsh, she cannot possibly have gone off with him. Therefore, where is she ? "

I looked at my watch. " We're eight minutes late in starting," I said.

Mrs. Bradley nodded.

" You have solved the problem of the identity of this mysterious lover, of course ? " she said, after a pause.

" Oh, yes," I replied. " Lowry."

" I think not," she said. " In fact, I know not."

" Oh ? " I said, racking my brains. But nothing came except the thought of Sir William Kingston-Fox.

" Not—the Manor House ? " I suggested. She looked surprised, but rather pleased, I thought.

" Clever child," she said. " Yes. From the Manor House, as you so discreetly put it. How did you know ? "

" It was a mere guess," I replied modestly. " How did you get to know ? "

" Well, obviously Cora McCanley would not be attracted by a poor man," she said.

" No, of course not," I agreed, thinking of Cora's many quarrels with Burt over money matters.

" So I thought about everybody in the village and wrote down a list of all those men who would have sufficient money to attract the young woman. Then I used my powers of observation and deduction, such as they are, and fixed upon—our mutual friend." She looked at me curiously. " But I can't imagine how *you* got hold of the same idea," she said.

" Well," I modestly replied, " of course I have not the advantage of living under the same roof as the gentleman in question, but I hope I can use my common-sense."

" Queer," said Mrs. Bradley. " He used to be

absolutely wrapped up in Margaret," she continued,
" but, I don't know—since that quarrel about the dog
last July matters have been different. Well, to cut the
story short, dear child, I have received from his own
lips an account of how he had arranged to go to London
and meet Cora at the Whittier Hotel in the Strand.
At the last minute he changed his mind——"

" Funked the publicity, I suppose," I interpolated.

" —and telephoned Cora to say he wasn't coming."

" Telephoned ? " I exclaimed.

" Yes. And Cora answered, and agreed that it was
too risky. She then invited him to come on the Tuesday
evening to the Bungalow, and he promised to go."

" But he *didn't* go ! " I exclaimed. " He couldn't
have gone, because he was with us, patrolling the sea-
shore, until one o'clock in the morning."

" Exactly. He had no chance of letting Cora know
that he had been roped in for that, because he could
never get to the telephone at the Manor House without
one of the servants or one of us being at hand and able
to overhear what he said. So he trusted to luck that he
would be able to give you all the slip in the dusk and go
to the Bungalow after all."

I chuckled.

" Not very easy to manage," I said, " considering
that for safety's sake we all hunted in couples."

" It was impossible to manage it," said Mrs. Bradley, firmly, " and yet Cora has disappeared."

" Yes, but hang it all——" I began doubtfully.

" You still don't believe, then, that the poor girl is
dead ? " she asked. I shook my head. After all, I
had thought of it, on and off, for a whole week, so I

considered that my opinion was at least as valuable as her own. I had even discussed the thing with Daphne and we agreed in every particular.

" I think she's left Burt, and our lover-friend too, for some other man. After all, that is the police theory and it is Burt's own theory, and if she couldn't get the Manor House one, she must have made up her mind to another."

They put the lights out then, and the concert began with a part-song by the choir. Daphne played, and I conducted. I had not intended to conduct, but in the middle of the verse I could detect the tenors trying to force the pace, so I rose from my seat and kept the time for them. That is the sort of thing which makes one unpopular, of course, but what else can one do on these awkward occasions ? The choir sang a second song, a madrigal this time, and received a round of undeserved applause. The usual recitations, solos, concertina, and cornet solo items followed, and the local morris team gave a good show. I like those bells we wear, and I rather fancy myself in the braces. Very hot. So were we, by the time the dances were over.

The interval lasted for ten minutes, while Mrs. Coutts came from behind the scenes and talked to Sir William Kingston-Fox and, generally speaking, collared all the credit that was due elsewhere. Having shed my flannels and resumed mufti, I slid into my seat beside Mrs. Bradley, and waited, with a considerable amount of interest, for the play to commence. The play had been Mrs. Bradley's idea, and she had coached the players. I was amazed at the result. Margaret Kingston-Fox had the part of a young wife and William Coutts was her kid brother. They were to the life. The young husband was played by a professional actor, a friend of Mrs. Bradley. It was a stiffish part, of course, and you could spot the professional style. But it was Mrs. Gatty who was the eye-opener. As a mischief-making spinster aunt, she was supreme. She was screamingly funny, absolutely unselfconscious and she never once over-played the part. I've never known the village enthusiastic over one of our concerts before, but they wouldn't go home until they had had the sketch done right through for the second time.

" How on earth——? " I asked. Mrs. Bradley laughed.

" The poor woman only wanted to assert herself a little," she said. " She wanted the limelight, child. Now she has got it. She won't qualify for admission to an asylum just yet."

" By Jove," I said, in the intervals of clapping Mrs. Gatty, who was taking her fifth curtain, " you are a wonderful woman, you know."

" Yes, I know," she replied. I dropped the subject, of course. You can't do yourself justice when you try to compliment people who have that kind of impression about themselves. I said, rather nastily :

" And you don't know where the body is ? "

" Bodies are," corrected Mrs. Bradley, as we rose to the National Anthem. I walked beside her as far as the gates of the Manor House.

" We shall have to search the stone quarries. It's the only thing."

" How are we going to get it done thoroughly ? "

" Say you've lost a wàd of Treasury notes there," I

suggested, grinning, " and you'll get the quarries positively combed."

She took up the idea with enthusiasm, and next day the news spread like lightning.

" Of course, if you are right, it won't do for a child to find the body," I said doubtfully. I hadn't thought of that until the moment of mentioning it.

" Don't worry," replied Mrs. Bradley. " The bodies —plural, dear child !—are not in the stone quarries. My aim was to distract the attention of the village from the place where the real search will have to be made."

" And where is that ? " I asked. " Oh, of course, the sea-shore."

" No," replied Mrs. Bradley. " Use your bean—if any ! "

I gasped. The woman read Wodehouse. There was hope for her salvation, I felt. Well, perhaps that thought is a little risqué for a wearer of the cloth. Anyway, I regarded her with a new respect. No woman could be completely bats who could not only read but appositely quote our greatest living author. (Opinion expressed without prejudice, and merely in the interests of constructive criticism, of course.)

" Forward the Light Brigade ! " said I.

" To the churchyard," said Mrs. Bradley, with a grim chuckle.

" To the churchyard ? " I exclaimed, rather dashed at the woman's frightful blasphemy.

" Yes, yes," said Mrs. Bradley, impatiently. " I'm giving this elusive murderer of girls credit for possessing brains. A churchyard is such an obvious place in which to bury a dead body that very few people would think of looking there for evidences of murder."

" But—but where?" I babbled wildly, torn between the most frightful curiosity I've ever known, and a conscience-stricken conviction that old Coutts ought to be on the spot to cope with the rather frightful situation which was beginning to take the chair.

" Of course, I'm not going to do anything illegal," said Mrs. Bradley, impatiently. " But before I lose my wad of Treasury notes in the stone quarries, we must get an exhumation order. And we ought to have it at once. The body has been buried too long already. I don't want squabbling over the identification of the corpse."

" But you can't exhume the whole churchyard ! " I exclaimed, probably ungrammatically.

" Of course not, dear child," said Mrs. Bradley, patiently this time. " Meg Tosstick's grave will be sufficient, I expect."

Well, it was, of course. On the night, or rather, in the very early morning, after the villagers had searched for Mrs. Bradley's wallet—and found it, of course— trust the old lady to do a job thoroughly—a party of us, including old Coutts and myself, Ferdinand Lestrange, a representative of the Home Office, and a fairly stout squad of police, including the police doctor, watched the exhumation of Meg Tosstick's body. Only it wasn't Meg Tosstick's body. It was Cora McCanley's.

CHAPTER XII

PERMUTATIONS AND COMBINATIONS

" Oh," I said, a great light beginning to dawn, of course, " so when you said, all those days ago, that you were on the track of the person who murdered that poor girl, you meant Cora, not Meg ? "

" I did," replied Mrs. Bradley. She spoke complacently, as well she might, for if she had not thought of looking for Cora McCanley in the new grave where Meg Tosstick had been buried, I don't suppose anybody else would have done so, and the disappearance of Cora would have been another of those unsolved mysteries that the Sunday papers seem so keen about.

" I suppose the murderer hid Cora's body until Meg was buried, and then changed the corpses, trusting that the new grave would tell no tales of having been re-opened," I said, getting my mind to work on the problem.

" I think the murderer minimised every possible risk," said Mrs. Bradley, obliquely.

" But where is Meg's body ? " I asked.

" In the sea, I expect," said Mrs. Bradley. " But we can shelve that point. Let the police get on with it. I have provided them with the body they asked me for, and now it is up to them to find the one which has disappeared. Bob Candy is our immediate object of

consideration. Ferdinand is confident. He is more confident than I am, as a matter of fact. I shall be very glad
when the trial is over, because then we can get Bob to
talk, and that will assist us very considerably in solving
several points whose solution at present eludes me."

" To talk ? " I said.

" To talk," repeated Mrs. Bradley, firmly. " Once he
has been acquitted he will be in a position to tell us the
truth."

" But he *has* told us the truth," I said.

" Not the whole truth," said Mrs. Bradley. " One
could not expect it. I had some hopes at the beginning
that he would tell it to you, but those hopes were
doomed to disappointment."

I was still hotly on Bob's side, of course. I had been
several times to visit the poor lad, and I could not believe that he had committed murder.

" He swore to me on the Bible that he had never
thought of murder," I said, excitedly. Mrs. Bradley
waved her skinny yellow claw at me.

" Then I think it was very, very cruel of you to
allow the poor child to perjure himself," she said.
" We shall have him attempting to commit suicide
before the trial if you go overburdening his already
heavily burdened and not very powerful mind. A nice
thing for my poor Ferdinand to attempt—the defence
of a would-be suicide who has been charged with
murder ! You are a selfish and mutton-headed little
boy, Noel Wells ! " She then softened towards me, of
course. No woman can remain angry for long with a
younger man. I have often noticed that.

" Do use your brains sometimes, dear child," she

said, very kindly. " I know it hurts, but persevere."

There could be no reasonable doubt of my perse-
verance, in that and other directions. I was even making
headway with old Coutts about speeding up my marriage with Daphne. But I could not share Mrs. Bradley's cock-eyed point of view about Bob. If she could
not make up her mind whether he was guilty or innocent she had no right to interfere with the course of
justice. *I* was sticking up for Candy because, in my
heart of hearts, I believed him innocent.

Mrs. Bradley said, after a pause :

" Don't you see that the murder of Meg led on
directly, and, in a sense, inevitably to the murder of
Cora ? Don't you see that there was never any reason
strong enough for Bob to kill Meg of his own accord ?
Either he is innocent or else he had to be induced by
someone else to commit the murder."

" Oh, I see that well enough," I said eagerly.
" He didn't commit the murder, therefore he was not
induced to do so. You know that I still believe him
innocent of the murder, don't you ? "

" First," said Mrs. Bradley, taking no notice of my
remarks, " whoever murdered Cora had planned the
murder very carefully, and wanted to distract attention
from it. That is quite certain, isn't it ? "

" Yes. You mean those bogus letters and things ? "

" It was not a bogus letter," Mrs. Bradley reminded me, " if you are referring to the missive
received by Burt. It was a genuine letter, written by
Cora for a special purpose, and it fulfilled that purpose,
but not quite as Cora had intended that it should. It
was written with the idea of indicating to Burt that

she was in a different locality from the one where her body actually was at the time of posting the letter. Only, you see, her body was dead, not alive, when the letter was posted. That bit of the story was the one which Cora did not foresee. I don't imagine her lover foresaw it, either."

"But why did her lover kill her?" I asked. We seemed tacitly agreed to refer to Sir William by this pseudonym.

" The question is not ' Why did he kill her ? ', but ' Did he kill her ? ' isn't it ? " asked Mrs. Bradley.

The woman was tiresome, of course. She grimaced at me, and wagged her yellow forefinger, and continued :

" He amused himself with her, and fooled her into believing that the two of them would go off together, probably just for the length of time that her engagement with *Home Birds* might be expected to last. Cora was fond of Burt, in a way, you see, and would not want to leave him for good and all. But we have no positive indications that it was her lover who killed Cora McCanley. Cora belonged to a definite type of uneducated female. Such girls have no outside interests and they have no faculties within themselves for creating amusement or interest of any kind. They are usually very prodigal of their charms, within limits, and are curiously insensitive to a man's failings provided he has good-humour and a certain amount of money. Hoodwinking the preoccupied Burt was probably Cora's sole means of entertaining herself in this somewhat one-horse village. To take an instance of what I mean. You remember the night that William Coutts was left with Cora while Burt and Yorke went down to the village for some books, don't you ? "

" Gatty on the roof of the Bungalow, you mean ? "
I asked, with my usual keenness.

" Yes. What impression did you receive of Cora's
state of mind ? "

" Well, when I got there," I said, weighing the
thing, " she seemed to me frightfully jumpy."

" Yes. And she certainly did not believe the noises
had been made by boys on the roof, did she ? "

" No," I said, " I don't suppose she did."

" Why do you think she was so scared, Noel ? "

" Well, William was scared too," I remonstrated.

" Yes, of course. Fear is much more catching than
any other disease that I know," said Mrs. Bradley.
" But will you admit that Cora may have believed it
was her lover on the roof, and that Burt would discover
him when he returned with Yorke from the station ? "

" What, Gatty ? " I said, amazed. " By Jove, that
would account for Mrs. Gatty being so weird in her
ways, wouldn't it ? You know, the unfaithful husband
stunt, and so on. And yet you can't somehow visualise
little Gatty in the rôle of Don Juan, can you ? Besides,
you agreed that the lover came from the Manor House,
and Gatty——"

Mrs. Bradley sighed, although I couldn't at the
moment detect any reason for it.

" I am not talking about Gatty," she said, in a
pained tone.

" But it was certainly Gatty on the roof," I riposted
lightly. " You can't deny that."

" I have no wish to deny it," said Mrs. Bradley
wearily, I thought. The woman was getting old, of
course.

" It was Gatty on the roof. That has been proved. The point I am trying to make is that Cora fancied it might be, not Gatty, but this lover of hers. Got it, dear child ? "

" Oh, yes, yes. Of course," I said, grasping the thing in a flash, of course, immediately it was put to me in an intelligent manner. "Then he couldn't have been very heavy, could he, and yet I should have thought——"

Mrs. Bradley weighed the point.

" We might test that," she said thoughtfully. " Besides, I would be glad of an excuse to go up to the Bungalow. I want to see how Edwy David has taken the news. He must have heard by now. Go back to the vicarage and get William Coutts, and I will go to the Moat House and collect Mr. Gatty."

I, too, was intensely curious to note how Burt had taken the news of Cora's murder, but, as our rather curious quartette ascended the steep, rough track that led past the stone quarries to Burt's bungalow, I experienced decided qualms about asking him to take part in Mrs. Bradley's little test. Her idea was to get Burt, Gatty, and myself to climb on the roof, and, at a given signal from her, to take it in turns to crawl about above the dining-room. William Coutts was to be in the dining-room and record in a notebook all the differences he could detect in the amount of noise, scraping or anything else that went on above his head. He was to number the climbers 1, 2, and 3, without knowing the order in which we were to perform our antics up above, and was to put a cross beside the number whose sounds were most similar to the sounds made by Gatty on the night in question.

William was fearfully bucked. Burt was morose. He
informed us all that he had not been a scrap surprised
at the news. He had been perfectly certain that Cora
was deceiving him because she had become a model of
wifely virtue during the past summer. My words, of
course, not his. His would belong more properly in
Restoration comedy than to a simple chronicle of our
Saltmarsh happenings. He betrayed no sign of grief,
beyond a certain preoccupation and a good deal of
irritability, and consented readily, if profanely, to
crawl about his roof at Mrs. Bradley's bidding and to
allow Gatty and me to do so. He addressed Gatty
quite civilly and offered us drinks all round. Mrs.
Bradley accepted them for us, but stipulated that the
trial was to take place first.

It was a beautiful day. The weather had steadily
improved since the murders, I don't know why, of
course, and I sprawled in the broad sunshine with my
seat in a kind of broad guttering between two slopes of
roof, my back against the sunny side and my long legs
up the shady side. The slope was gradual, the sun was
hot, and I tilted my hat over my face and waited for
the signal. Burt was number one on the list, Gatty
was the second player, I was last. After about five
minutes, the signal came. I cautiously lowered my legs,
heaved my body first to a squatting and then to a
kneeling position, and wormed my way across to the
slope above the dining-room. Gatty had confessed to
the wearing of tennis shoes on his nocturnal ramble,
and so the three of us were similarly shod. As I crawled
along, I could see into Burt's back garden. There on
the step was the coloured man, Foster Washington

NM

Yorke. He had a woodman's axe in his hands again, and he was splitting a billet of wood. There was something kingly about the bloke, and I should have liked to watch him at his work. As it was, however, silence was essential to our plan. I tried to attract his attention, but at that moment Mrs. Bradley came round the corner of the Bungalow and invited him to desist.

I crawled about a bit, and tried to be as cat-like as possible, but got my hands and trousers pretty filthy, and lost my footing once, and slithered quite a long way down the tiles, my foot coming to rest in the guttering. Then I descended, and we charged in to check William's notebook.

There was not enough difference for him to be able to tick any one of us as being more like Gatty than the others. Burt weighed thirteen stone nine, Gatty a mere ten one, and I went about eleven twelve.

"She couldn't know it was *not* her lover trying to find out whether the coast was clear," I said.

"As long as you're satisfied," said Mrs. Bradley. She thanked Burt, and signed to me to take the other two away. I didn't like the idea of that. If Burt had murdered Cora, as I was beginning to feel sure he had, it certainly was not the game to leave a frail little old woman alone with him while they discussed the thing. So, urging the others on, I waited, out of earshot, it is true, but prepared for Burt if he started anything. He didn't start anything, of course, and, after about ten minutes' conversation with him, Mrs. Bradley came away. He waved to us with grim geniality from his gate as we started to descend the hill.

"Any proof?" I asked.

" Proof ? " said Mrs. Bradley.

" That Burt killed Cora," I said.

" Oh, no. Did you expect any ? He didn't kill her, you know," said Mrs. Bradley.

" Well, he's fearfully callous about it," I said.

" Yes. I should be more suspicious, perhaps, if he were more obviously upset," said Mrs. Bradley, drily. " Wouldn't you ? "

It was a new idea to me. I turned it over in my mind as we descended the hill.

" Did you see the negro servant chopping wood ? " asked Mrs. Bradley.

" Yes," I said. " A fine-looking fellow, isn't he ? "

" Yes," replied Mrs. Bradley. She said no more until we arrived at the gates of the Manor House. " What is the feeling about coloured people in Saltmarsh, I wonder ? " she said. " Don't go asking questions about it round the village. I don't want the poor man ill-treated on the assumption that he is the murderer. I must try and find out——" she paused. " You couldn't get Mr. Coutts to preach a sermon about it, I suppose, could you ? " she said. " Then I should have something to work on, and people wouldn't connect my remarks with the murders."

Old Coutts, who is always grateful for tips, gladly embodied the point of his Sunday evening remarks. I agree with Mrs. Coutts. You really can't call his Sunday evening efforts preaching a sermon. I went into the Mornington Arms on the Monday evening, and the bar hummed with discussion. The general conclusion seemed to be that negroes were all right and one could treat them as brother Christians, but—— The stumbling block seemed to be the colour bar in marriage. Nobody was in favour of marrying a negro woman, and the idea that their daughters might marry negro husbands caused more foaming at the mouth than the beer which most of the protagonists were imbibing pretty freely. True to my unspoken promise, I asked no questions, but merely carried on the vicar's arguments as the discussion came my way.

" Well ? " said Mrs. Bradley. I told her the general feeling.

" And now what about Cora ? " I asked.

" Ah, that's up a different street," replied Mrs. Bradley. She was thoughtful for a moment, and then she said suddenly :

" Meg's funeral was on the Friday, wasn't it ? "

" On the Friday. Yes," I replied.

" I said he minimised the risk of discovery," said Mrs. Bradley, as though talking to herself, " but he took a fearful chance between the Tuesday and the Thursday, didn't he ? "

" Did he ? " I asked. She cackled.

" Spill the news," I said. She cackled again.

" I'm wondering how to do it," she said. " I am not a vindictive woman," she went on, " and I don't believe in hanging. Sometimes I wish I did. Sometimes I would give anything to be able to see no more than one single point of view. And sometimes I wish I believed in hell, Noel, my dear."

She ended all with a screech that the Bottomless Pit could scarcely hope to equal. A most extraordinary woman.

CHAPTER XIII

BATS IN THE JURY BOX

The trial of Robert Candy for the murder of
Margaret Tosstick began on October 20th, which
happened to be a Tuesday, and ended at mid-day on
the following Saturday. I obtained leave from old
Coutts to stay in the town until the trial was ended, and
promised to write every day and let him know how
things were going. It was eleven weeks and a day since
the murder of Meg Tosstick, and exactly eleven weeks
since the murder of Cora McCanley. As we had expected,
Bob was accused of murdering both mother and child,
and he pleaded not guilty on both counts. The inquest
on the exhumed body of Cora McCanley, which had been
held on the day following the exhumation, had resulted
in a verdict of murder by person or persons unknown,
although a small but rowdy school of thought, not in
our own village of Saltmarsh, but in Much and Little
Hartley and the purlieus of Lower Bossingbury, were
of the strong opinion that poor Bob was the culprit here
as well, and had all three murders to his account.
Even Mrs. Gatty, now happily restored to normal and
the proud president of the new Saltmarsh and District
Amateur Dramatic and Operatic Society, told me that
once you began thinking over Bob's ancestry, you didn't
know where you were. There was a lot of truth in it, of
course, but fortunately Bob had an alibi for that

Tuesday, which even the police now considered must have been the day of Cora McCanley's death. He had been employed all day at the vicarage getting the garden into some sort of order, for the bishop was expected, I remember, and Mrs. Coutts had a feeling that he would accept an invitation to stay for two or three days. I presume that news of the murder choked him off, for he never came at all. Anyway, that was Bob's alibi, and it lasted until opening time at the Mornington Arms on that Tuesday evening. After six-thirty the whole of the Mornington Arms' staff were prepared to swear to Bob, especially as he even shared a bedroom with the other barman, Peachey, who lay awake that night with a poisoned finger, poor fellow.

I had often attended Petty Sessions, of course, but never a big trial. I was horribly nervous. What if they should find Bob guilty ? It would be perfectly beastly to think of his hanging—perfectly beastly. I studied Sir Ferdinand Lestrange. I am a fair lip-reader. I could see him quoting Horace to his junior. You know the bit, I expect. His junior replied with a bit of—well, Terence, I think. Burt would have appreciated it, anyhow.

The jury were a leery-looking lot, and included five women. Just as well, I thought. Women are so much more practical than men. I felt certain that these good ladies would be able to devise a better fate for poor Bob than standing him over a beastly trap door with a noose round his neck.

I wasn't listening much. I was trying to think what the judge would look like in a black cap. . . . But he wasn't going to put on the black cap in this case. . . . I began to take in what the counsel for the prosecution was saying. He was a big, florid man, and he had a curiously soft and yet perfectly audible voice, and his words dripped, like honey and venom mixed, into the minds of his hearers. I began to think Bob *must* have done it. Still, I comforted myself with the thought that when Sir Ferdinand got up, I should be equally certain that Bob had not. I was not deceived, of course. Sir Ferdinand was wonderful. Of course, the whole thing struck me as being a kind of cricket match between counsel, with the judge as keeper of the score and the jury as umpires. And a frightfully confusing business the umpiring was, I should think. I did not take down the thing in shorthand, but it seemed to me that the great stunt was to confuse the witnesses and get them to contradict themselves. Old Lowry, fat as ever, quite as chinful and even more hairless, was the chief witness for the defence. His evidence, elicited by Sir Ferdinand, was to the effect that no living man would have had time to get up those three dozen bottles of beer, transport them to the jug and bottle department and go upstairs and strangle Meg Tosstick within the time limit sworn to by three independent witnesses (who were produced in due course), Charles Peachey, Mabel Pusey and the saloon barmaid, Susan Galt. A plan of the Mornington Arms, showing the route from the cellar under the garage to the doorway of the jug and bottle department with the distances clearly marked in feet and inches, was passed to the jury. Then the prosecution dealt with Lowry, and tried to force him to declare the minimum of time ever taken

(*a*) by Candy and the knife and boots together to bring up beer, (*b*) by Candy alone,

(*c*) by Peachey and the knife and boots,

(*d*) by Peachey alone,

and elicited the somewhat moot point that he had never timed any of the above by watch, clock, stop-watch, or other mechanical device, and so could not possibly swear that a quarter of an hour was *not* sufficient time for Candy to have dealt with the bottles and committed the murder. The prosecution further discovered that the barmaid, Mabel Pusey, could not swear that fifteen minutes was the exact time taken by Candy. She was compelled, under rigorous cross-examination, to admit that the time Candy was absent from the bar might have been twenty minutes. On the other hand again, she protested, it might just as easily have been twelve. This voluntary cry-from-the-heart did not suit the prosecution, I suppose, and Mabel was allowed to stand down. Poor girl ! She was considerably flustered, but had done what she could for Bob. " If Bob gets off all right, he ought to marry Mabel," I thought to myself. Another bit of Lowry's evidence was an account of the affection which Bob undoubtedly had had for the dead girl. As the prosecution were putting jealousy and thwarted love as the motive for the crime, however, this went about fifty-fifty with the jury, I suppose, but Sir Ferdinand evidently thought it was worth while to bung it in, even if the prosecution could score off it. As a matter of fact, he made a rather nice thing of it in his closing speech. I suppose these counsel have to be looking ahead the whole time. Fearfully wearing, of course.

Motive and opportunity were the prosecution's main lines of attack, and they scored pretty heavily, I should say. There was also a nasty bit when the prosecuting counsel, leaning forward, asked Bob what the row was about between himself and the Lowrys on the Sunday night before the Bank Holiday and the murder. Mrs. Bradley and I had both hoped that Ferdinand would not put Bob in the box, but I suppose it looks bad if the prisoner does not make his statement, and Sir Ferdinand was out for a dyed-in-the-wool, no-stain-on-the-character-of-my-unfortunate-and-much-maligned client decision. So he risked it. Bob, glowering (which was a pity with so many women on the jury), replied that the quarrel was a private matter. The prosecuting counsel, with a nasty smile, pressed the point. Bob suddenly met his eye squarely and replied :

" I were complaining about the food."

" You were complaining about the food, were you ? " asked the counsel. The jury wrote this down.

" I were," repeated Bob, stolidly. His grim expression lightened. " Hadn't been so bad for years."

" I understood that you asked permission to visit the girl Tosstick in her bedroom, and that you became angry when the permission was refused," said the prosecution counsel, silkily.

" Maybe you're right," said Bob. " It's the food I remember best."

" Pore feller," said a woman, rather audibly. Thus encouraged, I suppose, Bob stuck to the food and nothing would budge him. Sir Ferdinand began to look happier. His junior read the note that he scribbled and grinned meaningly at the jury.

The matter of the baby was gone into next. It was a pity, I think, from the point of view of the prosecution, that they had been compelled to accept the theory that Bob had murdered the baby, because they could not get very far with it. The Lowrys had explained that, by the wish of the girl-mother, nobody had set eyes on the baby except herself and Mrs. Lowry. Mrs. Lowry explained that not even her husband had seen the baby. No, the child was not deformed. . . . Luckily for Bob, the jury, one and all, were looking at Mrs. Lowry as she gave her evidence, and not at him. If ever a poor wretch on trial for his life looked thoroughly guilty, it was Bob Candy. He glowered, and seemed to be swearing to himself. He looked evil enough to have murdered a dozen babies.

Sir Ferdinand rose to make hay. He wanted to know what had become of the body of the baby. He wanted to know how and when it had been proved that the baby had been murdered at all, apart from whether the prosecution could prove that the accused man had murdered it. Might it not have been claimed by its natural father ? Had any attempt been made by the prosecution to discover whether it was living with its natural father ? Had any attempt been made—here there was what is known as a sensation in court—had any attempt been made to prove that the baby had ever been born at all ?

A doctor who had been present at the post-mortem was able to assure Sir Ferdinand that the deceased girl had certainly been delivered of a child. Pressed by Sir Ferdinand, he admitted that it was beyond him to declare whether the baby had been born alive or dead.

The judge, in his summing-up, rather stressed the baby. He was noted for his leniency to murderers of the working class type, I believe. The point that, while the body of the mother had been found lying in the bed where she had been done to death, whereas no trace of the baby could be found, was in favour of the prisoner. He was accused of murdering mother and child. Of course, the jury must use their judgment and decide whether the prisoner was guilty of both murders or only of one, or of neither of the murders. If they believed that the baby had not been murdered, but was either born dead or had been taken by the father or by some other interested person, they could say so. They must weigh up the motive imputed to the prisoner and see whether, in their opinion, it was sufficiently strong to cause him to take the life of the girl he had intended to marry. They must weigh up the opportunity and re-member that all-important time-limit they had heard learned counsel discussing so ably. They were to ask themselves whether any other person might have had a stronger motive or a more favourable opportunity for committing the murders for which the prisoner at the bar had been charged. (Well, of course, they had heard nothing about old Coutts, or Mrs. Coutts, so that wasn't too simple for them ! But still, really and truly, it seemed to me that the judge said everything except actually to put the words " Not Guilty " into their mouths.)

Mrs. Bradley was seated beside me in the court on that last exciting Saturday morning. As soon as the jury had retired, I turned to her and said that I sup-posed it was all over, bar actually conducting old Bob in triumph back to Saltmarsh. She shook her head.

" I should not care to predict the result," she said.

" There are five women on the jury, and women are notoriously hard on sexual crimes. For Bob's sake I wish the jury had been all men. He would certainly have been acquitted. Women are still an unknown quantity on a jury. Of course, the seven men may bully them into giving in. It is surprising the way in which women will allow themselves to be bullied out of their rights by the opposite sex."

I could not help thinking that if the opposite sex had any notions of bullying Mrs. Bradley they were in for a thin time, but I did not say so. We waited for nearly two hours and then the jury returned.

Guilty of both murders.

So the black cap was needed after all, and I was able to see how the judge looked in it. A little older, and a little more sad, I thought. I was absolutely stunned, of course. It had never occurred to me for one single instant that we should not be taking Bob back with us to Saltmarsh. The poor fellow cried when the judge put on the black cap. He was led away, still weeping, and rubbing away the tears with the sleeve of his jacket. It was horrible.

Mrs. Bradley slid her skinny arm in mine when we got outside.

" Never mind, Noel," she said quietly. " We shall appeal, of course, and if the poor boy doesn't throw up the sponge and begin confessing or any rubbish of that sort, we shall get him off. The verdict was directly contrary to the summing-up, you noticed. I'm not coming back to Saltmarsh for about ten days. At the end of that time I will return armed to the teeth. Perhaps the verdict is the best thing that could have happened, as things stand. Poor Bob ! That dreadful manner of his was all against him. He stood there *looking* such a thug ! "

" How inconsistent your sex is," I exclaimed. " You believe him innocent now the court declares him guilty ! "

" Oh, no," rejoined Mrs. Bradley. " I have always believed him innocent. Did you spot the witness who was lying ? "

" No," I said.

" I did," she said, with a kind of fat satisfaction in her dulcet voice. " Good-bye, dear child. Don't pine. In ten days, or maybe less, I shall be in Saltmarsh with Jove's thunderbolts. Look after Daphne, whatever happens. Good-bye."

Daphne cried for nearly an hour when I returned to Saltmarsh with the sad news of Bob's conviction. Even Mrs. Coutts seemed rather dashed. The Lowrys were mobbed at the station by villagers anxious to hear the news. Burt came down to the vicarage and we told him. He was thoughtful, and didn't use any strong language. He said at last :

"Do you think he could have done for Cora as well?"

" Impossible ! " we all said. After all, we ourselves had provided Bob's alibi for the Tuesday.

" Oh," said Burt, " that's all right, then. If I knew for certain who had killed Cora I would——" The rest of the sentence was quite unprintable, but even Mrs. Coutts made no adverse comment except for a grim tightening of her lips, and a clenching of her nervous hands.

The Gattys were the next to hear the news from us.

" Poor fellow ! Poor young fellow," was the burden of their song.

We got all the visitors out of the house at last, and Daphne said :

" I couldn't say so in front of all those people, because I suppose it would be contempt of court or something, but I still think those Lowrys did it ! I hate that fat, bald-headed old man ! "

" That's no reason for thinking he murdered Meg Tosstick," I retorted. " Besides, neither of the Lowrys went near the pub at the time of Meg Tosstick's murder, and neither of 'em left the pub on the morning, afternoon, or evening of Cora McCanley's death. You can't fix it on them, dearest, however much you dislike them."

" Well, who *did* do it, then ? " she persisted. We went over the whole thing again ; hammered out all the suspects and their alibis, just as we had done so many times before.

" Uncle is easily the likeliest," said Daphne dolefully. I chewed it over until far into the night. I mean, dash it all, he so absolutely *was*, you know ! And what about Cora McCanley ? If he had seduced one girl, why not another ? Ah, but he had an alibi for the Tuesday. I knew that. We had been together all that day, and during the night we had patrolled the shore, of course. If only somebody could find out *all* Cora's movements on the afternoon and evening of her death, I felt we might get somewhere. But at Wyemouth Harbour railway station she had simply disappeared. We could trace her to the booking office but not a step beyond. I knew that Mrs. Bradley felt sure she had returned to the Bungalow, but there was no proof of it.

I went to the Bungalow next day and talked to Burt about it. A risky thing to do, of course, but it occurred to me that if we could only discover the murderer of Cora, it would give us just that much firmer ground of appeal for Bob. One of these psychology stunts, I mean, of course. Burt was surprisingly mild and very sympathetic.

" Of course I don't want the bleeding fellow to be hanged if he's innocent," he said. " But I tell you what it is, Wells. When I find Cora's murderer, I'm going to get my hands round his throat first, and then I'm going to knock the neck off my last bottle of Veuve Clicquot, and then I'm doing a dive into the stone quarries before I'm arrested."

The remark was a bit of a revelation to me, of course, in more ways than one. To begin with, Burt was now giving us every indication that his feeling for Cora McCanley had been very much stronger than we had ever imagined. Secondly, I had always laboured under the—I think rather excusable—delusion that the term " the Widow," used in describing champagne, was some kind of a—complimentary, of course—reference to Queen Victoria.

But my conversation with Burt got me no further. I was not at all keen on mentioning Sir William's name in connection with Cora, and, in any case, if Cora had indeed been murdered on the Tuesday, Sir William could not possibly have been concerned in her death.

As I walked home, however, another horrible thought struck me. If Cora had been murdered *later* than the Tuesday, the squire had no more of an alibi than, say, Lowry, for instance, or myself, or old Coutts . . . !

CHAPTER XIV

TWENTIETH-CENTURY USAGE
OF A SMUGGLERS' HOLE

Mrs. Bradley was better than her word. It was exactly
five days after the result of Bob's trial had been
announced in the evening papers, that she returned to
Saltmarsh. That is to say, it was on the late afternoon of
Thursday, October 29th, that she walked into the vicarage and informed us that, in the opinion of everyone in
legal circles whose opinion she had been able to hear—
and their name, it appeared, was pretty well legion, of
course, as her son was in the thick of things—Bob's
appeal could not fail.

" A verdict in the teeth of the summing up is usually
reversed on appeal, I believe," said old Coutts, who, of
course, knows nothing at all about it—a fact which his
wife was very quick in bringing to his notice. I do dislike that woman. When she is in the right I dislike her
rather more than when she is in the wrong.

Mrs. Bradley had received a cordial invitation from
Sir William to continue in residence at the Manor
House until the mysteries of Saltmarsh were thoroughly cleared up. He had been much entertained
by Mrs. Bradley's brilliant deductions as to the where-
abouts of Cora McCanley's body, and his theory, often
and loudly expressed, was that Bob was innocent, and

that the murderer of Cora had also murdered Meg and
the baby.

Next morning, at about eleven o'clock, I was not
too pleased to receive a summons from Sir William
to visit the Manor, " with all my shorthand at my
finger-tips."

Daphne and I were inspecting the store of apples in
the loft, when the message came. It is a useful work, that
of inspecting the storage of apples, and I was annoyed
at being called away to other matters.

To my astonishment, the Chief Constable of the
County was with Sir William and Mrs. Bradley, and
Sir William's first move, after bunging my name and
station at the great man, was to clear out and leave
the three of us in possession of the library. I was given
a nice notebook, a set of beautifully sharpened pencils, and a comfortable, workmanlike seat at the big
table. The other two sat in armchairs on either side of
the fire.

" Now, Mr. Wells," said the Chief Constable, beaming. He looked like an inspector of schools, or like the
gently smiling crocodile of the classic. They *are* awfully
alike, you know, both in appearance and character.

I hitched my chair forward rather nervously, and
grinned.

" At your service, sir," I replied, suitably I hope.

" You have been sent for to act as Mrs. Bradley's
secretary. You are under pledge of secrecy on account of
everything that is said in this room from now onwards,
until you are released from that pledge," he said.
(I have been released from it by now, of course, or
I should not be discussing these matters.)

Oм

I bowed, feeling rather like a League of Nations Conference on the White Slave Traffic, of course.

" Please take down everything that is said, in your beautiful shorthand, Noel, my dear, and later, when you have read it over to me, transcribe it into your nice legible longhand," said Mrs. Bradley kindly. " Are you ready ? "

Well, they talked, of course, and I took down. That's about all it amounted to.

" You think, then," the Chief Constable began, " that the unfortunate lad will be acquitted ? "

" If the police could possibly discover the murderer of Cora McCanley, I think it would be certain," Mrs. Bradley replied. " The bodies of Meg Tosstick and the baby have not been found yet, I take it ? "

" No. The police have followed up every possible clue. I don't think they have left a single stone un-turned," the Chief Constable replied, " but, so far— nothing ! "

Mrs. Bradley grimaced, I suppose, at this. I didn't look up from my notebook, so, of course, I can't be certain, and there was a longish pause. At last she said :

" The criminal is rather a remarkable person. Let me outline to you what I think he has done. I am assuming, by the way, that we are dealing with one criminal who committed both crimes ; not with two murderers."

" You say ' he,' as though it could not be a woman's crime," said the Chief Constable.

" My mind is open on the point," said Mrs. Bradley, " I don't see why it shouldn't be a woman's crime. Of course, Cora McCanley was a big girl and Meg

Tosstick a little one, but both appear to have been stunned before they were strangled."

" Oh, so Cora was strangled too," I thought to myself, as I waited for the next remark to take down.

" Yes. Surprise is a great factor, of course, in a strangling crime," said the Chief Constable. " And there are such things as drugs, of course, or the victim being attacked during sleep. She had quite a lump on the back of her head, as you say. She may certainly have been stunned first."

" During sleep," said Mrs. Bradley, thoughtfully. There was a long pause. Then she went on, " You mean that she was sleeping beside her murderer, and that he attacked and killed her ? "

It occurred to me that Mrs. Bradley was determined to shield Sir William.

" Well," said the Chief Constable, slowly, " if she had a lover, you see, and was expecting to go off with him—I wonder *where* she was killed ! That's what the inspector and his people have been trying to get at. But the trail stops dead at Wyemouth Harbour Station."

" The Pier-head Station ? " asked Mrs. Bradley.

" Oh, no. The main line Central Station," replied the Chief Constable. " She took a ticket for London, as we should have expected her to do if her story of going to join the touring company were true. The next thing we know for certain is that she did not join the company. We can't prove whether she actually went to London or not. It's as though, when Cora McCanley stepped past the barrier to board the London train, she stepped into thin air."

" Have you considered the possibility of her having crossed the line by the footbridge and boarded a train which was returning to the Pier-head Station ? " asked Mrs. Bradley.

" But what could she do at the Pier-head Station ? " demanded the Chief Constable. " She could do nothing but swim, unless she chartered a boat."

" Surely she could have returned to the Bungalow by way of the seashore, if she wished ? " said Mrs. Bradley.

" She could. Your argument, then, is that she returned almost immediately to Saltmarsh ? "

" That is what I think. You see, you have to take the girl's temperament into account. Hoodwinking her partner would be the chief appeal to her. She was bored, you see. To have a lover under Burt's very nose would tickle her sense of the humorous more than actually going off with someone."

" I see. Then you think she walked along the sands from Wyemouth Harbour Pier-head Station—or, of course, she could have walked along the cliffs if the tide were full—we can check the state of the tide, of course—and risked running full tilt into Burt ? "

" I think she felt pretty secure," said Mrs. Bradley, " so far as Burt was concerned. Have you heard of the smugglers' passage from the Mornington Arms to Saltmarsh Cove ? "

" I've heard of it, yes. Why ? "

" I happen to know," said Mrs. Bradley, " that Burt, who is rather an extraordinary young man, spent a good deal of his spare time in digging a transverse to that old tunnel from his bungalow."

She gave me time to get this down, and then asked me for a sheet of paper and a pencil. She sketched quickly and badly, but comprehensibly, a plan of the chief houses in Saltmarsh and dotted in the old tunnel and Burt's new bit.

"Like that, wasn't it, Noel?" she asked, handing it to me. I assented and the Chief Constable studied it.

"You see," said Mrs. Bradley. "I think Cora walked as far as the Cove—(knowing that the chances were at least a thousand to one against her meeting anybody she knew)—dived into the Cove, followed the passage—(whose entrance at the Cove end is so cleverly concealed that I spent two hours there with a powerful electric torch before I located it)—reached the transverse to the Bungalow, went along the transverse, and was actually under or in the Bungalow when she was murdered."

"But—but they always slept together!" I yelped, as soon as I had dashed the theory on to paper. Both the polite conversationalists stared at me as though I had gone mad.

"They what?" said the Chief Constable, concentrating upon the somewhat salient point I had indicated to them.

"Always slept together. They've both told me so at different times. You know, shared a bed," I said.

"This is important, isn't it?" asked the Chief Constable.

"Well, it is important in view of the fact that Burt and Cora had a serious quarrel on the morning of the day she was murdered," said Mrs. Bradley. "But it is not particularly important in this instance, because Burt was one of the night watchers at the Cove, wasn't he, Noel ? "

" Oh, yes, of course. I had forgotten that," I said, feeling a fool.

The Chief Constable produced papers and a note-book. He donned horn-rimmed glasses and, looking rather like Mr. Pickwick, perused the literature he had dug out of his dispatch case. " Burt seems to confess to the quarrel," he said at last. " Yes," he went on, " he certainly seems to confess to the quarrel. It was very bitter, apparently, and was with reference to the stinginess of Burt in withholding the greater portion of his income from McCanley. He gives as his reason for behaving thus that she was extravagant."

Mrs. Bradley nodded.

" Cora was angry about having so little money," she ventured. I could see, of course, that she did not intend to give Burt away about the smuggled books, if she could help it ; and, after all, if the man had seen the error of his ways, it was surely right to guard him from punishment.

" Very angry, it seems," said the Chief Constable. " She made Burt very angry, too. In the end he chased her with the intention, as he very frankly admits, of wreaking vengeance upon her person, whereat Cora rushed to the edge of the stone quarries and threatened to throw herself over if he did not instantly and finally give up the intention of beating her."

" Quite a melodramatic scene, in fact," said Mrs. Bradley. I could not help feeling rather relieved that William Coutts had missed this bit.

" Exactly," said the Chief Constable. " So melodramatic that I don't suppose for one instant that anything of the sort happened at all. I'll get the inspector
along to question Burt about this underground passage
business. I had never thought of Cora McCanley having
been murdered in the Bungalow itself. Of course,
during what one may call the suspicious hours of that
Tuesday, Burt seems to have a pretty complete alibi."

" Well, as the doctor who examined Cora's exhumed
body refuses to commit himself as to the time that death
took place, we don't know whether Burt's alibi *was*
complete, do we ? " asked Mrs. Bradley, quietly.

" If you will be kind enough to excuse me," said the
Chief Constable, slowly digesting this point—" I will
just step into the hall and telephone the Wyemouth
Harbour inspector and his people. They will be glad
to get on to Burt again. They have been very suspicious
of him all along, I know."

" One moment," said Mrs. Bradley. She hesitated,
and then continued, " Of course, I cannot control your
actions, but may I suggest that Burt is not your man ? "

" No ? " said the Chief Constable, surprised. " But
everything points to it, and if his alibi is *not* as good as
it seems we have no check on him before seven-thirty
p.m., you see."

" Not quite everything points to it," said Mrs.
Bradley. " To begin with, what do you think Cora
McCanley's object was in affecting to go to London to
join that touring company ? "

" To free herself from Burt in order to meet her
lover," said the Chief Constable. " I thought the
whole argument rested on that assumption."

" Yes, it does," said Mrs. Bradley. " Think it out, dear Sir Malcolm. Think it out, before you telephone the police."

" You are not suggesting to me that Cora and her lover spent the night, or that part of the night which passed before she was murdered, in Burt's bungalow without Burt's knowledge ? " asked Sir Malcolm.

" That would certainly be Cora McCanley's idea of girlish fun, and a very good idea of it, too," said Mrs. Bradley. " Oh, I'm sorry about Cora ! She was bored and became naughty, just like a child, and her punishment was far too heavy for her sin ! "

" Sin ? " I said, when I had dotted down the above.

" Think it out, child, think it out," said Mrs. Bradley waving her hand.

" But you don't call that kind of behaviour sinful," I said.

" *I* don't," said Mrs. Bradley. " But some people do."

They both nodded. Then Mrs. Bradley said :

" If I were you, Sir Malcolm, I should ask the inspector to find out how tired Burt was that night, or rather, early morning, when he returned home."

" If he felt anything at all like I did," I said, " he was pretty anxious to get to bed."

" That's an idea ! " said the Chief Constable, disregarding my contribution to the discussion. " I'll just leave it at that, then."

" I should," said Mrs. Bradley. " After all, if you really think the murderer was Burt, you still have to ask yourself what he did with the body between the

time the murder was committed and the time it was
put into Meg Tosstick's coffin."

" Yes, that coffin business," said the Chief Constable,
scratching his jaw, " is a regular facer, isn't it ? The
sheer damned impudence of it really tickles me ! I can't
think how you deduced it, though."

" It was obvious really," said Mrs. Bradley. " The
whole thing turns on the murder of Meg Tosstick. I
hope they reprieve young Candy."

" Ah, what do you think about young Candy ? "
asked the Chief Constable.

" The result of the trial, do you mean ? "

" No. I wondered whether you yourself had come to
any conclusion, quite apart from the trial and its very
unfortunate result, as to his innocence or guilt."

" As I have said to Noel here," replied Mrs. Bradley,
" I believe either that Candy was absolutely innocent,
or else that Candy was incited to the murder by someone who knew the poor lad so well that he or she, the
inciter, could deduce exactly what Bob's reactions
would be to the suggestion that Meg, his sweetheart,
had permitted herself to be seduced by a negro and had
borne a half-caste child."

" What ! " shouted Sir Malcolm and I, in one
breath. Mrs. Bradley turned to me.

" Don't you remember, Noel, that you managed to
find out for me what the village as a whole thought of
mixed marriages ? Don't you remember Mr. Coutts'
sermon on brotherly love, and the subsequent discussion among the villagers, skilfully fanned and guided by
yourself ? "

She turned to Sir Malcolm.

"The whole difficulty, to my mind, of connecting the first murder with anybody at all was the seemingly insurmountable difficulty of accounting for the time when it was done."

"The time?" said Sir Malcolm. "Do you mean that you didn't agree with the doctor's evidence of the time of death?"

"Oh, I don't mean that," Mrs. Bradley hastened to assure him. "I never disagree with expert witnesses upon principle."

"Upon principle?" said Sir Malcolm, puzzled.

"Yes. I am sometimes called in the capacity of expert witness myself," Mrs. Bradley explained. "I mean that it puzzled me to think that the murder was committed eleven days after the baby's birth. I could not help considering that if Bob, or the baby's father, killed Meg Tosstick when all the village knew that she had had an illegitimate child, some other reason, besides the facts of seduction and illegitimacy, must have caused that murder. For two or three weeks, faced with the twin facts, seemingly contradictory, that the murder must have been committed by Bob and yet Bob would have had much less motive *then* to kill Meg, eleven days after the birth of her child, than, say, six months earlier, when he received the shocking news that she was pregnant, I was forced to the conclusion that some other factor had entered into the case. I have come to the conclusion that Bob may have been incited to murder Meg by being told by someone who had an interest in causing Meg's death, that she had been seduced by Foster Washington Yorke, Burt's negro servant, and had borne a half-caste baby. I also deduce, partly from the disappearance of the baby, that this was a lie."

" From the disappearance of the baby ? " said the Chief Constable.

" Partly, yes. If you will get on the telephone now to Mrs. Lowry, and ask a few questions about the baby, I think that you will at least discover it was not a little half-breed."

" But, my dear Mrs. Bradley," the Chief Constable objected, " the police have already driven the unfortunate Lowrys, both man and wife, the one to blasphemy and the other to hysterics, by their repeated questionings. I am sure we can get nothing further from the Lowrys. Still, I can try, if you like."

" By the way, Sir Malcolm," I said, looking up, " I know both the Lowrys have a good alibi for the Bank Holiday murder, but what about the Tuesday ? "

He smiled paternally, and turned out his despatch case again.

" Naturally," he said, " the inspector and his people have been very severe with the Lowrys, as the first murder occurred in their house, although, as you say, they were not on the spot at the time, and can in no way be held responsible for what happened during their absence. But, my dear fellow, there is nothing at all to connect them in any way with the murder of Cora McCanley."

" What ? " said I, thinking of Daphne's dislike of the fellow. " Not with that secret passage leading direct from the Mornington Arms to that transverse passage made by Burt for his—own amusement ? " I ended weakly, catching Mrs. Bradley's eye. I had been about to give Burt away. Unintentionally, of course.

" Well," said Sir Malcolm, shuffling the papers until he found the one he wanted, " both the Lowrys went to the bank at Wyemouth Harbour in the morning, and had lunch at a hotel there. That's all checked. In the afternoon Mr. Lowry had a nap in the summer house—sworn to by the gardener and gardener's boy— and Mrs. Lowry marked some new linen, assisted by two of the maids. At four-thirty they had tea, turned on the wireless, invited the men and maids in to listen with them, and from opening time until closing time they were both kept very busy indeed. How's that ? "

He went out to the telephone again, and returned in five minutes, during which time Mrs. Bradley sat staring into the fire. He was obviously amused when he came back.

" I wish we'd betted on the nigger babby," he said, seating himself again. Mrs. Bradley looked startled.

" You don't mean that it *was* a brown one ? " she asked incredulously. The Chief Constable, smiling gently, kept nodding his head like a mandarin.

" Right first pip ! " he observed, with almost boyish inelegance, of course, but rather expressively. Mrs. Bradley shook her head as forcibly as he was nodding his.

" I tell you, my dear Sir Malcolm," she said gently but firmly, " that it is absolutely and utterly impossible that the child should have been a half-caste."

" Well, to convince you, I might put the point to Foster Washington Yorke," said Sir Malcolm good-humouredly. It generally puts people in a good humour,

I notice, to catch Jove nodding—Mrs. Bradley, in this case, of course. " But the gentle blackamoor would simply deny it blandly, and, that being so, and ourselves being unable to produce the child, where are we ? "

" Exactly one step further on the road than we were before," said Mrs. Bradley, firmly.

" But this good woman Lowry tells me, now, that the only reason they had for refusing to allow the baby to be seen was to save that poor girl Tosstick's feelings. Apparently she turned hysterical at the very suggestion that she should receive visitors after her confinement, and so, out of pity, they kept people out, and kept the poor girl's secret."

" Of course," said Mrs. Bradley, " they kept people out because it paid them to do so. That baby strongly resembled somebody who wanted his identity kept secret."

" It certainly would not be the Lowrys, if they weren't on the make somehow," I said, remembering Lowry's commission on our cocoanuts at the fête. The Chief Constable scratched his jaw.

" Of course, there's something in it," he admitted. " You mean the Lowrys found it was decidedly to their interest to keep the identity of that baby's father dark "—he grinned at the feeble pun—" and have been primed with this information about the negro parentage of the child by the real father ? "

I looked at Mrs. Bradley. She pursed her little beaky lips at me, so, of course, I kept my mouth shut. There was a long silence. Sir Malcolm broke it.

" I wonder *when* the baby disappeared," he said.

" The day that it was born," said Mrs. Bradley, in a small voice.

She and I sat on, discussing the thing, after the Chief Constable had gone. He had taken a longhand copy of my shorthand verbatim report with him.

" Well, Noel, my child ? " she said.

" Hang it all," I said, " it's more of a mess than ever, isn't it ? "

" I don't think so," she replied. She sat very upright in her chair and sighed deeply.

" Truth, truth ! Where art thou, lovely many-sided, single hearted one ! " she observed, apparently to a tall vase on the revolving book-case. " I know all about it, every single thing, and I don't want to prove it. Noel," she said, switching her gaze on to me as I still sat at the table and played with my pencil, " if or when you commit a murder, mind you do absolutely nothing when the deed is over. Go on with your ordinary life, present a bland, ingenuous countenance to the world, alter none of your habits, let there be no inconsistencies, and, above all, my dear boy, don't be clever."

I goggled, of course.

" Sez you ! " I observed, not inappositely, I flatter myself.

" I mean it," she said. " The murderer—I am not talking about Candy, who *must* be reprieved, whether his hand actually committed the crime or not, but about the real murderer of both Meg Tosstick and Cora McCanley—the murderer must have had an accomplice. These two choice spirits have followed just about one-half of my prescription, but they tripped up on the other half."

" Please expound," I said.

Mrs. Bradley smiled. She reminded me of a sånd lizard basking in the sun. She replied, good-naturedly :

" The murderer did very nearly nothing, and the accomplice was clever, too. He went on with his ordinary life, showing no fear. He altered only one of his habits, but that one alteration was so very inconsistent with what I could gather of his ordinary behaviour, that it caused me almost immediate suspicion. Oh, and they were both a bit too clever, you know. They must have realised that I am getting old and tired, Noel, my dear."

She hooted, as usual, just as I was going to offer manly sympathy, so I cut short my condolences. Then I said :

" I wonder how long it would have been before Cora's death was discovered, if it had not been for you ? "

She shook her head.

" I don't know," she said. " Of course, time was important to the murderer, once Cora's body was buried in Meg's coffin. The longer the lapse of time, the less chance there would be of identification, you see."

" Funny that the bodies of Meg Tosstick and the child have not been found," I said.

" Oh, Meg's body must have been washed up somewhere by now," said Mrs. Bradley. " I believe the police have been called upon to identify nearly a dozen drowned bodies, strangled and not, but, of course, identification is almost impossible and not really very important now."

" Look here, Mrs. Bradley," I said, after a pause, " what *about* Burt ? "

" What *about* him ? " she repeated, puzzled.

" Yes," I said. " I know you have told me he didn't murder Cora, but how can you be sure ? I mean——" I went on, without giving her a chance to butt in with some of her leg-pulling stunts that make me forget what it is I have set out to say—" you have told the Chief Constable that you believe Cora was murdered actually in the Bungalow itself. You have shown, very reasonably, I admit, that she could have returned to the Bungalow by way of the shore, or the cliffs, and the smugglers' passage without being seen. But you have not shown how her lover could have come to her there and murdered her ; whereas, if she did return, as you have said, what could be more natural than that Burt should have killed her that night when he returned from that patrolling of the sea-shore ? "

" Lots of things," said Mrs. Bradley, drily. " First, I cannot believe that Burt would kill a woman."

" He could beat one, anyway," I said.

" Oh, my dear boy ! " said Mrs. Bradley, laughing. " Besides, I don't think the beatings Cora McCanley received from Burt can have upset or hurt her very much, or she would have left him. She always had plenty of opportunity to do so if she chose. Her charms were decidedly of the marketable type. No, it was lack of money that Cora always complained about, nothing else."

" Well ? " I said, letting it pass.

" I believe Burt would kill a man," she said, calmly.

" You mean the lover ? "

" I mean the lover. The lover was afraid of Burt. Cora wasn't. Do you see a motive for Cora's death ? "

" Not altogether," said I, groping dimly.

" You remember the quarrel between Burt and Cora ? "

" Yes."

" And the reason for it ? "

" Money again ? " I suggested.

" I don't think so. I think they quarrelled because Burt had found out that Cora had a lover and wanted to know his name. But that is mere guesswork on my part. Go on," said Mrs. Bradley.

" She thought she might be able to tap the lover, found she couldn't, and threatened to give him away to Burt. She would get off with a hiding from Burt, but the lover would be manhandled by Burt and perhaps chucked into the stone quarries. The lover may even have been hidden somewhere, listening to the quarrel."

" Full marks, this time," said Mrs. Bradley, patting me on the shoulder. " I couldn't have done it better myself. After all, one could hear the voices of Cora and Burt a mile off when both of them were angry. You remember that Margaret Kingston-Fox heard them, for instance, and she is the last person one imagines eavesdropping."

" But you gave me all the tips," I said, blushing modestly, and referring to her praise of my efforts.

" Yes, well, it may easily have happened, that way," said Mrs. Bradley. " Is that the telephone I can hear ? "

It was. A maid came in to say so. Mrs. Bradley was wanted on the telephone. I waited. She came in looking rather worried.

" Sir Malcolm has kindly rung up to inform me that
Pm

the end of the passage which opens into the cellars of the Mornington Arms is blocked up. Bricked in, he says. He has questioned the whole staff and the two Lowrys, but nobody remembers the bricking-up being done. It is obviously old work, and has not been disturbed for years. If further proof were needed that the passage has not been used from the end which comes out at the inn cellar, the bricks are covered with the cobwebs of years ! "

" So nobody could possibly get from the inn to the Bungalow along the secret passage," I said. " But then, we never thought anybody did. It was only Cora, and she came from the Cove end," I continued, feeling my way through the maze.

" We had better go and worry Burt again, I suppose," said Mrs. Bradley briskly. " Will you accompany me ? "

" With pleasure," I exclaimed. A thought struck me. " I wonder what Foster Washington Yorke was doing on the night that Cora was murdered ? " I said. Mrs. Bradley looked at me with sheer admiration in her keen black eyes.

" Child," she said, " go right to the top of the class. By heaven, Holmes, this is wonderful ! "

She slapped me very heartily and painfully between the shoulder-blades.

" In forty-five minutes, or less, I hope and trust that your intelligent question will be answered to your satisfaction," she said. " And mine," she added, on a grim note.

Burt was out when we arrived at the Bungalow. This served our purpose pretty well, as we were able to interview Foster Washington Yorke undisturbed. He was not chopping wood this time. He was doing some washing—shirts, I think, but whether his own or Burt's, I could not say. He smiled politely when he saw us, and removed his dark brown hands from the tub.

" Finish the good work," said Mrs. Bradley, seating herself on a scullery chair. " I suppose you can talk and work, can't you ? "

" Ef youse come to ask me questions about po' Miss Cora, madam," said the negro, unexpectedly and emotionally, " no, Ah can't work and talk about her."

He bent to his task and sloshed the shirts about in a heartfelt sort of way. He had been fond of Cora, of course.

" Ah'll done go and hang 'em on de line now," he said. " Den we'll talk, if you please." His manner had changed for the worse, it seemed to me. However, he brought another chair so that I could sit down. He himself leaned against the door-post, folded his arms across his splendid chest and surveyed us with a fair amount of hostility.

" And now, what, folks ? " he said, insolently. Mrs. Bradley leaned forward.

" You recollect which day it was that Miss Cora went away, Mr. Yorke, don't you ? "

" Ah does that." He recited, almost mechanically, like a child who has learned a lesson, " Miss Cora done go to catch the 3.30 train from Wyemouth Harbour on Tuesday, August 4th, de day after de Bank Holiday. Ah nebber seen Miss Cora no mo'."

Mrs. Bradley fixed him with her dreadful gaze. " What about Tuesday night ? " she asked quietly. The negro shook his head.

" Ah nebber seen Miss Cora no mo' after she done leave this house to catch her train," he repeated, stolidly.

" Oh ? Look here, Foster, what were you doing on that Tuesday night ? "

" Doing nothing," said the negro, sullen as a child who is being found out.

" It won't do," said Mrs. Bradley, patiently. " Listen, Foster. Miss Cora died in this house. I want to know where you were when she died."

CHAPTER XV

BLACK MAN'S MAGGOT

For a moment I thought the negro had not understood the purport, so to speak, of Mrs. Bradley's words. Then I saw his gritted teeth as his mouth widened into a grin of surprise and terror.

" Miss Cora nebber died in dis hyer house," he said, almost in a whisper. His eyes rolled horribly in his head with fear. Mrs. Bradley said rapidly in French :

" Oh, heavens ! I forgot these people are afraid of ghosts ! " Foster's anguished gaze rested on me. His big mouth was trembling. He looked a sorry spectacle.

" Mister Wells, pray to de Lawd ! Oh, mercy, pray to de good Lawd fo' me ! " he said. Sweat glistened on his brow. He was in anguish. I put out my hand and touched him. His hand was quite cold.

" My dear fellow," I said, " it's quite all right. Quite all right. Don't be alarmed."

His teeth were chattering with fright. Mrs. Bradley said in French :

" Give him the Swastika from your watch-chain to hold. Be quick."

I complied. The poor man held it as though it were a talisman. It was, I think, to him. Gradually his shiverings ceased. He shook himself as though ridding himself of some clinging, clammy presence. Then he said :

" I done tell all I know."

" Good," said Mrs. Bradley.

" You don't tell Mr. Burt. De debbil's in dat man."

We promised. He sat on the edge of the mangle and told us his story. Briefly it was that, having seen Cora off to the station and, after tea, Burt to the patrolling stunt that we all turned out for that night, it struck the negro that, as his employer was pretty certain to be late home, he might as well go into Wyemouth Harbour by bus and have a couple of hours at the pictures. He had left the Bungalow at a quarter to seven, he said, and he arrived back at just after eleven. He had seen the big picture, but had not stayed longer for fear Burt should return from the sea-shore before he himself arrived home from Wyemouth Harbour.

" Now," said Mrs. Bradley at this point of the story, " what did you see when you came home ? "

" Nothing," replied the negro.

" Think again," said Mrs. Bradley. " Did you come in by way of the front door or the back door ? "

" Sho', Ah entered by de back door, same as Ah does always," replied Yorke.

" Was it exactly as you left it ? "

A light seemed to dawn on the negro.

" Now yo' done say dat," he replied, " Ah remembers having to use de front-door key after all, because de back door am locked and bolted. I done say to myself, ' You fergit, and leabe de house by de front door, yo' fool nigger.' "

" And did you leave the house by the front door ? " asked Mrs. Bradley, keenly.

" Ef Ah done dat, Ah gone done it in my sleep,"

said the negro emphatically. " Ah didn't nebber in my life use the front door, 'cept Ah come in with Mr. Burt or Miss Cora."

" Ah," said Mrs. Bradley. " Well, now, Mr. Yorke, who usually locked the back door at nights ? Was it you, or Miss Cora, or Mr. Burt ? "

" Ah lock dat back door soon as we'm all fixed in fer de evening," replied Foster. " Ah takes no chances wid folks"—he shivered, and rolled his eyes— " walking in at dat back door and coming peeking ober my shoulder after de sun goes down. Mr. Burt lock de front door when dey go up to bed. Ah don't nebber hab no sorter truck wid dat front door. Dat's why Ah surprised myself walking in and out dere dat Tuesday."

" What did you do when you returned ? " asked Mrs. Bradley.

" I done get de supper fo' Mr. Burt, but he ain't wanting no supper."

" Too tired ? " said I, remembering what I myself had felt like after six hours' patrolling of that wretched beach.

" He took a coupla three whiskies, hot, into him," said Foster, " then he done go up to bed."

" At what time was this ? " Mrs. Bradley asked.

" Dat was half past one o'clock in de mawning to a tick," replied Yorke. " Ah looked at dat clock up dere special. Mr. Burt done took off his boots and threw 'em at dis po' nigger, and he cuss good and plenty, and den he go 'long to bed. Den Ah done go to bed again, too. Ah bin in bed once. Den Ah go to bed again."

Mrs. Bradley nodded, and rose to go.

" Thank you, Foster," she said. She paused at the back door. " Do you often go to the pictures in Wyemouth Harbour ? " she asked. The negro grinned.

" Seem like Miss Cora she mean me to go dat ebening, anyway," he said. " She gib me a ten shillun note and tip me de wink. ' He done go to de pub to-night, 'cause he can't sleep good widout Ah'm in de bed wid him or else he's full ob sperrits,' she say. ' You done go make a night ob it, too, down Wyemouth Harbour, yo' black ole image.' "

" Well ? " said Mrs. Bradley, as we walked down the hill together. " What about that ? "

" Something in what you said about Cora returning to the Bungalow that night," I said. " She was the person who locked the back door, I suppose ? "

" Yes. A curious trick for her mind to play her," said Mrs. Bradley. " The desire for concealment and secrecy, you see. I don't suppose she realised for an instant that she had done it."

" The negro might have done it," I hazarded.

" Most unlikely," said Mrs. Bradley. " It was a settled habit with him to use the back door, you see, when he went in and out. He would have locked it, but not bolted and barred it, against his return."

" You don't think Burt did it in the early evening ? " I asked.

" You are determined to hug your delusions to the last, dear child," she said. " Where do you suppose he hid the body ? Even the secret passage was not safe enough for that, you see. No, no. I am pleased with our last little bit of work, though. We clear the way to the truth, dear child."

" Are you going to get the police to check up Yorke at the pictures ? " I asked.

" I don't think so," she replied.

" But suppose he didn't go ! " I exclaimed. " He was very anxious to tell us that Cora had given him leave to go. Suppose he were in the house when she returned to it, and thought she was an apparition, and fell upon her, and strangled her——"

" And hid her dead body in the underground passage and bundled it down to the churchyard without Burt's knowledge, and dug up poor Meg Tosstick, and substituted Cora, and took Meg's dead body to the seashore and cast it into the water, and——"

" You're pulling my leg," I said.

" Surely not ! " said Mrs. Bradley, in mock amazement.

" You mean," I said, " that Foster Washington Yorke wouldn't handle dead bodies ? "

Mrs. Bradley cackled, and patted me ironically on the back.

I talked things over with Daphne again that night when the others had gone to bed. Suddenly she got jumpy and said she could hear something outside the window. I laughed and said it was only a rose tapping against the glass. She said it was not. I went to the window and drew aside the curtain. A face was pressed against the glass. I suppose I gave an exclamation. I know I was rather startled. Daphne screamed. Old Coutts came tearing downstairs to see what was up. Together we went to the front door, and called out to know who was there. Daphne was just behind us. She would not stay in the room alone.

It was Foster Washington Yorke. The thought that a murder had taken place in the Bungalow had proved too much for the poor chap. He had come to the vicarage for shelter. We hardly knew what to do. In the end, I had to have young William in my room and we gave the negro a camp bed in William's room. A bit thick on me, of course, and the whole incident had not exactly strengthened Daphne's nervous system, but the poor black was in such a state of frenzy that we thought it best to humour him and send him back in the morning.

I woke up once in the night, and, the partition wall being thin, I could hear him softly moaning and praying. The poor fellow must have been in the dickens of a state. It was rather dreadful to think what he must be going through. One conclusion which I came to was that it was useless and ridiculous to suspect him of the murder. He would never have had the nerve for it. It was a comfort to think that there was some other male in Saltmarsh besides myself who would not have had the nerve to commit the murder of Cora McCanley.

CHAPTER XVI

MRS. GATTY FALLS FROM GRACE, AND MRS. BRADLEY LEADS US UP THE GARDEN

At this interesting juncture, Mrs. Gatty decided to start her games again. It must have been frightfully disheartening for Mrs. Bradley, of course. The first inkling we received at the Vicarage of Mrs. Gatty's lapse was by word of mouth from William Coutts.

" I say," said William, bursting into the dining room where Daphne, and I, during the enforced absence— thank heaven !—of Mrs. Coutts at a Bazaar Committee Meeting, and of the old man at a local football match, were working out colour schemes and furnishings from a Maple's catalogue—" the old dame's broken loose again. We've been chasing her all over Saltmarsh. She's got hold of an ox-goad and she's prodded old Brown in the seat with it ! "

" What old dame ? " said I, thinking wildly of Mrs. Bradley.

" Mrs. Gatty," said William. He was flushed, dirty, of course, and grinning. " She thinks she's a sanitary inspector now, and she's going round condemning all the ash-pits."

" A sanitary inspector ? " I said.

" Rather," said William. " And she told old Lowry at the pub that he kept his coals in the bath. She wouldn't go away until he'd taken her along and proved that he didn't." William chuckled. "I suppose just because the bathroom the Lowrys use for themselves is on the ground floor—well, *of course* they have to let the visitors use the upstairs ones !—she thinks the Lowrys don't wash. So old Lowry informed her that he lies and soaks for about two hours at a time and Mrs. Lowry bore him out. So Mrs. Gatty's given him a certificate of purity signed William Ewart Gladstone, and old Lowry says he's going to frame it. She's going round now demanding to look at everybody's ears to see whether they wash them ! " He whooped with extreme joy. " I hope she asks to see Aunt Caroline's ears ! "

Daphne was not smiling.

" I say, Noel," she said, in a troubled voice, " it's rather awful, isn't it ? I mean, she was a bit funny before, but that awful Mrs. Bradley seems to have made her worse ! "

Well, honestly, it did seem like it. Even the murders paled into insignificance before Mrs. Gatty's latest exploits. Her old mania of comparing people with animals returned with renewed force. She waited until Burt was stuck, trying to get Daphne's kitten out of our apple tree, and then she planted a bun on the ferrule of her umbrella and offered it to him and called him a brown bear. She informed Margaret Kingston-Fox that she was a shy-eyed delicate deer, and insisted upon referring to old Burns the financier as Lady Clare. She offered him a chrysanthemum to put in his hair because the season for roses was past. If it had been anybody but Mrs. Gatty, one would have said that our legs were being pulled. But, of course, we knew Mrs. Gatty of old. She dogged me, for instance, all over the the village one morning, bleating like a sheep, and informed me, at the top of her voice, and to the great entertainment of a crowd of schoolchildren—it was Saturday, of course—that I had changed for the better. As, before this, she had always compared me with a goat, not a sheep, I presume that some kind of scriptural allusion was intended. I escaped by taking to my heels, pursued by the shouts of the children and Mrs. Gatty's insane bleating.

I met Mrs. Bradley later—on the following Monday— and commiserated with her on the failure of the cure. She cackled, as usual, and informed me that there was no doubt Candy would be released. He would probably have to undergo a medical examination, she told me.

" And now," she continued, blandly, " I am ready to lecture for you, Noel, my dear."

I looked rather surprised, I expect. I remembered having once given her the gist of one of my lectures— the one on Sir Robert Walpole, if I remember rightly —but, try as I would, I could not recollect having asked her to lecture to us. Still, I supposed that, in a moment of mental aberration, I must have done so ; therefore I coughed to break the rather dead silence which had followed her announcement, and expressed my pleasure, thanks and gratification as heartily as I could.

" When ? " I said, trembling inwardly, of course.

" When do you hold your meetings ? " she demanded. It was Monday, as I say, when she asked. Oh, yes, of course it was Monday. Bob Candy was returned to Saltmarsh, the hero of the hour, on the following Friday, and was sent off to Kent, with the barmaid Mabel and Mabel's brother Sidney, to recuperate at Mrs. Bradley's expense. The idea was for a friend of Mrs. Bradley—a Kentish landowner—to find him a job later on. This was done, by the way, and Bob's story ended happily, so far as I know.

" The lectures are on Wednesdays," I replied. She beamed.

" Wednesday week, then, dear child."

" And the—er—the subject ? " I stuttered, hoping, of course, for the best.

" Ah, the subject," said Mrs. Bradley, looking a bit dashed. " Of course. Yes. The subject." She brightened. " How do you think they would like to hear me on ' Ego and Libido ' ? "

I choked a bit, swallowing it, and passed a humid forefinger round the inside of the dog-collar.

" Ah, well, perhaps not. It's really rather elementary," she said. " What about ' Pride and Prejudice in their Relationship to Racial Health ' ? "

" Well, er——" I said desperately.

" Well, look here," said Mrs. Bradley. " We'll leave it until to-morrow. I'll get up something, never fear."

" They aren't awfully easily interested, you know," I said, feebly. " I mean, we generally have lantern slides, and even then they hoot and raise catcalls sometimes, and I *have* known them to chuck things at the screen."

" Ah, I couldn't have that," said Mrs. Bradley. She paused. " Does the vicar turn up ? " she asked. (Well, he doesn't, of course.)

" He will for *your* lecture, I have no doubt," I said, hoping, again, for the best.

" And Mrs. Coutts ? " said Mrs. Bradley.

" I'll rake her in," I said, hurriedly.

" And I myself will get Edwy David Burt to come along, and I think we ought to have Sir William and Mr. Bransome Burns——"

" He's staying rather a long time at the Manor House, isn't he ? " I asked ; rather rudely, of course, for it was none of my business how long Sir William kept his guests. Mrs. Bradley laughed like a hyena.

" So am I staying rather a long time, dear child," she pointed out. She poked me in the ribs.

" Sorry," I mumbled, sheering off a pace or two. I blushed. Rather a brick, of course. But, really, I had become so much accustomed to her presence in and about the village that I had forgotten that she was, in that sense, Sir William's guest.

" Never mind, dear child," she said gaily. " We meet at Philippi."

I broke the news of the lecture to the members of the vicarage household at tea that evening. Their reactions were characteristic, of course. Old Coutts grinned ruefully.

" I suppose I must turn up and help keep order," he said.

" We'd better start with a tea, or else we shan't get anybody, and that would be frightfully awkward for the poor old dear," said Daphne, who, of course, is full of the milk of human kindness and drips it about rather after the manner of a punctured cocoanut—that is to say, where it is neither expected nor desired.

" Don't you worry," said William sturdily. " They'll come, if it's only to throw eggs. She's been talking to some of 'em about the way they bring up their bally offspring."

" William ! " said Mrs. Coutts, sharply.

" Well, anyway, she has ! " said William defiantly. " What's she going to talk about, Noel ? "

" Well, that's just the point," I said, weakly. Mrs. Coutts sat up very straight and parked the tea-pot, with which she had been about to fill my cup, on its parent china stand.

" You understand," she said, with frightful venom, " I hold you responsible."

I didn't get this at first.

" Eh ? " I said, with my winning smile.

" Yes," said Mrs. Coutts, " if That Woman speaks upon an Indelicate Topic, I shall hold you personally responsible. So mind ! " She picked up the tea-pot and cascaded the brew into my cup.

" Hello," said William, opening his eyes wide, " has she been talking to you, too, Aunt, about bringing up kids ? "

" Go out of the room, William ! " thundered old Coutts. William, hastily snatching a chunk of bread and butter, went.

" Really," I said, " I think—don't you think—I mean, you're a bit premature, Mrs. Coutts. After all, why should she talk about anything peculiar ? Besides, I am sure that Mrs. Bradley would never dream of lecturing upon any topic which is—well, not lecturable upon."

I tried the winning smile again, but it came unstuck

half-way. I don't know why. I mean, I'm not *afraid* of Mrs. Coutts. Daphne came to my rescue.

" You can always rise and protest, Aunt," she said austerely, " if you don't approve of the lecture."

" Quite, quite," said old Coutts, rising from the table. Mrs. Coutts stacked up the tray in frightful silence, and waited rather pointedly for my cup. I got up and rang the bell. When tea was cleared, Mrs. Coutts hopped it to the Girls' Guildry and Daphne and I collared cake out of the sideboard and went in search of William.

At intervals during the next day I tried in vain to get from Mrs. Bradley the subject of her lecture. She would tell me nothing definite. All she would do was to hint that the lecture would certainly draw crowds if I would fix up, in place of the usual notice, a card indicating that a Mystery Lecture would be given by Mrs. Beatrice Lestrange Bradley, in the Village Hall at 9.0 p.m. on the Wednesday week.

" But we always start at seven-thirty. You see, we wash out the Women's Prayer Meeting and Devotional on lecture nights," I said. She waved all that aside.

" We have dinner just before that," she said. " Surely, dear child, you are not suggesting that I miss my dinner ? "

" No, of course not," I said, " but isn't nine o'clock rather the other extreme ? "

" No," said Mrs. Bradley. " It must be quite dark while my lecture is going on. The hall must be dark, and it must be pitch dark outside."

" But we can draw the blinds and things," I pointed out. " We always do darken the hall for lantern

Q T

lectures. By the way, do you want somebody to manage the slides for you ? ''

She shook her head.

" There is only one slide," she said. "It can be fixed at the commencement of the lecture and left until the end."

I began to regret that I had not put my foot down and boldly refused her offer to lecture. We usually get a sprinkling of youths from other villages at our lectures and they are apt to be a nuisance. Our best chance, I thought, was to fill the hall with as many of our own people as we could. To this end, I spent the Wednesday morning in going round the village soliciting promises of attendance at the lecture. As it happened, the notice had tickled the fancy of some of our people, and even Burt announced his intention of being present.

"And I'll have to bring my nigger with me," he said. " Hanged if I can get the coon to stay in the house alone for a single instant, since he spent the night at your place. I can't think what's the matter with the fellow. He misses Cora, you know. That's about the fact of it. These blighters are like dogs for that. Besides, Mrs. Gatty has been round frightening him. Is she quite mad ? ''

So on the Wednesday evening at about ten minutes to nine, the front rows of the village hall were filled with a fairly complete collection of the local nobs and semi-nobs. There were Sir William and Margaret and Bransome Burns, the Gattys, our vicarage party, except William who had been sent to bed, and Mrs. Coutts who was remaining indoors to see that he stayed there, the doctor and his wife and two daughters, Burt, and quite a sprinkling of the more respectable element of the village and most of the servants from the hall, the pub and the Moat House. At the back were the people whom our weekly winter efforts were really intended to benefit—the louts, mutts and hobbledehoys of our own village and the neighbouring hamlets. In short, the hall was about three-quarters full.

At nine o'clock precisely, Mrs. Bradley mounted the rostrum and commenced her lecture. She had asked particularly that the hall might be in complete darkness except for the light of the magic lantern, so that we could not see her, we could only hear her really beautiful voice coming across out of the void, so to speak. There was dead silence when she began. Except for occasional gasps and whistles of surprise and an exclamation from a rather hysterical servant girl, and Mrs. Gatty's absurd interruption and somebody popping out quietly towards the end, there was complete silence until the great thrill. She waited until all the lights were extinguished, and her one lantern slide, a plan of Saltmarsh and the surrounding country, had been thrown on to the screen, before she began her remarks. Then she said :

" To-night I am going to show you the mistakes made by persons who had a hand in committing the Saltmarsh murders. At the end of my lecture I think that everybody in this hall will know the author of the deaths by violence of Margaret (Meg) Tosstick, of this village, and Cora McCanley, of the Bungalow, Saltmarsh Quarries. In front of you on the screen there is a rough plan of the scene of operations. I will explain what is meant by the various markings on that plan.

MRS. BRADLEY'S LANTERN SLIDE

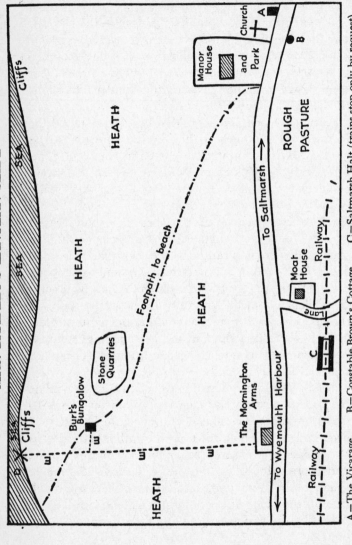

A=The Vicarage.   B=Constable Brown's Cottage.   C=Saltmarsh Halt (trains stop only by request).
D=Saltmarsh Cove.   EEE=Smugglers' underground passage (including piece constructed by Burt).

" To your extreme right, as you look at the screen, you will see a square. That represents Saltmarsh vicarage. Moving your gaze from right to left, you will perceive a cross which represents the church, and then a rectangle, which represents the residence of Sir William Kingston-Fox. I think you call it the Manor House. To the left of the plan there is another square, rather larger than the first. This is the Mornington Arms Hotel. The main road through the village of Saltmarsh is represented by a broad ribbon-like marking running below all the above-named buildings. On the other side of this road and almost opposite the church, you will see a much smaller square than either of the others. This represents the cottage of Constable Brown. Up a short and narrow side turning, a mere lane, further to the left and on the same side of the main road as Constable Brown's cottage, there is a rectangle which marks the site of the Moat House, the residence of Mr. and Mrs. Gatty.

" At the top of the plan you will see a wavering line which represents the sea coast. The small cross there marks the cave known as Saltmarsh Cove. It is an old smugglers' hole, as most of you know, and an underground passage was constructed in about the year 1704 to connect the Cove with the Mornington Arms, which was then called the Pagg and Nancy, after a famous smuggler and his sweetheart. This passage to the Pagg and Nancy, which was made to meet the problem of getting contraband liquor to the inn in the old smuggling days, is represented by a closely-dotted line and the dotted line which leads from the Cove, past the Bungalow, where Miss McCanley lived, to the edge of

Sir William Kingston-Fox's estate, represents the foot-path which leads past the stone quarries. An arrow, pointing along the coast to your right, would show direction of the current called Deadman's Drift.

" I shall not have very much occasion to refer to the plan during the course of my lecture, but I am going to leave it up in front of you, so that you may the more easily follow the movements of the persons about whom I have to tell you."

There was a slight pause. Somebody shuffled his feet ; a chair creaked as somebody changed her position ; somebody cleared his throat. They were nervous, not fidgety, noises. The whole atmosphere reminded me of a fearful row at school once when the head pi-jawed us before he expelled a chap. There was the same tense-ness, the same feeling of wondering how much the old man knew about one's own sins . . . Mrs. Bradley braced her belt about her, so to speak, and having fired off the sighting shots, as it were, got down to business.

" I warn you," she said, " that you will find my next remark very unpalatable. But I am going to ask you to receive it patiently and accept it as the truth. It seems to me that the whole Mystery of Saltmarsh, as the newspapers have called it, rests upon the fact that this unpalatable truth which I am going to utter was not recognised, even by the police, for an important clue—which means a key, you know—to the dreadful things which have happened here since the beginning of August. Briefly, your comrade, and my young friend, Robert Candy, may have been the agent who strangled Margaret Tosstick on the evening of August Bank Holiday, August 3rd."

There was an uncomfortable rustling, but nobody said a word. She continued :

" I am calling my lecture, ' Mistakes the Murderer Made.' I am not referring to Robert Candy, but to the murderer of Cora McCanley and the murderer of Meg Tosstick."

I heard Burt whisper a terrible oath, but Mrs. Bradley's voice was hypnotic, and, shifting his great shoulders uneasily against the back of his chair, which was next to mine, he settled down again into immobility.

" The first mistake the murderer made," said Mrs. Bradley, " was in arranging for Robert Candy to kill Meg Tosstick eleven days after her baby was born. His second mistake was that the baby was never seen, apparently, except by Mrs. Lowry, who had acted as midwife at the birth of the child ; therefore several wild rumours, which circulated about the village very freely and were believed by certain very credulous and rather foolish people, could not be disproved, except by Mrs. Lowry, and she seems to have been sworn to secrecy."

I thought of Mrs. Coutts and the underlying causes of the siege of the vicarage. I thought, too, of the girl's ruin being laid at the door of Sir William Kingston-Fox. I could feel people trying to pierce the blackness in which Mrs. Lowry sat, invisible.

" The murderer's third mistake," said Mrs. Bradley, " was to kill his second victim on the day after the first murder. His fourth lay in refusing to allow Cora McCanley to go to London and do something at the London terminus silly enough or flighty enough, or daring enough to make certain that she would be noticed. As soon as it was found impossible to ascertain whether Cora McCanley had ever arrived at the London terminus to which she took a ticket on that particular Tuesday, it became a matter for consideration whether she had ever actually left Saltmarsh. Then the police discovered that she had never joined the theatrical company which was her supposed objective. Thus it became increasingly conjecturable whether she had ever left Saltmarsh. From that, the question arose, ' Where was she, if she were still in Saltmarsh ? '

" That question was answered by the discovery of her body in Meg Tosstick's grave. It was mere chance that that melodramatic action of changing the bodies did not count as another of the murderer's mistakes. Suppose that the body of Meg Tosstick had been found before we came to the conclusion that the name of the buried girl did not correspond with the name on the tombstone ! The police would then have exhumed the body and discovered that it was not Meg's but Miss McCanley's, and that it also had met death by strangling. I have made various tests, and I discover that flotsam thrown into the water opposite Saltmarsh Cove and thereabouts is washed up two or three days later on to the spit of land known as Dead Man's Reach, some two miles down the coast westwards ; that is, to the right of that rough plan. By the most extraordinary coincidence, the tides, the wind and the awful weather must have combined to take the body out to sea. It has not yet been found ; or, if found, it has not yet been identified. The murderer may have worked this out.

He is a clever person. But I think he was taking a big risk. His argument probably ran something like this :

" ' Cora McCanley has disappeared from Salt-marsh. Some interfering busybody has put the police on her track. So if I throw her body into the sea and it gets washed up and identified, where am I ? On the other hand, if Meg Tosstick's body gets washed up, the chances are that as no description of Meg has been circulated, the body won't be identified, particularly as it will have been in the sea for a day or two.'

" So he risked it, and it came off ; and, but for the most fortuitous set of circumstances "—(thus Mrs. Bradley on her own marvellous bits of reasoning and deduction !)— "it would have continued to come off, at any rate for several months. By that time, any possible connection of the murderer with the crime would have vanished.

" Now, those fortuitous circumstances were as follows :

" You remember, perhaps, that I stated the murderer's first mistake had been to cause Robert Candy, for whom, please, I feel quite as much sympathy as you do, to kill his sweetheart eleven days after her baby was born. Now, that kind of crime for that kind of reason is almost unheard-of. There was no earthly reason, so far as one could see, why Bob Candy, having familiarised his mind with the fact that his sweetheart had betrayed him, and having shown neither scorn nor resentment when he heard that the child was born, should suddenly, without apparent warning, seize an opportunity to strangle the girl he had loved. It was so unreasonable an action that one felt an amazing amount of curiosity about it. One weighed the known facts, wondering all the time whether the police had not arrested the wrong man. But the more one looked at the facts, the more apparent it became that Bob was probably the technically-guilty person."

This time there was an interruption. From the second row—I know where it was, because it came from immediately behind me—Mrs. Gatty's unmistakable voice said menacingly :

" That will do, Croc. That will do. The pig shall lie down with the young she-bear ; she was no longer Lady Clare ; and all the beasts of the field shall be blind for the space of two moons. I, Moto-Kari, the wise owl, have spoken it. Go away, you boys ! "

She was prodded into silence by old Gatty, I suppose. Anyway, she shut up, after that, and Mrs. Bradley was able to continue her remarks. In five minutes, or less, the audience was as much absorbed in what she was saying as though there had been no interruption. Mrs. Gatty went to sleep, I believe. I could hear her deep, rather noisy breathing, behind me, and once old Gatty grunted as though her head on his shoulder was becoming too heavy to be blithely and carelessly supported.

" It was obvious from the first," Mrs. Bradley continued, " that poor Meg Tosstick was being terrorised, presumably by the father of her child. Now, the biggest mistake that the murderer of Cora McCanley (and the *responsible* murderer of Meg) made, was this. He changed his habit of mind. When a man or woman changes a mental habit, one of two things has happened. Either there is an ulterior motive for that change, or else that person's spiritual outlook has completely altered. The change to which I am referring was a change from meanness to generosity—perhaps the most unusual change which ever takes place in the nature of man. It is, indeed, such an unusual change that we psychologists always regard it with what I consider to be a very legitimate and comprehensible amount of doubt and suspicion when it is brought to our notice.

" Now, I brought to the investigation of these Salt-marsh crimes an open and unprejudiced mind. I did not know any of you, when I first came to stay here, with the exception of Sir William Kingston-Fox and his daughter. The fact that I knew nothing about you was more of a disadvantage than an advantage, because it meant that almost all the information about you which it was possible for me to acquire had to be acquired from other people, many of whom showed considerable prejudice and bias in what they told me. A good deal of the most valuable information now in my possession was given to me without the donors being aware of the importance of their remarks. It might be of interest to some of you to be given a few examples of the kind of thing I mean. Let us take, for instance, the matter of that secret passage which connected the Cove with the Mornington Arms. You may, or may not know, that the end of the passage which terminates in the cellars of the Mornington Arms is now blocked up. Mr. Lowry informs us that it was blocked up when he succeeded his father at the Mornington Arms, and that he remembers, very vaguely, its being blocked up when he was a tiny boy. Now when I tell you that I know for a fact that Cora McCanley was murdered in her own home, and that Mr. Burt, for a joke, once spent several months tunnelling a transverse to that tunnel so that he could reach the Cove underground from his bungalow if he wished to do so, you will see that it was of importance to Mr. Lowry to prove that the exit at his end was blocked. But did Mr. Lowry prove it ? No. The supposition that that exit was, and had, for years and years been blocked up, came out quite casually when I was talking with one of Sir William Kingston-Fox's servants some time ago, and this supposition was proved to be a fact only quite recently, after police investigations.

" To take another instance :—there was the affair of Mr. Burt and the vicar. You remember that the vicar was attacked by two men with blackened faces whom he supposed were poachers. It was entirely fortuitously that it came to my notice that Mr. Burt kept a negro manservant, and so I traced Mr. Burt's little joke to its perpetrator. So far as the murder of Meg Tosstick was concerned, that incident was of primary importance, because it then suggested to me that Robert Candy was goaded into murdering Margaret Tosstick by hearing that she had been seduced by Burt's negro servant and had borne a half-breed baby."

There was a sudden violent interruption. Foster Washington Yorke stood up, I should say, and his chair fell back on to the person behind, who shrieked.

" Dat's a lie ! Dat's a lie ! " shouted the negro, apparently, by the sound, trying to fight his way to the front of the hall. Several people tried to collar him, of course. At least, judging from the row that was going on, they did. Suddenly in the midst of the tumult the door nearest to me opened, and some biggish person slid out without a sound. I felt a terrific draught from the open door, but I could not identify the slinking figure. Mrs. Bradley had a megaphone with her, I should think, because the village hall was suddenly filled with her voice, amplified and booming. It said, in a tone of absolute confidence and authority :

" Keep your seats, ladies and gentlemen. Quiet, please."

She got quiet. Then her voice—her ordinary voice this time—said steadily :

" Ladies and gentlemen, someone has just left the hall. There is a cordon of police waiting for him outside. Please remain exactly where you are. Any person or persons making any attempt either to create a disturbance or to leave the hall until I receive a prearranged signal from the police, is liable to arrest as an accessory either before or after the fact of the crime. Please keep your seats."

" Tell us who done it ! " shouted the voice of someone bolder than the rest.

" Ladies and gentlemen," said Mrs. Bradley, " I warn you solemnly that any demonstration in this hall to-night under the circumstances—the peculiar circumstances—will be regarded by the police as a breach of the peace."

" Oh, blast the police ! " shouted Burt, hysterically. " Turn the lights up, somebody, and let me get at him ! " He swore, loudly and terribly.

" Turn up the lights ! " shouted several voices.

The lights were switched on by old Coutts. I felt him get up and squeeze past me. As soon as I had got

over the first blindness, after the intense darkness of
the hall, I turned round to see who had left the hall
in that furtive manner. While I was still blinking at the
empty chair in the row behind me, Mrs. Bradley said :

"Listen, ladies and gentlemen."

We all listened. There was the sound of a car on the
road outside. About five farm labourers were holding
Burt on to his chair.

"They've got him," she continued, gravely.

"Who ? " asked several voices.

"The police," said Mrs. Bradley, wilfully mis-
understanding the question, I suppose.

I had been wondering how on earth we were going
to get the hall cleared in an orderly way, but suddenly
the doors were in the possession of the police, and those
excellent chaps took matters into their own hands, and
we were freed from all trouble and anxiety. At last
nobody but Mrs. Bradley, the Gattys, old Coutts, Sir
William, Bransome Burns, Margaret Kingston-Fox
and I were left in the hall.

"Of course, that man took advantage of the disturbance caused by Foster Washington Yorke. I
thought perhaps he would," Mrs. Bradley said. "I
didn't want him to go too soon. It was interesting to
see the point at which he cracked, though. Did you
notice ? "

"You were saying something about that blocked-up
passage, weren't you ? " I said. Suddenly Mrs. Gatty
began to giggle wildly.

"The bathroom ! The bathroom ! " she shouted.

CHAPTER XVII

MRS BRADLEY STICKS HER PIG

"Precisely," said Mrs. Bradley. "The bathroom. That was the last link, and a very important one. I wanted to be certain about it before I handed some of the rest of my conclusions to the police."

"Excuse me," said Sir William, "but what about an adjournment? They'll be wanting to lock up this hall for the night, won't they, Coutts?"

"Quite," said old Coutts. "Will you all come along to the vicarage? It isn't far out of your way. I daresay my wife would be glad to hear the full story. Besides, I confess that I haven't yet fathomed the identity of the murderer. Stupid, I know. . . ."

"Oh, if you want me to tell it as a story——" said Mrs. Bradley, with her famous cackle. We all assured her that we did. I too, had not discovered who it was who had dived out of the hall and into the arms of the police.

Daphne and I managed to loiter behind the others as we walked along the main road home. Unfortunately, it is a very short distance from the village hall to the vicarage.

When we were seated in the vicarage dining-room, which, fortunately, was large enough to house the entire gathering, including William Coutts, who took cover behind the settee and gazed imploringly at me when he caught my eye, Mrs. Bradley told us the whole story as she had built it up brick by brick and argument by argument.

"As I explained in the village hall just now," she said, "I couldn't believe that an impulse to kill Meg Tosstick would have come naturally to Candy. For a long time I could imagine no argument which would have been strong enough to goad him to the deed. At last, with Noel's and Mr. Coutts' help, I established that the feeling in the village against mixed marriages was very strong—therefore, I wondered whether that fact explained Bob Candy's action, if indeed he was the murderer. An interesting feature, too, was the fact that nobody ever saw Meg's baby except its mother and Mrs. Lowry. So my next problem was to find out why such secrecy had been maintained. At first I confess, I was inclined to think that somebody in the position of, say, lord of the Manor—she grinned at Sir William—" or shepherd of the village souls "—she leered at old Coutts—" had been bribing Mrs. Lowry to keep a secret for him. I could not help suspecting that the newly-born baby very strongly resembled somebody who did not want his identity to be known. New-born babies often bear a far more striking resemblance to one or other of their progenitors than do infants of five or six months old. That is a recognised fact.

"Of course, when everybody was refused admission to the mother's bedroom, one of two things was likely. Either the girl herself felt the shame of her position very keenly—if she did, it was a false shame, I should like to add—" here Mrs. Coutts began to get white round the nostrils. Mrs. Bradley looked her blandly in the eye, nodded in a birdlike manner as though to indicate that she had given Mrs. Coutts one to get on with— which she had, of course—and continued—" or else it was feared that she would give away the name of the father.

" We know now that both these reasons may have been true ; but the most important reason for keeping people away from the mother and child was that the day after it was born the baby must have disappeared. Do you remember, Noel, that I asked you several times whether you considered Bob Candy capable of murder ? " she broke off, turning to me.

I nodded.

" Oh, yes," I replied. " I thought you meant he had murdered Meg Tosstick."

" I did not necessarily mean he had murdered Meg Tosstick. I meant that in any case, murder or no murder, he had distinctly homicidal tendencies, a very bad heredity, and that the man who had wronged both Bob and Meg may have known of these, and feared death at Bob's hands. It was absolutely essential to the father's safety, perhaps, that Meg should die before she had a chance of betraying him to Candy. He may have hoped that she would die in childbirth. She did not. And she produced a child so startlingly like its father in appearance——"

" Poor little thing," interpolated Daphne.

" —that, even if he denied Meg's assertions, he knew no one would believe him when once they had seen the baby. So first he may have planned to do away with the evidence of his paternity. By some means he got rid of the newly-born infant, we will suppose, and

RM

for a day or two perhaps he felt safe. Then he realised that Mrs. Lowry could not keep Meg Tosstick hidden away from the world for ever, and that directly the girl's confinement was absolutely concluded people would want to know what had happened to the baby ; and the girl would tell them. He dared not say that the mother had smothered it or overlaid it or killed it in the madness of puerperal fever, because then the child's body would have to be seen by a doctor, and then the very secret which he wanted kept would immediately come to light. . . .

" Oh, another rather curious, but very significant point ! You remember that I began telling the villagers about information I lighted on more by luck than judgment ? Well, here is an example. As the woman at the inn was always called Mrs. Lowry I took it for granted at first that Mr. and Mrs. Lowry were man and wife. Then it struck me that there was a most extraordinary physical resemblance between them, and I came to the conclusion that ' Mrs.' was probably a courtesy title, and that they were really brother and sister. I have worked on that assumption during the later stages of the investigation, and it has explained several points insuperably difficult to correlate with the rest of the facts. Do you follow what I mean ? "

" Of course they are brother and sister," said Mrs. Coutts, frostily. " I could have told you that weeks ago if you had come to me."

" Fortunately Mrs. Bradley could do without your assistance, Aunt, you see," said Daphne, who simply cannot resist having a jab at the woman if it is humanly possible.

There ensued a good slab of domestic back-chat, of course. When we were all quiet again, and while Daphne was still putting out her tongue at me, because, for once, I was on Mrs. Coutts' side and Daphne knew it, Mrs. Bradley resumed her remarks.

" Matters came to their first head, I imagine, when Mr. and Mrs. Coutts here sent away the pregnant girl ; and to their second head, if I may express myself clumsily," she said, " with the trouble at the inn on the Sunday immediately preceding the August Bank Holiday. Bob Candy, you remember, had to be forcibly prevented from breaking into Meg Tosstick's bedroom because he was determined to find out whether she was being ill-treated by the Lowrys."

" They locked him in the woodshed until he cooled off, didn't they ? " I asked.

" Oh, the night he came round to say that he wouldn't play in the cricket match against Much Hartley ? " said old Coutts. " I remember. Yes, yes, quite." His manner was a nice mixture of gentlemanly detachment and professional sympathy.

" Yes. Having worked him up to the required state of baffled fury," continued Mrs. Bradley, "one or other of the Lowrys—the woman, I expect—told him the lie about the negro parentage of Meg's baby—the lie that so much upset poor Yorke in the village hall just now."

" Yes, he *was* upset, wasn't he ? " said Sir William.

" His moral sense outraged, do you think ? " asked Gatty.

" His sense of justice, I expect," said Coutts. " After

all, it *was* a lie. He was *not* the baby's father." He coughed.

" Simpler than all those explanations is the real one," said Mrs. Bradley. " Yorke is a sensitive, nervous man, and has a horror of being lynched. All negroes who have lived in countries where the colour line is drawn, have what the language of my profession might call a ' mob-law' complex, you know. But about Candy : almost immediately the Lowrys had told Bob that lie about the parentage of the child, giving him sufficient time to brood over what he had heard and work himself up into the requisite state of nervous ferocity, but not giving him a sufficient interval in which to cool off and think better of it, Lowry, devilishly pretending to be sorry for the poor youth, offered him a whole day's holiday. Now I contend that the Lowrys knew quite well that Bob would make some attempt to get into communication with Meg and see the baby some time during that day's holiday while everyone else at the inn was absent at the August Bank Holiday fête. That part of the business, and the consequent suspicion which rested on Bob, was dastardly.

"Of course, Bob never saw the baby. The prosecuting counsel at the poor youth's trial actually said that he would not be a bit surprised if it was in attempting to coerce Meg into showing him the baby so that he could know the worst, that Bob went too far and strangled the girl. ' He thought,' said Counsel 'that she was determined to keep from him all evidence of her shame.'

" The matter of the time-limit at Bob's disposal, that quarter of an hour in which it was thought that he must have committed the crime, was attacked so thoroughly by the defence at Bob's trial that it need not be thrashed out now. Even the girl Mabel, who is almost insanely pro-Bob, allowed to Wells and myself that he would have had time to get those bottles up and also commit the murder. The theory of the prosecution, that Bob had previously got the bottles ready in order to leave himself time to commit the murder—(or, as he probably planned, poor boy !—time to slip up and ' have it out with Meg ')—also deserved consideration. If they believed that the murder was pre-arranged, they were right to assume that Bob would want to allow himself plenty of time.

" You remember what I said in the village hall just now about the improbability of a mean man becoming generous ? " she went on. We assented, of course. " Well, I heard about Lowry's meanness from two distinct and unconnected sources. I heard, quite independently, that Lowry was mean to the village children when they brought him empty bottles, and that he obtained a commission on getting the cocoanuts for the shy at the village fête. Mrs. Gatty and Noel Wells respectively, were my informants." She grinned at us impartially.

" Another example of casually acquired but important information, of course," I said.

" Very important indeed," said Mrs. Bradley. " Yes, well, I could not reconcile with that information the very definite fact that Lowry had given shelter to a girl who had lost her situation and her character, and had even been turned out of doors by her own father." She paused and smiled. " I *did* hear that Saltmarsh was the fortunate possessor of a very charitable vicar," she said, wickedly, " but all attempts to substantiate the rumour that he was paying for Meg Tosstick's keep at the Mornington Arms absolutely failed."

" So I should hope ! " exclaimed Mrs. Coutts, sharply. Mrs. Bradley laughed, and Mrs. Gatty said spitefully :

" The rumour was almost strong enough to break all the glass in the vicarage windows, anyhow, my dear Mrs. Camel ! "

Mrs. Coutts' thin lips closed tightly together. She looked down her nose in a way that we inmates of the vicarage had learned to behold with dread. Needless to say, it cut no ice at all with either Mrs. Gatty or Mrs. Bradley, and the latter continued :

" Do you remember, Noel, asking me once whether Lowry could have committed murder by proxy ? "

" What ? " said several of us together.

" Oh, come," said Mrs. Bradley with her terrifying cackle.

" But *Lowry* ! " we all said. There was a fairly lengthy silence while we digested it. Of course, it was pretty obvious as soon as she said it. There's a game one plays at parties which makes me feel much the same. You all sit round with pencils and paper and an expression of anguished concentration while some silly blighter plays well-known airs on the piano. You have to write down the titles of as many of the airs as you can, and there is a frightful prize for the best result and the worst player, who is invariably me, has to pay some ghastly forfeit. Well, when they read out the titles, you know, I find I really knew them all the time, but just couldn't seem to put a name to them.

Well, I felt just the same about this murderer business. All along I had felt that Lowry's name was on the very tip of my tongue, and as soon as Mrs. Bradley actually pronounced it I sort of realised, as it were, that I had known it all along. Daphne was openly, blatantly and really rather vulgarly triumphant.

" I knew it ! I knew it ! " she shrieked. " Didn't I say he was a horrid fat pig ! "

We shut her up, of course. It wasn't decent to talk like that. After all, the man would be hanged soon enough, and I have never agreed with those who would speak ill of the dead.

" But you don't really mean that Lowry killed Meg Tosstick and Cora McCanley ? " asked little Gatty.

" Remember the word ' proxy,' Mr. Gatty," I said, feeling fearfully bucked, of course, to think that I had put my finger on the spot. " Mrs. Bradley's point is that Lowry incited Candy to murder Meg by telling him that she had had an affair with the negro and that her illegitimate child was a half-breed."

" Ah ! " said Gatty. " Clever work, of course. But wasn't that taking rather a lot for granted, Mrs. Bradley ? "

" It was," replied Mrs. Bradley, with her dry cackle.

" But, of course," said I, fearfully conscious that Daphne was drinking me in, " these inn-keepers have to be pretty good psychologists. Can't keep an inn unless you've got your wits about you, can you, Mrs. Bradley ? "

" Surely not," said the little old woman, making no attempt, as a lesser personality would have done, to snatch the laurel wreath from my head and bung it on her own. It was my little hour, and she let me get away with it. A bit sardonic of her, really, I suppose. The ' sufficient rope ' idea, I expect, if the truth were known, although the word ' rope ' in a tale of murder is a bit sinister, of course. But little Gatty wanted his money's worth.

" Well, what about Cora McCanley, then?" he demanded, " Did he prevail upon someone to murder her too ? "

" Well, to understand all the points in connection with the murder of Cora McCanley," said Mrs. Bradley, " we have to consider, not only the peculiar psychology of the murderer, but the psychological and physiological type to which Cora McCanley belonged. Right from the very first I could not understand how she could bear to spend long months in that lonely bungalow without any amusement or mental relaxation whatever. I soon came to the conclusion that she was not without amusement, and immediately I suspected the presence, in or near Saltmarsh, of a lover. But how was it, I asked myself at first, that a jealous stag among men like Burt should be unaware of what was going on ? Their last quarrel, which was partly overheard by William Coutts, assured me that Burt was not deceived.

" The smugglers' passage explained a good deal of what otherwise would have been mysterious in Cora's actions. That she had a lover seemed to me absolutely certain, but I could not decide how they managed to meet secretly, until I heard about the smugglers' passage. The passage was their secret way, the Cove their meeting place. When Burt was out on his smuggling excursions, which some of you do not know about,

Cora and her lover met, very comfortably, in the Bunga-low itself. At the first sign of Burt's return, the lover made his escape. He went by the underground passage if Burt came overland home, and out of the skylight if Burt returned by way of the underground passage. There he crouched on the roof until the coast was clear. Then, as soon as Cora gave the signal, he would drop from the roof to the ground—see the advantages of a bungalow over a house !—and would made his escape past the stone quarries and back to the Morning-ton Arms and so home. You realise the importance of the position of the Mornington Arms ? It was built well away from the village and the village's gossiping tongue."

" Then when Cora heard Mr. Gatty on the roof that night, she must have thought Low—her lover had gone mad," I said.

" She must have been frightfully alarmed when Burt fired his revolver," said William.

" Go to bed, William," said Mrs. Coutts, apparently aware for the first time of his presence in the select group. William was about to argue the point when Daphne said :

" Yes, come on, Bill. I'm coming as well. We'll talk through the wall if you like. We've heard all the thrills." So off they went. I formed the impression that Mrs. Bradley was glad to see the back of them. I rather gathered that their youthful presence cramped her style a bit.

" You don't think that Cora and Lowry were at the Bungalow enjoying themselves together while Burt and Yorke were savaging me by the Cove, do you ? " enquired old Coutts.

" Impossible, Bedivere ! " snapped the woman, handing her spouse the marital back-chat, as usual.

" Why impossible ? " asked old Gatty. " Quite a sensible idea."

" If you want to know," said Mrs. Coutts, " I saw them dancing together in Sir William's park. I saw them distinctly."

" You would," I thought, remembering her habit of snooping round, and her perfectly beastly mind.

" They were very well-conducted, too," went on Mrs. Coutts, as though she felt she was scoring off somebody. " I remember thinking that they set a very good example to everyone there, if only the village could be induced to profit by a good example," she concluded bitterly. " Their behaviour compared very favourably with that of nearly every other person in the park."

" I don't doubt it for an instant," said Mrs. Bradley, politely. " I suppose you remained in the park all the evening ? "

I avoided Mrs. Bradley's eye, which seemed to be seeking mine, in case I should begin to giggle. Not that I am an hysterical subject, of course, but I do sometimes giggle at the wrong time.

" All the evening," said Mrs. Coutts, unwillingly. She seemed to resent Mrs. Bradley's questioning, although she had been all over her at one time, of course.

" All the evening until you went home and found that Mr. Coutts was missing from home," I reminded her. Old Coutts glowered. He hated to be reminded of that evening. I suppose he did get pretty badly knocked about by Burt and Yorke.

" But about the murder of Cora McCanley," said little Gatty. " I take it that Cora and Lowry left the park together at about the same time as Mrs. Coutts went back to the vicarage, and——"

" Oh, no ! " I burst out. " Mrs. Bradley has already shown that Cora was murdered on the Tuesday."

" Ah," said little Gatty, showing his wolf's fangs. " Then I will try again. Lowry, the inn-keeper, was Cora McCanley's lover, wasn't he ? "

The Coutts and Mrs. Gatty assented. Mrs. Bradley smiled like the crocodile that welcomes little fishes in, and Sir William scowled at the carpet. Only Bransome Burns, the financier, made no sign at all. He hadn't, all along, of course.

" Well, Cora McCanley was blackmailing him for some reason——"

" Burt kept her short of money," I interpolated.

" Ah," said Burns, waking up, " silly game, blackmail. Always get the worst of it in the end."

" Well, she did, rather, didn't she ? " I said. " Getting done in, I mean. Funny both the girls were strangled."

" Why ? " asked Mrs. Bradley.

" Well, you would think the second murder would have been done a different way."

" Oh, murderers usually repeat themselves," said Mrs. Bradley.

" Yes, but in this case," I said, intending to remind her that possibly we were talking of two murderers, not one ; but Gatty interrupted me.

" She was blackmailing him on the Tuesday when he joined her at the Bungalow, then ? "

" How could he know it was safe to join her at the Bungalow ? " asked Mrs. Gatty.

" Why, Burt was at the Cove and along the beach with us on that guarding and patrolling stunt, and Yorke was at the cinema in Wyemouth," said I.

" Yes, very well. He strangled Cora and dragged her body up that secret passage to the inn——" said old Gatty.

" But he couldn't ! " interrupted Margaret Kingston-Fox, who had been following the story with very close attention.

" Why not ? " asked Mrs. Gatty, to everybody's surprise.

" Because it was bricked up, and had spiders' webs all over it," said Margaret. All those present knew that, of course, by this time, because Mrs. Bradley had announced it at the lecture.

" You forget Mrs. Gatty's health and cleanliness campaign," said Mrs. Bradley, laughing.

" What ? " I said. " Do you mean that that was a put-up job ? "

" Completely," said Mrs. Gatty, beaming. " Mrs. Bradley said she had to know whether that passage had an outlet at the inn."

" You see, Noel," said Mrs. Bradley, turning to me, " when that bomb was dropped about the blocked-up end to the smugglers' passage, I thought for one wild instant that my whole theory of the crimes was wrong. It seemed to me that the passage must open into the inn. Then it occurred to me that if I had proof that the passage had a new exit, also in the inn, my case would be stronger than before. Besides, I had felt all along that the outlet in the cellar, which is now under the garages, you remember, was much too public a way for anybody to be able to use in safety. So Mrs. Gatty and I put our heads together, and it was her brilliant idea that if a man wanted to be away from the world for a longish period of time, the best thing for him to do would be to lie and soak in his bath. When Mrs. Gatty discovered that the Lowrys' own private bathroom was on the ground floor of the inn, it was all over bar the shouting. The fact that Lowry and Mrs. Lowry were brother and sister and not man and wife was sufficient to explain everything else."

"Well, I'm damned," I said. Apparently Mrs. Coutts was, too, for she never said a word, and she is usually on to a little strong language like a terrier on a rat.

We sat and drank it in about the passage.

"Then they got Meg Tosstick's body to the sea along the passage," I said, " and the baby, too——"

"He went along the passage to kill Cora McCanley in the Bungalow," said old Gatty, who seemed to be getting quite a sleuth-hound, " and brought her body back to the inn the same way—as I said just now."

"So that's that," said Sir William.

"Not quite," said Mrs. Bradley, " I've a piece of positive proof about the use of the smugglers' passage which may interest you. You remember the substitution of Cora McCanley's body for that of Meg Tosstick in the coffin, don't you ? Well, of course, the substitution was made at the inn. At this point Lowry showed an amount of audacity which really deserved to come off. But, acting upon his own initiative, the police inspector had got on to the undertaker who was given the job of arranging Meg Tosstick's funeral. It took him some time, because the undertaker was not a local man. He did not come from Wyemouth Harbour, either, as most people believed, but from a place called Harmington in the next county. He got the job, he thought, because he was some sort of connection of Lowry. It was a motor-funeral, you remember, so that distance was no object, and in any case the town the undertaker came from is less than twenty miles away. The advantage of that particular town was that, for Lowry's purpose, it was sufficiently obscure.

" Well, greatly to their credit, the police got on to this man, and persuaded him to try and recall the build and features of the girl whose body he had screwed down in the coffin. He was shown photographs of about fifteen young women, including those of Meg and Cora, and, despite the evidences of strangulation with their resultant disfigurement, he unhesitatingly picked out Cora as the girl whose coffin he had actually supplied. He gave us the measurements then. Oh, it was Cora, without a doubt, for whom Meg Tosstick's coffin was made. They proved it to the hilt. You remember what a fine big girl she was, compared with Meg ? "

CHAPTER XVIII

THE LAST STRAW

We gasped.

" What ? " said old Coutts. " *We* actually buried the wrong girl ? "

" Oh, yes," said Mrs. Bradley. " If it had come off, you see, it would have been a splendid move to avoid discovery. No difficult and dangerous digging up of graves in the churchyard at night. No risk that the undertaker would recognise that the girl for whom the coffin was prepared was not the girl whose sweetheart had been arrested for murder——"

" But what on earth made you think of having the body exhumed ? " demanded Sir William.

" Well," said Mrs. Bradley, " granted all the rest of the story, including the fact of the secret passage, it was the obvious thing to do, wasn't it ? The only thing I cannot understand, dear people, is why on earth you have all jumped to the conclusion that Lowry was the murderer. Why, you can't really imagine a girl like Cora McCanley falling in love with Lowry ! Lowry is incestuous, he is cowardly, and he was blackmailed into assisting the murderer. But the actual murderer of Meg Tosstick and Cora McCanley——"

" No, no ! " shrieked Mrs. Coutts, and fainted.

It was the second time in our respective existences that I had clasped Mrs. Coutts to my breast. Heaven knows I didn't want to, but noblesse oblige, of course. I looked round helplessly. She was no light weight, and she hung on my arms, which were clasped strongly but inelegantly round her waist, more like a sack of flour than the languishing lily with whom I have heard a fainting lady compared.

The settee was cleared and we laid her down. She was a rather unnerving bluish colour, and her lips were drawn back from her teeth almost in a snarl. Mrs. Bradley stepped forward, knelt by the couch and did all the things that people in the know do do on these, to me, positively demoralising occasions. But it was not the slightest use. Mrs. Coutts was dead.

People withdrew, of course, as decently and quietly as they could, and I was going, too, when old Coutts, who, with myself and Mrs. Bradley, had remained behind in the room, grabbed me by the arm.

" Stay with me, Wells," he said. " I suppose we must telephone for a doctor."

Mrs. Bradley, to whom the suggestion seemed to be made, shrugged her shoulders.

" I can write the certificate if you like," she said. " I am qualified to do so."

" Yes. . . . Thank you," said old Coutts.

He sat down and put his hands to his face.

" This is my fault," he said. Mrs. Bradley sat down, too, and motioned me to a seat.

" Let us not talk of faults," she said gently. " Perhaps I am at fault, too. I knew that I was going to cause her death. I had to choose between killing her through shock, or as an alternative——"

Old Coutts lifted his head.

" As an alternative ? " he repeated heavily.

" Letting her stand her trial," said Mrs. Bradley.

" She did commit the murders, then ? " Coutts asked. He did not seem in the least surprised.

Mrs. Bradley inclined her head.

" And she would have committed others," she said. " That is why I had to make a choice." She looked gravely and sadly at the body. " I have made it," she concluded. " There was Daphne to consider. . . . "

" Yes . . . " said old Coutts. " Thank you." He got up and stumbled out of the room. We could hear him walking up and down his study. Up and down . . . up and down.

" I had better tell you everything, Noel, I think," said Mrs. Bradley. " Poor boy. You look tired."

" I'm ill," I said. I went outside, and, for some reason, was horribly sick. When I came back, fit for society but shaking at the knees, Mrs. Coutts' body had been covered. I could make out its thin, rigid, pathetic outline under a dark-blue bed-cover.

" She murdered Meg Tosstick on the Monday, Cora McCanley on the Tuesday and made an attempt on Daphne Coutts on the following Saturday week. You remember the incident at the organ ? As soon as you told me about that, I knew all the rest. The vestry door was the clue."

" But that wasn't Mrs. Coutts, surely ? " I said. " Why, she was prostrate in bed with one of her fearful headaches when we arrived home."

" She was prostrate in bed with a heart attack brought on by rage, excitement, and the expenditure
Sм

of nervous and physical energy," said Mrs. Bradley. " Did you know her heart was weak ? "

" Well, more or less, I suppose," I said.

" And, of course, her nervous system had been in a state of attrition for years," said Mrs. Bradley. " Terrible. Poor, poor woman."

She sounded so genuinely sorry that I gazed in astonishment. After all, this was the " poor, poor woman " who would have allowed Bob Candy and the innkeeper, Lowry, to be hanged for her crimes.

" Mr. Coutts allowed temptation to overcome him in the matter of Meg Tosstick while she was a servant in his house," said Mrs. Bradley in a level voice that did not comment, criticise or condemn, " and, of course, Mrs. Coutts found it out. Do you remember the first time she came back from the inn when she had seen the mother and the newly-born child ? "

" Oh, yes, I remember her coming in," I said. I did, of course, very vividly. " But you are wrong about one thing. She did not see the mother and baby. The Lowrys refused her admittance."

" I know she *said* they did," said Mrs. Bradley. " But I am sure that was an untrue statement. They did let her in, and it was she who ordered them not to admit anyone else because the baby took after her husband in appearance. She had a fairly firm hold over the Lowrys, remember."

" A hold over them ! " I said. This, of course, was a new one to me.

" They were incestuous," said Mrs. Bradley. She paused. " I suppose it is because we have inherited the Jewish code of morals that incest is considered to be a sin," she continued, watching my face. " Biologically I believe there is no weighty reason against it. However, most people regard it as a somewhat undesirable social foible, and Mrs. Coutts certainly put pressure on the Lowrys—blackmail, some people would call it—when she discovered that they were brother and sister and had indulged at some time or another in an illicit relationship."

" Oh, yes. She *would* find it out, if there was anything nasty going on," I said, bitterly. " She loved evil. It fascinated her, I think."

" She had her punishment," said Mrs. Bradley, seriously. " She found out that Meg Tosstick was with child, and she guessed that it was her own husband who had seduced the girl."

" Didn't she know for certain ? " I asked.

" Not until the birth of the child, I think. The resemblance then was unmistakable. Some new-born babies bear a most extraordinary resemblance to one of their progenitors, as I said ; this resemblance tends to become less marked as the child grows older. I am sure that Meg did not confess, and I don't think Mr. Coutts was very likely to do so, was he ? "

" His life was pretty much of a hell as it was," said I. " I don't suppose he wanted to make matters worse."

" Yes, it must be hell to be compelled to lead the existence of a monk when one's urge for procreation is very strong," said Mrs. Bradley. " That was the trouble, of course."

" But surely——" I said awkwardly, lacking her beautifully scientific detachment—" Cora McCanley, I mean——"

" Oh, Mr. Coutts was not Cora McCanley's mysterious lover," said Mrs. Bradley. " Nor was Sir William Kingston-Fox." She smiled wickedly at me. I could have kicked myself for jumping to conclusions. " Don't you remember telling me what a long holiday Mr. Bransome Burns was spending in these parts ? " she said " Burns was a financier. That, to the impecunious Cora, meant a good deal, of course. She had dug enough money out of Burns to go for that jaunt to London that I spoke about, and had made up her mind to go. Then, as I told you—only you were convinced I was talking about Sir William—Burns telephoned to put her off, and she arranged to hoodwink Burt, and, later, return to the Bungalow. The idea of deceiving Burt, with whom she had quarrelled violently, appealed to Cora, just as I said before, and the story I told of her return and the manner of it was also true. I don't know how long she had been at the Bungalow waiting for Burns, who couldn't get away from you all on the seashore that night, when Mrs. Coutts arrived by way of the underground passage *from the inn.* Cora must have been fearfully annoyed at first, and then fearfully alarmed. Mrs. Coutts strangled her to death after having stunned her with the poker. Do you remember Burt's poker ? And do you remember that the Chief Constable told us Cora had had a blow on the back of the head ? "

I nodded, and shuddered, of course ; I remembered how I myself had picked up that poker once with the intention of knocking out Burt with it.

" And, of course, if anybody had seen Mrs. Coutts on her way back from the Bungalow that evening, she had her reason ready. She pretended she had gone out to look for you all and persuade you to come home, didn't she ? Do you remember that ? Only, she gave the wrong time, I expect, to her husband. She went to the Bungalow much earlier than she said, and she had to race back to the inn to get hold of Lowry and tell him he must remove Cora's body."

" I remember how fearfully knocked out she was on that Tuesday might," I said. " It's a wonder her heart stood the strain of the two murders, isn't it ? "

" Well, yes and no," said Mrs. Bradley. " She probably considered that she was doing the will of God in ridding the earth of what she considered to be two dreadfully depraved and wicked people. She knew that Cora was an actress, and she knew that the vicar had yielded to temptation in the form of Meg Tosstick. She grew suspicious even of little Daphne, you remember, and it is a very good thing, Noel, that you were sentimental enough to mount guard over the girl as you did. Of course, as the mania took root, there is no doubt that she would have considered herself a crusader against all sexual intercourse. She was the wrong age, my dear Noel, to make the discovery that her husband had deceived her. It was an awful tragedy, that meaningless death of poor Cora McCanley."

" Do you think Coutts will get over it ? " I asked.

" Yes, when the trial of Lowry is over, I am sure he will," said Mrs. Bradley. " He's had a shock, but it isn't as though he was fond of her, you see."

" Then how did Lowry come in ? " I asked.

" He was paid by Mr. Coutts to look after Meg Tosstick," said Mrs. Bradley, " and I think it was his own idea, not Mrs. Coutts', to change the bodies of the two girls when she had made him drag the body of Cora to the inn. Do you realise he had no alibi (except that supplied by his sister) after the bar opened on that Tuesday evening ? ''

" And the baby ? " I said.

" Oh," said Mrs. Bradley, " the baby is alive some-where, I have no doubt. Mrs. Coutts wanted to kill it, I expect, but found she couldn't. Women are strangely inhibited from killing children, Noel, my dear."

THE END

APPENDIX

MRS. BRADLEY'S NOTEBOOK

July 7th : To Saltmarsh, at the invitation of Sir William Kingston-Fox, Ferdinand's schoolfellow. Nice of the man to ask me. Shall be bored stiff, I expect.

July 9th : Not so dull as I expected.
Sir William fulfilled boyhood promise of good looks and uncontrolled temper. I like the daughter. A very charming child. But why on earth does the man propose to marry her to Bransome Burns ? Burns is keen on the match. Horrible !

July 15th : To-day I met some of the local celebrities, including the vicar's wife and a certain Mrs. Gatty. Interesting contrast in mental defectiveness. Must have a go at Mrs. Gatty and see what can be done. Exhibitionist. Mrs. Coutts a bad case of sadism plus inverted nymphomania, I think. Very curious and interesting, but I doubt whether my attentions would be received in the spirit in which they would be offered. She won't upset the general public unduly if she does not break loose. Woman has brains, of course, and is a remarkably fine pianist. Got herself pretty well under control, at present. Obviously does not know the strength of the devil within her. Let us hope nothing ever happens to unchain him.

July 17th : The village humming with news this morning. Some unfortunate girl has had an illegitimate child. I didn't know people bothered about such things nowadays.

July 28th : It is not the illegitimacy which is causing the excitement, but the facts that (1) the girl won't name the baby's father and (2) she won't allow anybody to see her or the child. I met the curate to-day. A nice, rather weak-chinned youth. I also met the rest of the vicarage household. A jolly little boy of fourteen or so, a remarkably beautiful young girl at whom the curate casts the most ridiculous sheep's eyes the whole time—bless their hearts !—and the vicar. Heigho ! The devil a monk would be ! Took some pains to stir up Mrs. Coutts in order to test her reactions. She is absolutely unhinged on the subject of sexual relationships, and the vicar is horribly ill at ease. It would be quite in order to suspect that he is the father of the illegitimate child at the inn. *Mrs. Coutts has seen that child*, I am certain. Poor woman ! She is in hell.

July 29th : The girl was a maid-servant at the vicarage when the child was conceived. There can be no reasonable doubt of the vicar's implication. How tragic, and how immeasurably absurd !

My other patient, Mrs. Gatty, was rather extraordinarily amusing yesterday. Somebody locked her poor husband in the church crypt and she didn't want him released. There is another queer specimen in Saltmarsh, and that is Mr. Edwy David Burt, up at the Bungalow. And even our Mr. Burns is betraying unsuspected depths. I believe he has given up sighing for the moon (i.e. Margaret Kingston-Fox) and is consoling himself with a nice piece of cheese to whom I have not been able to fix a name. What a scandalmongering old woman I am ! It's living in the country does it ! Well, well !

August 2nd : My fat little exhibitionist excelled herself to-day. Very funny indeed.

August 4th : Village life is too exciting for me. Spent most of the night hunting for the vicar, only to discover to-day that he was chained up in the pound. Burt, of course, assisted by the negro servant. The same mental groove as the " Gatty in the crypt " incident. Out-Gattying Mrs. Gatty, in fact. No wonder the poor boy doesn't make a fortune at his job. No imagination. There is something startlingly reminiscent of crime in this banal repetition. I suppose Burt didn't murder that poor girl yesterday ?

August 6th : No, no ! It couldn't be Burt. Why has Cora McCanley disappeared from the Bungalow ? It is getting serious. What shall I do ?

August 17th : *Where is Cora McCanley ?* Of course it is Mrs. Coutts, but, poor woman, she is not responsible for her actions. The attack on little Daphne proves it. What on earth shall I do ? She can't go on killing people. Besides, I could not prove anything at present, even if I decided to inform the police. But there is no other solution to this frightful business.

Motive

Opportunity

Psychological factors.

All fit. But the woman is clever. All her wits about her at present. Terrified of discovery, too. Take the facts.

1. *Meg Tosstick*.

A. Time of the murder—9.0 p.m. to 10.30 p.m. on the night of Saltmarsh fête. Ideal opportunity. Everyone absent from the inn except those who were actually on duty all the time.

Question arises here. Did Mrs. Coutts commit the murder with her own hands, or did she prevail upon this poor boy Candy to strangle the girl ? My mind is open at present, but if she incited Bob, what was her argument, I wonder ? He would have killed Meg long enough ago if the fact of her seduction were sufficient to account for the murder. Shall get Wells to visit Bob and get his account of the way in which he spent the Bank Holiday.

And now for Burt. Indecent literature, I presume. Otherwise why was Burt so angry when the vicar seemed interested in Saltmarsh Cove, whose very name is associated with smugglers ? Burt is a " literary man," so smuggled books would be more in his line than smuggled beer. Psychological factor here, too. Besides, the landlord of the Mornington Arms has a secret of his own already, I fancy, and wouldn't risk breaking the law.

Shall take a strong line with Burt. Probably get myself thrown into the stone quarries. Heigho ! These violent inhabitants of peaceful villages !

August 20*th* : Wells just returned from visiting Candy in prison. Do not think Candy had any hand in the murder. In any case, Mrs. Coutts responsible, I am certain, because the thing comes to its head with the attempt on Daphne Coutts in the church. No one but Mrs. Coutts could have known

1. That Daphne was to be playing the organ that evening,
2. Where to find key of vestry,
3. That she would not excite suspicion if seen entering or leaving church at that time.

Of course, her husband would fit most of the evidence, but his psychological make-up quite wrong. Besides, if he had intended to kill Meg Tosstick he would have done it to save his face, i.e. *before* the birth of the baby. This applies to *all* males including Candy *unless* somebody—e.g. Mrs. Coutts—told Candy that Meg's seducer was the negro servant at the Bungalow. That might be the explanation if Candy committed the murder. Must find out attitude towards the Colour Question among villagers. Must get my invaluable Boswell, Captain Hastings, Doctor Watson, Noel Wells on to it. Child has a head like a turnip. I do not think the Bar suffered any great loss when he went into the Church. Nice enough youth, though. Little Daphne will do as she pleases with him.

August 24th : The village has made up its mind. The vicarage attacked to-day and the service disorganised. The vicar accused of being the father of Meg Tosstick's baby. Demands made for the production of the baby. I see Mrs. Coutts' hand in all this. On Saturday she produced a notice printed on the back of one or two of the Gattys' visiting cards which (presumably) have been left at the vicarage in times past. The notice reads : " Where is Meg Tosstick's baby ? "

The printing is rough enough, but the word " is " and the fact of the apostrophe " s " being in the right place, and the even more illuminating fact that Mrs. Coutts " discovered " these remarkable notices when nobody else was in the house, point clearly enough to their authorship. Anonymous writings are a feature of cases like hers. Sexual disorder, coupled with the mania for putting one's suspicions of others on to paper, very characteristic.

But what about Cora McCanley ? Where has Mrs. Coutts hidden the body ? She is the wife of the vicar. She ought to want a dead body buried in consecrated ground. That means the churchyard. Yes, but she *can't* have it buried. She murdered it. And there is no trace of it. Where could she put it ? Well, that depends upon where she killed it.

Bransome Burns used to go for long lonely walks. . . . I was pretty sure he was Cora McCanley's lover when he found that Margaret despised him.

Later : I've frightened him. He thinks I think he murdered Cora, and he's told me everything. They were to have met in London. She was to pretend to join this travelling company. But both fought shy in the end.

He was scared, I expect, of Burt, and she didn't trust Burns too far. They changed their minds, but Burns couldn't meet her at the Bungalow as arranged, and has not seen her since. Is obviously frightened. Wants to persuade me that he thinks she *did* go to the show and join the company after all.

August 25th : Shall inform the police of my suspicions.

August 26th : She could have thrown Cora's body into the sea.

Later : Or buried it in Meg Tosstick's grave, if she could get the people at the inn to change the bodies for the undertaker. But there is nothing at present—Why, of course, there is ! Whose suggestion was it, I wonder, that Meg should be cared for at the inn ? Suppose it came from Mrs. Coutts ! Suppose there is some very strong connection between Mrs. Coutts and the people at the inn ! The Lowrys, of course, must be related by blood as well as by marriage. They are very much alike in appearance.

August 27th : Solved it, I do believe ! Exhumation order asked for. Now for it.

August 29th, 5.0 a.m. : Cora's body, not Meg's, exhumed. The Lowrys *must* be implicated. The funeral took place from the inn, and the coffin had obviously been made for Cora, a much bigger and taller girl than Meg. Now, what hold could Mrs. Coutts have had over either or both of the Lowrys, that they should become accessories after the fact of the murder ? Oh, yes, I can answer that ! . . .

October 20th : Trial of Candy begins to-day.

October 24th : Candy found guilty of murdering mother and child. I must find some proof of Mrs. Coutts' guilt, I suppose, that will satisfy the authorities, *but I don't want the poor woman to be hanged.* If Candy is reprieved, I shall kill her by shock. She obviously has a weak heart, and sudden death is the best gift I can present to her. If she isn't hanged she will be sent to Broadmoor. I will kill her, unless Candy is not reprieved. In that case, I shall have to save him by denouncing her to the police.

October 25th : Good heavens ! I'm wrong about the whole thing ! The passage has no outlet at the inn. It has been bricked up these fifty years or so !

I must be right ! That passage must have a new outlet made by Lowry. He may have been a lover of Cora before Burns came upon the scene with his money and his more gentlemanly (! !) ways.

October 26th : Mrs. Gatty to the rescue. Marvellous woman ! The ground floor bathroom ! Now to twist Lowry's tail and save that wretched woman, if only Candy is reprieved.

October 29th : Candy set free. Sending him to Kent almost immediately.

November 5th, 2.30 a.m. : Guy Fawkes' Day. And I have committed my second murder.